DOVER · THRIFT · EDITIONS

Volpone and The Alchemist

BEN JONSON

DOVER PUBLICATIONS, INC.
Mineola, New York

DOVER THRIFT EDITIONS

GENERAL EDITOR: PAUL NEGRI
EDITOR OF THIS VOLUME: SUSAN L. RATTINER

Copyright

Theatrical Rights

This Dover Thrift Edition may be used in its entirety, in adaptation, or in any other way for theatrical productions, professional and amateur, in the United States, without fee, permission, or acknowledgment. (This may not apply outside of the United States, as copyright conditions may vary.)

Bibliographical Note

This Dover edition, first published in 2004, contains the unabridged texts of *Volpone; or, The Fox* and *The Alchemist*, as published in *The Chief Elizabethan Dramatists, Excluding Shakespeare*, Houghton Mifflin Company (The Riverside Press), Cambridge, Mass., 1911. An introductory Note and explanatory footnotes have been specially prepared for the present edition.

Library of Congress Cataloging-in-Publication Data

Jonson, Ben, 1573?–1637.
    Volpone ; and, The alchemist / Ben Jonson.
       p. cm. — (Dover thrift editions)
    ISBN 0-486-43630-6 (pbk.)
    1. Inheritance and succession—Drama. 2. City and town life—Drama. 3. London (England)—Drama. 4. Venice (Italy)—Drama. 5. Alchemists—Drama. 6. Extortion—Drama. I. Jonson, Ben, 1573?–1637. Alchemist. II. Title: Alchemist. III. Title. IV. Series.

PR2622.A1 2004
822'.3—dc22

2004049362

Manufactured in the United States of America
Dover Publications, Inc., 31 East 2nd Street, Mineola, N.Y. 11501

Note

GENERALLY REGARDED as the second most influential dramatist after William Shakespeare, Ben Jonson was born at Westminster in 1573. Before finding his niche as a playwright, he briefly followed his stepfather's trade of bricklaying, then served as a soldier in Flanders. By 1597, Jonson was a member of the Admiral's Company of actors, but his career was interrupted when he killed a fellow actor in a duel a year later. His first theatrical success came with *Every Man in His Humour* (performed 1598), a play in which Shakespeare acted a part. Jonson enjoyed great success with his satires and tragedies, and during the reign of James I, he turned his talents to masques and court entertainments. From 1605 until about 1617, Jonson was the leading literary figure in London. With the death of James, however, Jonson's popularity declined as well as his theatrical successes and his health. He briefly recovered with an appointment as chronologer to the city of London, but he lost that office and abandoned his attempts to regain his previous standing in the London theater. Jonson died August 6, 1637.

Jonson's major comedies, marked by a pungent satire and a brilliant command of language, express a strong distaste for the world in which he lived and a delight in exposing its follies and vices. *Volpone; or, The Fox*, one of Jonson's most popular plays, was first performed in 1605 or 1606 at the Globe Theater and remains one of the most biting satires on the more sordid aspects of human nature. A masterpiece of types, *Volpone* is a cynical commentary on the greed and vanity that formed a large part of the society it critiques. *The Alchemist* (performed 1610) revolves around the deception of three conmen who set themselves up as alchemists, and the numerous fools they dupe along the way. A superbly gifted writer with intellectual energy and literary acumen, Jonson exerted a great influence on his contemporaries as well as on subsequent generations of playwrights.

Contents

Volpone

The Alchemist

Volpone

DRAMATIS PERSONAE[1]

VOLPONE, *a magnifico.*
MOSCA, *his parasite.*
VOLTORE, *an advocate.*
CORBACCIO, *an old gentleman.*
CORVINO, *a merchant.*
BONARIO, *son to Corbaccio.*
SIR POLITIC WOULD-BE, *a knight.*
PEREGRINE, *a gentleman traveler.*
NANO, *a dwarf.*
CASTRONE, *an eunuch.*
ANDROGYNO, *an hermaphrodite.*

GREGE (*or Mob*)

COMMENDATORI, *officers of justice.*
MERCATORI, *three merchants.*
AVOCATORI, *four magistrates.*
NOTARIO, *the register.*

LADY WOULD-BE, SIR POLITIC'S *Wife.*
CELIA, CORVINO'S *Wife.*
SERVITORI, *Servants, two* WAITING-WOMEN, *&c.*

1. Many of the characters' names are in Italian, and their translations are the names of animals—Volpone: fox; Mosca: fly; Voltore: vulture; Corbaccio: raven; Corvino: crow. Bonario means "good-natured"; Nano means "dwarf"; Castrone means "gelding"; and Androgyno means "man-woman," from the Greek.

SCENE — *Venice*

THE ARGUMENT

V OLPONE, childless, rich, feigns sick, despairs,
O ffers his state to hopes of several heirs,
L ies languishing: his parasite receives
P resents of all, assures, deludes; then weaves
O ther cross plots, which ope themselves, are told.
N ew tricks for safety are sought; they thrive: when, bold,
E ach tempts th' other again, and all are sold.

PROLOGUE

Now, luck yet send us, and a little wit
    Will serve to make our play hit;
According to the palates of the season,
    Here is rhyme, not empty of reason.
This we were bid to credit from our poet,
    Whose true scope, if you would know it,
In all his poems still hath been this measure,
    To mix profit with your pleasure;
And not as some, whose throats their envy failing,
    Cry hoarsely, "All he writes is railing:"
And when his plays come forth, think they can flout them,
    With saying, he was a year about them.
To this there needs no lie, but this his creature,
    Which was two months since no feature:
And though he dares give them five lives to mend it,
    'T is known, five weeks fully penn'd it,

1

From his own hand, without a coadjutor,
  Novice, journeyman, or tutor.
Yet thus much I can give you as a token
  Of his play's worth, no eggs are broken,
Nor quaking custards with fierce teeth affrighted,
  Wherewith your rout are so delighted;
Nor hales he in a gull,[1] old ends reciting,
  To stop gaps in his loose writing;
With such a deal of monstrous and forc'd action,
  As might make Bethlem[2] a faction:
Nor made he his play for jests stol'n from each table,
  But makes jests to fit his fable;
And so presents quick comedy refin'd,
  As best critics have design'd;
The laws of time, place, persons he observeth,
  From no needful rule he swerveth.
All gall and copperas[3] from his ink he draineth,
  Only a little salt remaineth,
Wherewith he'll rub your cheeks, till, red with laughter,
  They shall look fresh a week after.

---

1. *gull*] an imposition, a trick.
2. *Bethlem*] or Bedlam, popular name for the Hospital of St. Mary of Bethlehem, the London insane asylum.
3. *copperas*] green vitriol, used in making ink.

ACT I

Scene I. — A *room in Volpone's house*

Enter VOLPONE, MOSCA.

VOLP.   Good morning to the day; and next, my gold!
        Open the shrine, that I may see my saint.

[MOSCA *withdraws the curtain, and discovers piles of gold, plate, jewels,*
etc.]
        Hail the world's soul, and mine! More glad than is
        The teeming earth to see the long'd-for sun
        Peep through the horns of the celestial Ram,
        Am I, to view thy splendour dark'ning his;
        That lying here, amongst my other hoards,
        Show'st like a flame by night, or like the day
        Struck out of chaos, when all darkness fled
        Unto the centre.[1] O thou son of Sol,
        But brighter than thy father, let me kiss,
        With adoration, thee, and every relic
        Of sacred treasure in this blessed room.
        Well did wise poets, by thy glorious name,
        Title that age which they would have the best;
        Thou being the best of things, and far transcending
        All style of joy, in children, parents, friends,
        Or any other waking dream on earth:
        Thy looks when they to Venus did ascribe,
        They should have given her twenty thousand Cupids;
        Such are thy beauties and our loves! Dear saint,
        Riches, the dumb god, that giv'st all men tongues,

---

1. *centre*] center of the earth.

3

            That canst do nought, and yet mak'st men do all things;
            The price of souls; even hell, with thee to boot,
            Is made worth heaven. Thou art virtue, fame,
            Honour, and all things else. Who can get thee,
            He shall be noble, valiant, honest, wise —

MOS.   And what he will, sir. Riches are in fortune
            A greater good than wisdom is in nature.

VOLP.   True, my beloved Mosca. Yet I glory
            More in the cunning purchase of my wealth,
            Than in the glad possession, since I gain
            No common way; I use no trade, no venture;
            I wound no earth with ploughshares, I fat no beasts
            To feed the shambles; have no mills for iron,
            Oil, corn, or men, to grind them into powder;
            I blow no subtle glass, expose no ships
            To threat'nings of the furrow-faced sea;
            I turn no monies in the public bank,
            No usure private.

MOS.   No, sir, nor devour
            Soft prodigals. You shall ha' some will swallow
            A melting heir as glibly as your Dutch
            Will pills of butter, and ne'er purge for it;
            Tear forth the fathers of poor families
            Out of their beds, and coffin them alive
            In some kind clasping prison, where their bones
            May be forthcoming, when the flesh is rotten:
            But your sweet nature doth abhor these courses;
            You loathe the widow's or the orphan's tears
            Should wash your pavements, or their piteous cries
            Ring in your roofs, and beat the air for vengeance.

VOLP.   Right, Mosca; I do loathe it.

MOS.   And, besides, sir,
            You are not like the thresher that doth stand
            With a huge flail, watching a heap of corn,
            And, hungry, dares not taste the smallest grain,
            But feeds on mallows, and such bitter herbs;
            Nor like the merchant, who hath fill'd his vaults
            With Romagnia, rich and Candian[2] wines,

---

2. *Romagnia ... Candian*] Romagna is a district in Northern Italy on the Adriatic Sea; Candia is the Isle of Crete.

Yet drinks the lees of Lombard's vinegar:
You will not lie in straw, whilst moths and worms
Feed on your sumptuous hangings and soft beds;
You know the use of riches, and dare give now
From that bright heap, to me, your poor observer,
Or to your dwarf, or your hermaphrodite,
Your eunuch, or what other household trifle
Your pleasure allows maintenance —

VOL.   Hold thee, Mosca,
Take of my hand; thou strik'st on truth in all,
And they are envious term thee parasite.
Call forth my dwarf, my eunuch, and my fool,
And let 'em make me sport.   [*Exit* MOS.]
                          What should I do,
But cocker[3] up my genius, and live free
To all delights my fortune calls me to?
I have no wife, no parent, child, ally,
To give my substance to; but whom I make
Must be my heir; and this makes men observe[4] me:
This draws new clients daily to my house,
Women and men of every sex and age,
That bring me presents, send me plate, coin, jewels,
With hope that when I die (which they expect
Each greedy minute) it shall then return
Tenfold upon them; whilst some, covetous
Above the rest, seek to engross me whole,
And counter-work the one unto the other,
Contend in gifts, as they would seem in love:
All which I suffer, playing with their hopes,
And am content to coin 'em into profit,
And look upon their kindness, and take more,
And look on that; still bearing them in hand,[5]
Letting the cherry knock against their lips,
And draw it by their mouths, and back again. —
How now!

3. *cocker*] to pamper.
4. *observe*] pay obsequious attention to.
5. *bearing . . . hand*] deceiving them by false hopes.

SCENE II. — *The same*

To him re-enter MOSCA, *with* NANO, ANDROGYNO, *and* CASTRONE.

NAN.   "Now, room for fresh gamesters, who do will you to know,
They do bring you neither play nor university show;
And therefore do intreat you that whatsoever they rehearse,
May not fare a whit the worse, for the false pace of the verse.
If you wonder at this, you will wonder more ere we pass,
For know, here[1] is inclos'd the soul of Pythagoras,
That juggler divine, as hereafter shall follow;
Which soul, fast and loose, sir, came first from Apollo,
And was breath'd into Aethalides, Mercurius his son,
Where it had the gift to remember all that ever was done.
From thence it fled forth, and made quick transmigration
To goldy-lock'd Euphorbus, who was kill'd in good fashion,
At the siege of old Troy, by the cuckold of Sparta.
Hermotimus was next (I find it in my charta).
To whom it did pass, where no sooner it was missing,
But with one Pyrrhus of Delos it learn'd to go a-fishing;
And thence did it enter the sophist of Greece.
From Pythagore, she went into a beautiful piece,
Hight Aspasia, the meretrix; and the next toss of her
Was again of a whore, she became a philosopher,
Crates the cynick, as itself doth relate it:
Since kings, knights, and beggars, knaves, lords, and fools
    gat it,
Besides ox and ass, camel, mule, goat, and brock,[2]
In all which it hath spoke, as in the cobbler's cock.[3]
But I come not here to discourse of that matter,
Or his one, two, or three, or his great oath, BY QUATER![4]
His musics, his trigon,[5] his golden thigh,

1. *here*] in Androgyno.
2. *brock*] badger.
3. *cock*] This interlude is based on Lucian's dialogue between a cobbler and a cock.
4. *Quater*] quatre, the four in dice.
5. *trigon*] a triangular lyre.

	Or his telling how elements shift; but I
	Would ask, how of late thou hast suffer'd translation,
	And shifted thy coat in these days of reformation.
AND.	Like one of the reform'd, a fool, as you see,
	Counting all old doctrine heresy.
NAN.	But not on thine own forbid meats hast thou ventur'd?
AND.	On fish, when first a Carthusian I enter'd.
NAN.	Why, then thy dogmatical silence hath left thee?
AND.	Of that an obstreperous lawyer bereft me.
NAN.	O wonderful change, when sir lawyer forsook thee!
	For Pythagore's sake, what body then took thee?
AND.	A good dull mule.
NAN.	And how! by that means
	Thou wert brought to allow of the eating of beans?
AND.	Yes.
NAN.	But from the mule into whom didst thou pass?
AND.	Into a very strange beast, by some writers call'd an ass;
	By others a precise,[6] pure, illuminate brother
	Of those devour flesh, and sometimes one another;
	And will drop you forth a libel, or a sanctifi'd lie,
	Betwixt every spoonful of a nativity-pie.[7]
NAN.	Now quit thee, for heaven, of that profane nation.
	And gently report thy next transmigration.
AND.	To the same that I am.
NAN.	A creature of delight,
	And, what is more than a fool, an hermaphrodite!
	Now, prithee, sweet soul, in all thy variation,
	Which body wouldst thou choose to keep up thy station?
AND.	Troth, this I am in: even here would I tarry.
NAN.	'Cause here the delight of each sex thou canst vary?
AND.	Alas, those pleasures be stale and forsaken;
	No, 't is your fool wherewith I am so taken,
	The only one creature that I can call blessed;
	For all other forms I have prov'd most distressed.
NAN.	Spoke true, as thou wert in Pythagoras still.
	This learned opinion we celebrate will,
	Fellow eunuch, as behoves us, with all our wit and art,

6. *precise*] puritanical.
7. *nativity-pie*] Christmas-pie.

To dignify that whereof ourselves are so great and special a
    part."
VOLP.   Now, very, very pretty! Mosca, this
    Was thy invention?
MOS.   If it please my patron,
    Not else.
VOLP.   It doth, good Mosca.
MOS.   Then it was, sir.

[NANO *and* CASTRONE *sing.*]

SONG.

"Fools, they are the only nation
Worth men's envy or admiration;
Free from care or sorrow-taking,
Selves and others merry making:
All they speak or do is sterling.
Your fool he is your great man's darling,
And your ladies' sport and pleasure;
Tongue and bauble are his treasure.
E'en his face begetteth laughter,
And he speaks truth free from slaughter;[8]
He's the grace of every feast,
And sometimes the chiefest guest;
Hath his trencher[9] and his stool,
When wit waits upon the fool.
  O, who would not be
  He, he, he?"

One knocks without.

VOLP.   Who's that? Away! Look, Mosca.
    Fool, begone!
                [*Exeunt* NANO, CAST. *and* ANDRO.]
MOS.   'T is Signior Voltore, the advocate;
    I know him by his knock.
VOLP.   Fetch me my gown,
    My furs, and night-caps; say my couch is changing
    And let him entertain himself a while
    Without i' th' gallery. [*Exit* MOSCA.] Now, now my clients

---

8. *free from slaughter*] with impunity.
9. *trencher*] plate.

        Begin their visitation! Vulture, kite,
        Raven, and gorcrow,[10] all my birds of prey,
        That think me turning carcase, now they come:
        I am not for 'em yet.

[*Re-enter* MOSCA, *with the gown, etc.*]

              How now! the news?
MOS.   A piece of plate, sir.
VOLP.   Of what bigness?
MOS.   Huge,
        Massy, and antique, with your name inscrib'd,
        And arms engraven.
VOLP.   Good! and not a fox
        Stretcht on the earth, with fine delusive sleights,
        Mocking a gaping crow? ha, Mosca!
MOS.   Sharp, sir.
VOLP.   Give me my furs.

               [*Puts on his sick dress.*]
             Why dost thou laugh so, man?
MOS.   I cannot choose, sir, when I apprehend
        What thoughts he has without now, as he walks:
        That this might be the last gift he should give,
        That this would fetch you; if you died to-day,
        And gave him all, what he should be to-morrow;
        What large return would come of all his ventures;
        How he should worshipp'd be, and reverenc'd;
        Ride with his furs, and foot cloths; waited on
        By herds of fools and clients; have clear way
        Made for his mule, as letter'd as himself;
        Be call'd the great and learned advocate:
        And then concludes, there's nought impossible.
VOLP.   Yes, to be learned, Mosca.
MOS.   O, no: rich
        Implies it. Hood an ass with reverend purple,
        So you can hide his two ambitious[11] ears,
        And he shall pass for a cathedral doctor.
VOLP.   My caps, my caps, good Mosca. Fetch him in.

---

  10. *gorcrow*] carrion crow.
  11. *ambitious*] also a reference to the word's etymological sense of "moving round."

MOS.   Stay, sir; your ointment for your eyes.

VOLP.   That's true;
        Dispatch, dispatch: I long to have possession
        Of my new present.

MOS.   That, and thousands more,
        I hope to see you lord of.

VOLP.   Thanks, kind Mosca.

MOS.   And that, when I am lost in blended dust,
        And hundreds such as I am, in succession —

VOLP.   Nay, that were too much, Mosca.

MOS.   You shall live
        Still to delude these harpies.

VOLP.   Loving Mosca!
        'T is well: my pillow now, and let him enter.

                                     [*Exit* MOSCA.]

        Now, my feign'd cough, my phthisic,[12] and my gout,
        My apoplexy, palsy, and catarrhs,
        Help, with your forced functions, this my posture,
        Wherein, this three year, I have milk'd their hopes.
        He comes; I hear him — Uh! [*coughing*] uh! uh! uh! O —

SCENE III. — *The same*

VOLPONE; *re-enter* MOSCA, *introducing* VOLTORE *with a piece of plate.*

MOS.   You still are what you were, sir. Only you,
        Of all the rest, are he commands his love,
        And you do wisely to preserve it thus,
        With early visitation, and kind notes
        Of your good meaning to him, which, I know,
        Cannot but come most grateful. Patron! sir!
        Here's Signior Voltore is come —

VOLP.   [*Faintly.*]   What say you?

MOS.   Sir, Signior Voltore is come this morning
        To visit you.

12. *phthisic*] phthisis, a progressively wasting or consumptive condition.

VOLP.	I thank him.
MOS.	And hath brought
	A piece of antique plate, bought of St. Mark,[1]
	With which he here presents you.
VOLP.	He is welcome.
	Pray him to come more often.
MOS.	Yes.
VOLT.	What says he?
MOS.	He thanks you, and desires you see him often.
VOLP.	Mosca.
MOS.	My patron!
VOLP.	Bring him near, where is he?
	I long to feel his hand.
MOS.	The plate is here, sir.
VOLT.	How fare you, sir?
VOLP.	I thank you, Signior Voltore;
	Where is the plate? mine eyes are bad.
VOLT.	[*putting it into his hands.*] I'm sorry
	To see you still thus weak.
MOS.	[*Aside.*] That he's not weaker.
VOLP.	You are too munificent.
VOLT.	No, sir; would to heaven
	I could as well give health to you, as that plate!
VOLP.	You give, sir, what you can; I thank you. Your love
	Hath taste in this, and shall not be unanswer'd:
	I pray you see me often.
VOLT.	Yes, I shall, sir.
VOLP.	Be not far from me.
MOS.	Do you observe that, sir?
VOLP.	Hearken unto me still; it will concern you.
MOS.	You are a happy man, sir; know your good.
VOLP.	I cannot now last long—
MOS.	(*Aside.*) You are his heir, sir.
VOLT.	(*Aside.*) Am I?
VOLP.	I feel me going: Uh! uh! uh! uh!
	I'm sailing to my port. Uh! uh! uh! uh!
	And I am glad I am so near my haven.
MOS.	Alas, kind gentleman! Well, we must all go—

1. *bought of St. Mark*] at one of the goldsmith's shops beside St. Mark's.

VOLT. But, Mosca —

MOS.   Age will conquer.

VOLT.   Prithee, hear me;
Am I inscrib'd his heir for certain?

MOS.   Are you!
I do beseech you, sir, you will vouchsafe
To write me i' your family. All my hopes
Depend upon your worship: I am lost
Except the rising sun do shine on me.

VOLT. It shall both shine, and warm thee, Mosca.

MOS.   Sir,
I am a man that hath not done your love
All the worst offices: here I wear your keys,
See all your coffers and your caskets lock'd,
Keep the poor inventory of your jewels,
Your plate, and monies; am your steward, sir,
Husband your goods here.

VOLT.   But am I sole heir?

MOS. Without a partner, sir: confirm'd this morning:
The wax is warm yet, and the ink scarce dry
Upon the parchment.

VOLT.   Happy, happy me!
By what good chance, sweet Mosca?

MOS.   Your desert, sir;
I know no second cause.

VOLT.   Thy modesty
Is loth to know it; well, we shall requite it.

MOS. He ever lik'd your course, sir; that first took him.
I oft have heard him say how he admir'd
Men of your large profession, that could speak
To every cause, and things mere contraries,
Till they were hoarse again, yet all be law;
That, with most quick agility, could turn,
And return; make knots, and undo them;
Give forked counsel; take provoking gold
On either hand, and put it up; these men,
He knew, would thrive with their humility.
And, for his part, he thought he should be blest
To have his heir of such a suff'ring spirit,
So wise, so grave, of so perplex'd a tongue,

And loud withal, that would not wag, nor scarce
Lie still, without a fee; when every word
Your worship but lets fall, is a chequin!² —
                                        Another knocks.

Who's that? one knocks; I would not have you seen, sir.
And yet — pretend you came and went in haste;
I'll fashion an excuse — and, gentle sir,
When you do come to swim in golden lard,
Up to the arms in honey, that your chin
Is borne up stiff with fatness of the flood,
Think on your vassal; but remember me:
I ha' not been your worst of clients.

VOLT.   Mosca! —
MOS.   When will you have your inventory brought, sir?
Or see a copy of the will? — Anon!
I'll bring them to you, sir. Away, begone,
Put business i' your face.   [*Exit* VOLTORE.]
VOLP.   [*Springing up.*] Excellent Mosca!
Come hither, let me kiss thee.
MOS.   Keep you still, sir.
Here is Corbaccio.
VOLP.   Set the plate away:
The vulture's gone, and the old raven's come.

SCENE IV. — *The same*

MOSCA, VOLPONE.

MOS.   Betake you to your silence, and your sleep.
Stand there and multiply. [*Putting the plate to the rest.*] Now
    we shall see
A wretch who is indeed more impotent
Than this can feign to be; yet hopes to hop
Over his grave.

2. *chequin*] zechin, or zecchino, an Italian gold coin.

[*Enter* CORBACCIO.]

                      Signior Corbaccio!
         You're very welcome, sir.

CORB.   How does your patron?

MOS.   Troth, as he did, sir; no amends.

CORB.   What! mends he?

MOS.   No, sir: he's rather worse.

CORB.   That's well. Where is he?

MOS.   Upon his couch, sir, newly fall'n asleep.

CORB.   Does he sleep well?

MOS.   No wink, sir, all this night,
   Nor yesterday; but slumbers.[1]

CORB.   Good! he should take
   Some counsel of physicians: I have brought him
   An opiate here, from mine own doctor.

MOS.   He will not hear of drugs.

CORB.   Why? I myself
   Stood by while 't was made, saw all th' ingredients;
   And know it cannot but most gently work:
   My life for his, 't is but to make him sleep.

VOLP.   [*Aside.*] Ay, his last sleep, if he would take it.

MOS.   Sir,
   He has no faith in physic.

CORB.   Say you, say you?

MOS.   He has no faith in physic: he does think
   Most of your doctors are the greater danger,
   And worse disease, t' escape. I often have
   Heard him protest that your physician
   Should never be his heir.

CORB.   Not I his heir?

MOS.   Not your physician, sir.

CORB.   O, no, no, no,
   I do not mean it.

MOS.   No, sir, nor their fees
   He cannot brook: he says they flay a man
   Before they kill him.

CORB.   Right, I do conceive you.

MOS.   And then they do it by experiment;
   For which the law not only doth absolve 'em,

----

1. *slumbers*] dozes.

         But gives them great reward: and he is loth
         To hire his death so.

CORB.   It is true, they kill
         With as much licence as a judge.

MOS.   .   Nay, more;
         For he but kills, sir, where the law condemns,
         And these can kill him too.

CORB.   Ay, or me;
         Or any man. How does his apoplex?
         Is that strong on him still?

MOS.   Most violent.
         His speech is broken, and his eyes are set,
         His face drawn longer than 't was wont —

CORB.   How! how!
         Stronger than he was wont?

MOS.   No, sir; his face
         Drawn longer than 't was wont.

CORB.   O, good!

MOS.   His mouth
         Is ever gaping, and his eyelids hang.

CORB.   Good.

MOS. .   A freezing numbness stiffens all his joints,
         And makes the colour of his flesh like lead.

CORB.   'T is good.

MOS.   His pulse beats slow, and dull.

CORB.   Good symptoms still.

MOS.   And from his brain —

CORB.   Ha? How? Not from his brain?

MOS.   Yes, sir, and from his brain —

CORB.   I conceive you; good.

MOS.   Flows a cold sweat, with a continual rheum,
         Forth the resolved corners of his eyes.

CORB.   Is 't possible? Yet I am better, ha!
         How does he with the swimming of his head?

MOS.   O, sir, 't is past the scotomy;[2] he now
         Hath lost his feeling, and hath left to snort:
         You hardly can perceive him, that he breathes.

CORB.   Excellent, excellent! sure I shall outlast him:
         This makes me young again, a score of years.

   2. *scotomy*] imperfect sight, with giddiness.

Mos.	I was a-coming for you, sir.
Corb.	Has he made his will?
	What has he giv'n me?
Mos.	No, sir.
Corb.	Nothing! ha?
Mos.	He has not made his will, sir.
Corb.	Oh, oh, oh!
	What then did Voltore, the lawyer, here?
Mos.	He smelt a carcase, sir, when he but heard
	My master was about his testament;
	As I did urge him to it for your good —
Corb.	He came unto him, did he? I thought so.
Mos.	Yes, and presented him this piece of plate.
Corb.	To be his heir?
Mos.	I do not know, sir.
Corb.	True:
	I know it too.
Mos.	[*Aside.*] By your own scale, sir.
Corb.	Well,
	I shall prevent him yet. See, Mosca, look,
	Here I have brought a bag of bright chequins,
	Will quite lay down his plate.
Mos.	[*taking the bag.*] Yea, marry, sir.
	This is true physic, this your sacred medicine;
	No talk of opiates to this great elixir!
Corb.	'T is *aurum palpabile*, if not *potabile.*[3]
Mos.	It shall be minister'd to him in his bowl.
Corb.	Ay, do, do, do.
Mos.	Most blessed cordial!
	This will recover him.
Corb.	Yes, do, do, do.
Mos.	I think it were not best, sir.
Corb.	What?
Mos.	To recover him.
Corb.	O, no, no, no; by no means.
Mos.	Why, sir, this
	Will work some strange effect, if he but feel it.

---

3. aurum palpabile . . . potabile] palpable, material gold, if not *aurum potabile*, or drinkable gold, which was the elixir.

CORB.   'T is true, therefore forbear; I'll take my venture:
       Give me 't again.
MOS.   At no hand: pardon me:
       You shall not do yourself that wrong, sir. I
       Will so advise you, you shall have it all.
CORB.   How?
MOS.   All, sir; 't is your right, your own; no man
       Can claim a part: 't is yours without a rival,
       Decreed by destiny.
CORB.   How, how, good Mosca?
MOS.   I'll tell you, sir. This fit he shall recover, —
CORB.   I do conceive you.
MOS.   And on first advantage
       Of his gain'd sense, will I re-importune him
       Unto the making of his testament:
       And show him this.   [*Pointing to the money.*]

CORB.   Good, good.
MOS.   'T is better yet,
       If you will hear, sir.
CORB.   Yes, with all my heart.
MOS.   Now would I counsel you, make home with speed;
       There, frame a will; whereto you shall inscribe
       My master your sole heir.
CORB.   And disinherit
       My son?
MOS.   O, sir, the better: for that colour[4]
       Shall make it much more taking.
CORB.   O, but colour?
MOS.   This will, sir, you shall send it unto me.
       Now, when I come to inforce, as I will do,
       Your cares, your watchings, and your many prayers,
       Your more than many gifts, your this day's present,
       And last, produce your will; where, without thought,
       Or least regard, unto your proper issue,
       A son so brave, and highly meriting,
       The stream of your diverted love hath thrown you
       Upon my master, and made him your heir;

---

4. *colour*] circumstance or appearance.

	He cannot be so stupid, or stone-dead,
	But out of conscience and mere gratitude —
CORB.	He must pronounce me his?
MOS.	'T is true.
CORB.	This plot
	Did I think on before.
MOS.	I do believe it.
CORB.	Do you not believe it?
MOS.	Yes, sir,
CORB.	Mine own project.
MOS.	Which, when he hath done, sir —
CORB.	Publish'd me his heir?
MOS.	And you so certain to survive him —
CORB.	Ay.
MOS.	Being so lusty a man —
CORB.	'T is true.
MOS.	Yes, sir —
CORB.	I thought on that too. See, how he should be
	The very organ to express my thoughts!
MOS.	You have not only done yourself a good —
CORB.	But multipli'd it on my son.
MOS.	'T is right, sir.
CORB.	Still, my invention.
MOS.	'Las, sir! heaven knows,
	It hath been all my study, all my care,
	(I e'en grow gray withal,) how to work things —
CORB.	I do conceive, sweet Mosca.
MOS.	You are he
	For whom I labour here.
CORB.	Ay, do, do, do:
	I'll straight about it. [*Going.*]
MOS.	[*Aside.*] Rook go with you,[5] raven!
CORB.	I know thee honest.
MOS.	You do lie, sir!
CORB.	And —
MOS.	Your knowledge is no better than your ears, sir.
CORB.	I do not doubt to be a father to thee.

5. *Rook go with you*] May you be rooked, or cheated.

MOS.	Nor I to gull my brother of his blessing.
CORB.	I may ha' my youth restor'd to me, why not?
MOS.	Your worship is a precious ass!
CORB.	What sayst thou?
MOS.	I do desire your worship to make haste, sir.
CORB.	'T is done, 't is done; I go. [*Exit.*]
VOLP.	[*leaping from his couch.*] O, I shall burst!

VOLP.   [*leaping from his couch.*] O, I shall burst!
Let out my sides, let out my sides —

MOS.   Contain
Your flux of laughter, sir: you know this hope
Is such a bait, it covers any hook.

VOLP.   O, but thy working, and thy placing it!
I cannot hold; good rascal, let me kiss thee:
I never knew thee in so rare a humour.

MOS.   Alas, sir, I but do as I am taught;
Follow your grave instructions; give them words;
Pour oil into their ears, and send them hence.

VOLP.   'T is true, 't is true. What a rare punishment
Is avarice to itself!

MOS.   Ay, with our help, sir.

VOLP.   So many cares, so many maladies,
So many fears attending on old age.
Yea, so often call'd on, as no wish
Can be more frequent with 'em, their limbs faint,
Their senses dull, their seeing, hearing, going,
All dead before them; yea, their very teeth,
Their instruments of eating, failing them:
Yet this is reckon'd life! Nay, here was one,
Is now gone home, that wishes to live longer!
Feels not his gout, nor palsy; feigns himself
Younger by scores of years, flatters his age
With confident belying it, hopes he may
With charms like Aeson,[6] have his youth restor'd;
And with these thoughts so battens, as if fate
Would be as easily cheated on as he,
And all turns air! Who's that there, now? a third!

                                  Another knocks.

---

6. *Aeson*] Jason's father, who was restored to life by the charm of Medea the witch.

MOS.	Close, to your couch again; I hear his voice.
	It is Corvino, our spruce merchant.
VOLP.	[*Lies down as before.*] Dead.[7]
MOS.	Another bout, sir, with your eyes [*Anointing them*]. Who's
	there?

SCENE V. — *The same*

MOSCA, VOLPONE. *Enter* CORVINO.

MOS.	Signior Corvino! come most wish'd for! O,
	How happy were you, if you knew it, now!
CORV.	Why? what? wherein?
MOS.	The tardy hour is come, sir.
CORV.	He is not dead?
MOS.	Not dead, sir, but as good;
	He knows no man.
CORV.	How shall I do then?
MOS.	Why, sir?
CORV.	I have brought him here a pearl.
MOS.	Perhaps he has
	So much remembrance left as to know you, sir:
	He still calls on you; nothing but your name
	Is in his mouth. Is your pearl orient,[1] sir?
CORV.	Venice was never owner of the like.
VOLP.	[*faintly.*] Signior Corvino!
MOS.	Hark!
VOLP.	Signior Corvino.
MOS.	He calls you; step and give it him. — He's here, sir.
	And he has brought you a rich pearl.
CORV.	How do you, sir?
	Tell him it doubles the twelve carat.
MOS.	Sir,

7. *Dead*] "Pretend that I'm dead."

___

1. *orient*] brilliant or lustrous, and therefore precious.

	He cannot understand, his hearing's gone;
	And yet it comforts him to see you —
CORV.	Say
	I have a diamond for him, too.
MOS.	Best show 't, sir;

He cannot understand, his hearing's gone;
And yet it comforts him to see you —

CORV.   Say
I have a diamond for him, too.

MOS.   Best show 't, sir;
Put it into his hand: 't is only there
He apprehends: he has his feeling yet.
See how he grasps it!

CORV.   'Las, good gentleman!
How pitiful the sight is!

MOS.   Tut, forget, sir.
The weeping of an heir should still be laughter
Under a visor.

CORV.   Why, am I his heir?

MOS.   Sir, I am sworn, I may not show the will
Till he be dead; but here has been Corbaccio,
Here has been Voltore, here were others too,
I cannot number 'em, they were so many;
All gaping here for legacies: but I,
Taking the vantage of his naming you,
Signior Corvino, Signior Corvino, took
Paper, and pen, and ink, and there I ask'd him
Whom he would have his heir! *Corvino*. Who
Should be executor? *Corvino*. And
To any question he was silent to,
I still interpreted the nods he made,
Through weakness, for consent: and sent home th' others,
Nothing bequeath'd them, but to cry and curse.

CORV.   O, my dear Mosca. (*They embrace.*) Does he not perceive us?

MOS.   No more than a blind harper. He knows no man,
No face of friend, nor name of any servant,
Who 't was that fed him last, or gave him drink:
Not those he hath begotten, or brought up,
Can he remember.

CORV.   Has he children?

MOS.   Bastards,
Some dozen, or more, that he begot on beggars,
Gypsies, and Jews, and black-moors, when he was drunk.
Knew you not that, sir? 't is the common fable,
The dwarf, the fool, the eunuch, are all his;

He's the true father of his family,
In all save me: — but he has giv'n 'em nothing.

CORV. That's well, that's well! Art sure he does not hear us?

MOS. Sure, sir! why, look you, credit your own sense.

[*Shouts in* VOLP.'S *ear.*]

The pox approach, and add to your diseases,
If it would send you hence the sooner, sir,
For your incontinence, it hath deserv'd it
Throughly and throughly, and the plague to boot! —
You may come near, sir. — Would you would once close
Those filthy eyes of yours, that flow with slime
Like two frog-pits; and those same hanging cheeks,
Cover'd with hide instead of skin — Nay, help, sir[2] —
That look like frozen dish-clouts set on end!

CORV. Or like an old smok'd wall, on which the rain
Ran down in streaks!

MOS.   Excellent, sir! speak out:
You may be louder yet; a culverin[3]
Discharged in his ear would hardly bore it.

CORV. His nose is like a common sewer, still running.

MOS. 'T is good! And what his mouth?

CORV.   A very draught.[4]

MOS. O, stop it up —

CORV.   By no means.

MOS.   Pray you, let me:
Faith I could stifle him rarely with a pillow
As well as any woman that should keep him.

CORV. Do as you will; but I'll begone.

MOS.   Be so;
It is your presence makes him last so long.

CORV. I pray you use no violence.

MOS.   No, sir! why?
Why should you be thus scrupulous, pray you, sir?

CORV. Nay, at your discretion.

MOS.   Well, good sir, be gone.

CORV. I will not trouble him now to take my pearl.

2. *Nay, help, sir*] said to Corvino, asking for his help in the abuse.
3. *culverin*] cannon.
4. *draught*] cesspool.

MOS. · · · · Puh! nor your diamond. What a needless care
Is this afflicts you? Is not all here yours?
Am not I here, whom you have made your creature?
That owe my being to you?

CORV. · · · · · · · · · · · · · · Grateful Mosca!
Thou art my friend, my fellow, my companion,
My partner, and shalt share in all my fortunes.

MOS. · · · · Excepting one.

CORV. · · · · · · · · · What's that?

MOS. · · · · · · · Your gallant wife, sir. · · · · *[Exit CORV.]*
Now is he gone: we had no other means
To shoot him hence but this.

VOLP. · · · · · · · · · · · · · My divine Mosca!
Thou hast to-day outgone thyself. Who's there?

· *Another knocks.*

I will be troubled with no more. Prepare
Me music, dances, banquets, all delights;
The Turk is not more sensual in his pleasures
Than will Volpone. *[Exit* MOS.*]* Let me see; a pearl!
A diamond! plate! chequins! Good morning's purchase.[5]
Why, this is better than rob churches, yet;
Or fat, by eating, once a month, a man —

[Re-enter MOSCA.*]*

Who is 't?

MOS. · · · · The beauteous Lady Would-be, sir,
Wife to the English knight, Sir Politic Would-be,
(This is the style, sir, is directed me,)
Hath sent to know how you have slept to-night,
And if you would be visited?

VOLP. · · · · · · · · · · · · · · · Not now:
Some three hours hence.

MOS. · · · · · · · · · · · · I told the squire[6] so much.

VOLP. · · · · When I am high with mirth and wine; then then:
'Fore heaven, I wonder at the desperate valour
Of the bold English, that they dare let loose
Their wives to all encounters!

---

5. *purchase*] booty.
6. *squire*] messenger.

MOS.   Sir, this knight
      Had not his name for nothing, he is *politic*,
      And knows, howe'er his wife affect strange airs,
      She hath not yet the face to be dishonest:
      But had she Signior Corvino's wife's face —
VOLP.   Hath she so rare a face?
MOS.   O, sir, the wonder,
      The blazing star of Italy! a wench
      Of the first year, a beauty ripe as harvest!
      Whose skin is whiter than a swan all over,
      Than silver, snow, or lilies; a soft lip,
      Would tempt you to eternity of kissing!
      And flesh that melteth in the touch to blood!
      Bright as your gold, and lovely as your gold!
VOLP.   Why had not I known this before?
MOS.   Alas, sir,
      Myself but yesterday discover'd it.
VOLP.   How might I see her?
MOS.   O, not possible;
      She's kept as warily as is your gold;
      Never does come abroad, never takes air
      But at a windore.[7] All her looks are sweet,
      As the first grapes or cherries, and are watch'd
      As near as they are.
VOLP.   I must see her.
MOS.   Sir,
      There is a guard of ten spies thick upon her,
      All his whole household; each of which is set
      Upon his fellow, and have all their charge,
      When he goes out, when he comes in, examin'd.
VOLP.   I will go see her, though but at her windore.
MOS.   In some disguise then.
VOLP.   That is true; I must
      Maintain mine own shape still the same: we'll think.
                                     [*Exeunt.*]

7. *windore*] window.

ACT II

SCENE I. — *St. Mark's Place; a retired corner before Corvino's house*

Enter SIR POLITIC WOULD-BE, *and* PEREGRINE.

SIR P.   Sir, to a wise man, all the world's his soil:
It is not Italy, nor France, nor Europe,
That must bound me, if my fates call me forth.
Yet I protest, it is no salt[1] desire
Of seeing countries, shifting a religion,
Nor any disaffection to the state
Where I was bred, and unto which I owe
My dearest plots, hath brought me out, much less
That idle, antique, stale, grey-headed project
Of knowing men's minds and manners, with Ulysses!
But a peculiar humour of my wife's
Laid for this height[2] of Venice, to observe,
To quote,[3] to learn the language, and so forth —
I hope you travel, sir, with licence?

PER.   Yes.

SIR P.   I dare the safelier converse — How long, sir,
Since you left England?

PER.   Seven weeks.

SIR P.   So lately!
You have not been with my lord ambassador?

PER.   Not yet, sir.

1. *salt*] frivolous.
2. *height*] latitude.
3. *To quote*] to make note of.

25

SIR P.   Pray you, what news, sir, vents our climate?
        I heard last night a most strange thing reported
        By some of my lord's followers, and I long
        To hear how 't will be seconded.

PER.   What was 't, sir?

SIR P.   Marry, sir, of a raven that should build
        In a ship royal of the king's.

PER.   [*Aside.*] This fellow,
        Does he gull me, trow? or is gull'd? Your name, sir?

SIR P.   My name is Politic Would-be.

PER.   [*Aside.*] O, that speaks him.
        A knight, sir?

SIR P.   A poor knight, sir.

PER.   Your lady
        Lies[4] here in Venice, for intelligence
        Of tires and fashions, and behaviour,
        Among the courtesans? The fine Lady Would-be?

SIR P.   Yes, sir; the spider and the bee ofttimes
        Suck from one flower.

PER.   Good Sir Politic,
        I cry you mercy; I have heard much of you:
        'T is true, sir, of your raven.

SIR P.   On your knowledge?

PER.   Yes, and your lion's whelping in the Tower.

SIR P.   Another whelp![5]

PER.   Another, sir.

SIR P.   Now heaven!
        What prodigies be these? The fires at Berwick!
        And the new star! These things concurring, strange,
        And full of omen! Saw you those meteors?

PER.   I did, sir.

SIR P.   Fearful! Pray you, sir, confirm me,
        Were there three porpoises seen above the bridge,
        As they give out?

PER.   Six, and a sturgeon, sir.

SIR P.   I am astonish'd.

---

4. *Lies*] stays.
5. *Another whelp!*] A lion is recorded to have been born in the Tower of London, Aug. 5, 1604, the first born in captivity in England.

PER.   Nay, sir, be not so;
I'll tell you a greater prodigy than these.

SIR P.   What should these things portend?

PER.   The very day
(Let me be sure) that I put forth from London,
There was a whale discover'd in the river,
As high as Woolwich, that had waited there,
Few know how many months, for the subversion
Of the Stode fleet.

SIR P.   Is 't possible? Believe it,
'T was either sent from Spain, or the archduke's
Spinola's whale,[6] upon my life, my credit!
Will they not leave these projects? Worthy sir,
Some other news.

PER.   Faith, Stone the fool is dead,
And they do lack a tavern fool extremely.

SIR P.   Is Mass Stone dead?

PER.   He's dead, sir; why, I hope
You thought him not immortal? — [*Aside.*] O, this knight,
Were he well known, would be a precious thing
To fit our English stage: he that should write
But such a fellow, should be thought to feign
Extremely, if not maliciously.

SIR P.   Stone dead!

PER.   Dead. — Lord! how deeply, sir, you apprehend it!
He was no kinsman to you?

SIR P.   That I know of.
Well! that same fellow was an unknown fool.

PER.   And yet you knew him, it seems?

SIR P.   I did so. Sir,
I knew him one of the most dangerous heads
Living within the state, and so I held him.

PER.   Indeed, sir?

SIR P.   While he liv'd, in action,
He has receiv'd weekly intelligence,

6. *'Twas either sent ... Spinola's whale*] Sir Politic believes the whale's presence in the
Thames River is some Spanish plot, perhaps directed by Archduke Albert, who ruled the
Spanish Netherlands in the name of Philip II, or General Ambrosio Spinola, leader of
the Spanish armies in Holland.

PER.

SIR P.

PER.

SIR P.

PER.

SIR P.

PER.

SIR P.

Upon my knowledge, out of the Low Countries,
For all parts of the world, in cabbages;
And those dispens'd again to ambassadors,
In oranges, musk-melons, apricots,
Lemons, pome-citrons, and such-like; sometimes
In Colchester oysters, and your Selsey cockles.

You make me wonder.

               Sir, upon my knowledge.
Nay, I've observ'd him, at your public ordinary,
Take his advertisement[7] from a traveller,
A conceal'd statesman, in a trencher of meat;
And instantly, before the meal was done,
Convey an answer in a tooth-pick.

                              Strange!
How could this be, sir?

                    Why, the meat was cut
So like his character, and so laid as he
Must easily read the cipher.

                       I have heard,
He could not read, sir.

                  So 't was given out,
In policy, by those that did employ him:
But he could read, and had your languages,
And to 't, as sound a noddle —

                   I have heard, sir,
That your baboons were spies, and that they were
A kind of subtle nation near to China.

Ay, ay, your Mamaluchi.[8] Faith, they had
Their hand in a French plot or two; but they
Were so extremely giv'n to women, as
They made discovery of all: yet I
Had my advices here, on Wednesday last,
From one of their own coat, they were return'd,
Made their relations, as the fashion is,
And now stand fair for fresh employment.

---

7. *advertisement*] information.
8. *Mamaluchi*] Italian form of mamelukes, slaves and warriors originally from Asia Minor, who for many years controlled the throne of Egypt.

PER.   [*Aside.*]   Heart!
    This Sir Pol will be ignorant of nothing. —
    It seems, sir, you know all.
SIR P.   Not all, sir; but
    I have some general notions. I do love
    To note and to observe: though I live out,
    Free from the active torrent, yet I'd mark
    The currents and the passages of things
    For mine own private use; and know the ebbs
    And flows of state.
PER.   Believe it, sir, I hold
    Myself in no small tie[9] unto my fortunes,
    For casting me thus luckily upon you,
    Whose knowledge, if your bounty equal it,
    May do me great assistance, in instruction
    For my behaviour, and my bearing, which
    Is yet so rude and raw.
SIR P.   Why? came you forth
    Empty of rules for travel?
PER.   Faith, I had
    Some common ones, from out that vulgar grammar,
    Which he that cri'd Italian to me, taught me.
SIR P.   Why, this it is that spoils all our brave bloods,
    Trusting our hopeful gentry unto pedants,
    Fellows of outside, and mere bark. You seem
    To be a gentleman of ingenuous race: —
    I not profess it, but my fate hath been
    To be, where I have been consulted with,
    In this high kind, touching some great men's sons,
    Persons of blood and honour. —
PER.   Who be these, sir?

9. *tie*] obligation.

Scene II.

To them enter Mosca *and* Nano *disguised, followed by persons with
materials for erecting a stage.*

Mos.　　Under that window, there 't must be. The same.

Sir P.　Fellows, to mount a bank. Did your instructor
　　　　In the dear tongues, never discourse to you
　　　　Of the Italian mountebanks?[1]

Per.　　　　　　　　　　　　　　Yes, sir.

Sir P.　　　　　　　　　　　　　　　　　Why,
　　　　Here shall you see one.

Per.　　　　　　　　　　They are quacksalvers,
　　　　Fellows that live by venting oils and drugs.

Sir P.　Was that the character he gave you of them?

Per.　　As I remember.

Sir P.　　　　　　　Pity his ignorance.
　　　　They are the only knowing men of Europe!
　　　　Great general scholars, excellent physicians,
　　　　Most admir'd statesmen, profest favourites
　　　　And cabinet counsellors to the greatest princes;
　　　　The only languag'd men of all the world!

Per.　　And, I have heard, they are most lewd[2] impostors;
　　　　Made all of terms and shreds; no less beliers
　　　　Of great men's favours, than their own vile medicines;
　　　　Which they will utter upon monstrous oaths;
　　　　Selling that drug for twopence, ere they part,
　　　　Which they have valu'd at twelve crowns before.

Sir P.　Sir, calumnies are answer'd best with silence.
　　　　Yourself shall judge. — Who is it mounts, my friends?

Mos.　　Scoto of Mantua,[3] sir.

---

1. *mountebanks*] from the Italian *monta in banco*, "to mount the bench," they were part street performer and part patent-medicine salesman.
2. *lewd*] ignorant.
3. *Scoto of Mantua*] a real performer, juggler and magician who visited England and performed before Queen Elizabeth.

SIR P.   Is 't he? Nay, then
I'll proudly promise, sir, you shall behold.
Another man than has been phant'sied[4] to you.
I wonder yet, that he should mount his bank,
Here in this nook, that has been wont t' appear
In face of the Piazza! — Here he comes.

[*Enter* VOLPONE, *disguised as a mountebank Doctor, and followed by a crowd of people.*]

VOLP.   Mount, zany. [*To* NANO.]
MOB.   Follow, follow, follow, follow!
SIR P.   See how the people follow him! he's a man
May write ten thousand crowns in bank here. Note,
                               [VOLPONE *mounts the stage.*]
Mark but his gesture: — I do use to observe
The state he keeps in getting up.
PER.   'T is worth it, sir.
VOLP.   "Most noble gentlemen, and my worthy patrons! It may seem
strange that I, your Scoto Mantuano, who was ever wont to
fix my bank in the face of the public Piazza, near the shelter
of the Portico to the Procuratia, should now, after eight
months' absence from this illustrious city of Venice, humbly retire myself into an obscure nook of the Piazza."
SIR P.   Did not I now object the same?
PER.   Peace, sir.
VOLP.   "Let me tell you: I am not, as your Lombard proverb saith,
cold on my feet; or content to part with my commodities at
a cheaper rate than I am accustom'd: look not for it. Nor
that the calumnious reports of that impudent detractor, and
shame to our profession (Alessandro Buttone, I mean), who
gave out, in public, I was condemn'd *a' sforzato*[5] to the
galleys, for poisoning the Cardinal Bembo's — cook, hath at
all attach'd, much less dejected me. No, no, worthy gentlemen; to tell you true, I cannot endure to see the rabble of
these ground *ciarlitani*,[6] that spread their cloaks on the
pavement, as if they meant to do feats of activity, and then

---

4. *phant'sied*] described, misrepresented.
5. a' sforzato] to hard labor.
6. ciarlitani] petty charlatans, imposters.

come in lamely, with their mouldy tales out of Boccacio,
like stale Tabarin,[7] the fabulist: some of them discoursing
their travels, and of their tedious captivity in the Turk's
galleys, when, indeed, were the truth known, they were the
Christian's galleys, where very temperately they eat bread,
and drunk water, as a wholesome penance, enjoin'd them
by their confessors, for base pilferies."

SIR P.   Note but his bearing, and contempt of these.

VOLP.   "These turdy-facy-nasty-paty-lousy-fartical rogues, with one
poor groat's-worth of unprepar'd antimony, finely wrapt up
in several *scartoccios*,[8] are able, very well, to kill their twenty
a week, and play; yet these meagre, starv'd spirits, who have
half stopt the organs of their minds with earthy oppilations,[9]
want not their favourers among your shrivell'd salad-eating
artisans, who are overjoy'd that they may have their half-
pe'rth of physic; though it purge 'em into another world, 't
makes no matter."

SIR P.   Excellent! ha' you heard better language, sir?

VOLP.   "Well, let 'em go. And, gentlemen, honourable gentlemen,
know, that for this time, our bank, being thus removed from
the clamours of the *canaglia*[10] shall be the scene of pleasure and delight; for I have nothing to sell, little or nothing
to sell."

SIR P.   I told you, sir, his end.

PER.   You did so, sir.

VOLP.   "I protest, I, and my six servants, are not able to make of this
precious liquor so fast as it is fetch'd away from my lodging
by gentlemen of your city; strangers of the Terra-firma;[11]
worshipful merchants; ay, and senators too: who, ever since
my arrival, have detain'd me to their uses, by their splen-
didous liberalities. And worthily; for, what avails your rich
man to have his magazines stuft with *moscadelli*, or of the
purest grape, when his physicians prescribe him, on pain of

7. *Tabarin*] a French charlatan of the early seventeenth century, whose jests were published.
8. scartoccios] folds of paper.
9. *oppilations*] obstructions.
10. canaglia] rabble.
11. *Terra-firma*] Continental possessions of Venice.

death, to drink nothing but water cocted[12] with aniseeds? O
health! health! the blessing of the rich! the riches of the
poor! who can buy thee at too dear a rate, since there is no
enjoying this world without thee? Be not then so sparing of
your purses, honourable gentlemen, as to abridge the natural course of life —"

PER.   You see his end.

SIR P.   Ay, is 't not good?

VOLP.   "For when a humid flux, or catarrh, by the mutability of air,
falls from your head into an arm or shoulder, or any other
part; take you a ducket, or your chequin of gold, and apply
to the place affected: see what good effect it can work. No,
no, 't is this blessed *unguento*,[13] this rare extraction, that
hath only power to disperse all malignant humours, that
proceed either of hot, cold, moist, or windy causes —"

PER.   I would he had put in dry too.

SIR P.   Pray you observe.

VOLP.   "To fortify the most indigest and crude stomach, ay, were it of
one that, through extreme weakness, vomited blood, applying only a warm napkin to the place, after the unction and
fricace;[14] — for the *vertigine*[15] in the head, putting but a
drop into your nostrils, likewise behind the ears; a most
sovereign and approv'd remedy; the *mal caduco*,[16] cramps,
convulsions, paralyses, epilepsies, *tremorcordia*, retir'd
nerves, ill vapours of the spleen, stoppings of the liver, the
stone, the strangury, *hernia ventosa, iliaca passio*;[17] stops a
dysenteria immediately; easeth the torsion[18] of the small
guts; and cures *melancholia hypocondriaca*, being taken
and appli'd, according to my printed receipt. (*Pointing to
his bill and his glass.*) For this is the physician, this the
medicine; this counsels, this cures; this gives the direction,
this works the effect; and, in sum, both together may be

12. *cocted*] boiled.
13. unguento] ointment.
14. *fricace*] an oil to be rubbed in.
15. vertigine] dizziness.
16. mal caduco] epilepsy.
17. hernia ventosa, iliaca passio] gassy hernia, cramps of the small intestine.
18. *torsion*] twisting.

term'd an abstract of the theoric and practic in the Aescula-
pian art. 'T will cost you eight crowns. And, — Zan Fritada,
prithee sing a verse extempore in honour of it."

SIR P.   How do you like him, sir?
PER.   Most strangely, I!
SIR P.   Is not his language rare?
PER.   But alchemy,
I never heard the like; or Broughton's[19] books.

[NANO *sings*.]

> Had old Hippocrates, or Galen,
> That to their books put med'cines all in,
> But known this secret, they had never
> (Of which they will be guilty ever)
> Been murderers of so much paper,
> Or wasted many a hurtless taper;
> No Indian drug had e'er been fam'd,
> Tobacco, sassafras not nam'd;
> Ne yet of guacum one small stick, sir,
> Nor Raymund Lully's[20] great elixir.
> Ne had been known the Danish Gonswart,[21]
> Or Paracelsus, with his long sword.[22]

PER.   All this, yet, will not do; eight crowns is high.
VOLP.   "No more. — Gentlemen, if I had but time to discourse to you
the miraculous effects of this my oil, surnam'd Oglio del
Scoto; with the countless catalogue of those I have cur'd of
th' aforesaid, and many more diseases; the patents and
privileges of all the princes and commonwealths of Chris-
tendom; or but the depositions of those that appear'd on my
part, before the signiory of the Sanita and most learned
College of Physicians; where I was authoris'd, upon notice
taken of the admirable virtues of my medicaments, and
mine own excellency in matter of rare and unknown secrets, not only to disperse them publicly in this famous city,
but in all the territories, that happily joy under the govern-

---

19. *Broughton's books*] Hugh Broughton, a Puritan divine and rabbinical scholar.
20. *Raymond Lully*] a Spanish mystic philosopher (ca. 1235–1316).
21. *Gonswart*] unidentified.
22. *Paracelsus*] famous 16th-century German doctor, who carried his familiar spirits in the handle of his sword.

ment of the most pious and magnificent states of Italy. But may some other gallant fellow say, 'O, there be divers that make profession to have as good, and as experimented receipts as yours:' indeed, very many have assay'd, like apes, in imitation of that, which is really and essentially in me, to make of this oil; bestow'd great cost in furnaces, stills, alembics,[23] continual fires, and preparation of the ingredients (as indeed there goes to it six hundred several simples, besides some quantity of human fat, for the conglutination, which we buy of the anatomists), but when these practitioners come to the last decoction, blow, blow, puff, puff, and all flies in fumo:[24] ha, ha, ha! Poor wretches! I rather pity their folly and indiscretion, than their loss of time and money; for those may be recover'd by industry: but to be a fool born, is a disease incurable.

"For myself, I always from my youth have endeavour'd to get the rarest secrets, and book them, either in exchange, or for money; I spar'd nor cost nor labour, where anything was worthy to be learned. And, gentlemen, honourable gentlemen, I will undertake, by virtue of chymical art, out of the honourable hat that covers your head, to extract the four elements; that is to say, the fire, air, water, and earth, and return you your felt without burn or stain. For, whilst others have been at the *ballo*,[25] I have been at my book; and am now past the craggy paths of study, and come to the flowery plains of honour and reputation."

SIR P.   I do assure you, sir, that is his aim.
VOLP.   "But to our price —"
PER.   And that withal, Sir Pol.
VOLP.   "You all know, honourable gentlemen, I never valu'd this *ampulla*, or vial, at less than eight crowns; but for this time, I am content to be depriv'd of it for six; six crowns is the price, and less in courtesy I know you cannot offer me; take it or leave it, howsoever, both it and I am at your service. I ask you not as the value of the thing, for then I should demand of you a thousand crowns, so the Cardinals Mon-

23. *alembics*] distilleries, also retorts.
24. *in fumo*] in smoke.
25. ballo] ball; dancing.

talto, Fernese, the great Duke of Tuscany, my gossip,[26] with
divers other princes, have given me; but I despise money.
Only to show my affection to you, honourable gentlemen,
and your illustrious State here, I have neglected the mes-
sages of these princes, mine own offices, fram'd my journey
hither, only to present you with the fruits of my travels. —
Tune your voices once more to the touch of your instruments, and give the honourable assembly some delightful
recreation."

PER.   What monstrous and most painful circumstance
           Is here, to get some three or four gazettes,[27]
           Some threepence i' the whole! for that 't will come to.

                         [NANO *sings.*]

               You that would last long, list to my song,
               Make no more coil, but buy of this oil.
               Would you be ever fair and young?
               Stout of teeth, and strong of tongue?
               Tart of palate? quick of ear?
               Sharp of sight? of nostril clear?
               Moist of hand? and light of foot?
               Or, I will come nearer to 't,
               Would you live free from all diseases?
               Do the act your mistress pleases,
               Yet fright all aches from your bones?
               Here's a med'cine for the nones.[28]

VOLP.   "Well, I am in a humour at this time to make a present of the
           small quantity my coffer contains; to the rich in courtesy,
           and to the poor for God's sake. Wherefore now mark: I ask'd
           you six crowns; and six crowns, at other times, you have
           paid me; you shall not give me six crowns, nor five, nor four,
           nor three, nor two, nor one; nor half a ducat; no, nor a
           moccinigo.[29] Sixpence it will cost you, or six hundred
           pound — expect no lower price, for, by the banner of my
           front, I will not bate a bagatine,[30] — that I will have, only, a
           pledge of your loves, to carry something from amongst you,

---

26. *gossip*] literally god-parent; usually, familiar friend.
27. *gazettes*] small Venetian coins.
28. *for the nones*] for the purpose.
29. moccinigo] a coin used in Venice, worth about ninepence.
30. *bagatine*] an Italian coin worth about one-third of a farthing.

to show I am not contemn'd by you. Therefore, now, toss your handkerchiefs, cheerfully, cheerfully; and be advertis'd, that the first heroic spirit that deigns to grace me with a handkerchief, I will give it a little remembrance of something beside, shall please it better than if I had presented it with a double pistolet."[31]

PER.   Will you be that heroic spark, Sir Pol?
         CELIA, *at the window, throws down her handkerchief.*
         O, see! the windore has prevented[32] you.

VOLP.   "Lady, I kiss your bounty; and for this timely grace you have done your poor Scoto of Mantua, I will return you, over and above my oil, a secret of that high and inestimable nature, shall make you for ever enamour'd on that minute, wherein your eye first descended on so mean, yet not altogether to be despis'd, an object. Here is a powder conceal'd in this paper, of which, if I should speak to the worth, nine thousand volumes were but as one page, that page as a line, that line as a word; so short is this pilgrimage of man (which some call life) to the expressing of it. Would I reflect on the price? Why, the whole world is but as an empire, that empire as a province, that province as a bank, that bank as a private purse to the purchase of it. I will only tell you; it is the powder that made Venus a goddess (given her by Apollo), that kept her perpetually young, clear'd her wrinkles, firm'd her gums, fill'd her skin, colour'd her hair; from her deriv'd to Helen, and at the sack of Troy unfortunately lost: till now, in this our age, it was as happily recover'd, by a studious antiquary, out of some ruins of Asia, who sent a moiety of it to the court of France (but much sophisticated), wherewith the ladies there now colour their hair. The rest, at this present, remains with me; extracted to a quintessence: so that, wherever it but touches, in youth it perpetually preserves, in age restores the complexion; seats your teeth, did they dance like virginal jacks,[33] firm as a wall: makes them white as ivory, that were black as —"

31. *pistolet*] a Spanish coin.
32. *prevented*] anticipated.
33. *virginal jacks*] small pieces of wood to which were attached the quills which struck the strings of the virginal.

SCENE III. — *The same*

To them enter CORVINO.

COR.   Spite o' the devil, and my shame! come down here;
         Come down! — No house but mine to make your scene?
         Signior Flaminio, will you down, sir? down?
         What, is my wife your Franciscina, sir?
         No windows on the whole Piazza, here,
         To make your properties, but mine? but mine?
                         Beats away [VOLPONE, NANO, *etc.*]
         Heart! ere to-morrow I shall be new christen'd,
         And called the Pantalone di Besogniosi,[1]
         About the town.
PER.   What should this mean, Sir Pol?
SIR P.   Some trick of state, believe it; I will home.
PER.   It may be some design on you.
SIR P.   I know not.
         I'll stand upon my guard.
PER.   It is your best, sir.
SIR P.   This three weeks, all my advices, all my letters.
         They have been intercepted.
PER.   Indeed, sir!
         Best have a care.
SIR P.   Nay, so I will.
PER.   This knight,
         I may not lose him, for my mirth, till night.
                                             [*Exeunt.*]

---

1. *Pantalone di Besogniosi*] Italian for "Fool of the Beggars."

SCENE IV. — A room in Volpone's house

Enter VOLPONE, MOSCA.

VOLP.   O, I am wounded!
MOS.   Where, sir?
VOLP.   Not without;
    Those blows were nothing: I could bear them ever.
    But angry Cupid, bolting from her eyes,
    Hath shot himself into me like a flame;
    Where now he flings about his burning heat,
    As in a furnace an ambitious fire
    Whose vent is stopt. The fight is all within me.
    I cannot live, except thou help me, Mosca;
    My liver melts, and I, without the hope
    Of some soft air from her refreshing breath,
    Am but a heap of cinders.
MOS.   'Las, good sir,
    Would you had never seen her!
VOLP.   Nay, would thou
    Hadst never told me of her!
MOS.   Sir, 't is true;
    I do confess I was unfortunate,
    And you unhappy; but I 'm bound in conscience,
    No less than duty, to effect my best
    To your release of torment, and I will, sir.
VOLP.   Dear Mosca, shall I hope?
MOS.   Sir, more than dear,
    I will not bid you to despair of aught
    Within a human compass.
VOLP.   O, there spoke
    My better angel. Mosca, take my keys,
    Gold, plate, and jewels, all 's at thy devotion;[1]
    Employ them how thou wilt: nay, coin me too:
    So thou in this but crown my longings, Mosca.

1. *at thy devotion*] at your service.

MOS.   Use but your patience.
VOLP.   So I have.
MOS.   I doubt not.
        To bring success to your desires.
VOLP.   Nay, then,
        I not repent me of my late disguise.
MOS.   If you can horn him, sir, you need not.
VOLP.   True:
        Besides, I never meant him for my heir.
        Is not the colour o' my beard and eyebrows
        To make me known?
MOS.   No jot.
VOLP.   I did it well.
MOS.   So well, would I could follow you in mine,
        With half the happiness! and yet I would
        Escape your epilogue.[2]
VOLP.   But were they gull'd
        With a belief that I was Scoto?
MOS.   Sir,
        Scoto himself could hardly have distinguish'd!
        I have not time to flatter you now; we'll part:
        And as I prosper, so applaud my art.   [*Exeunt.*]

SCENE V. — *A room in Corvino's house*

Enter CORVINO, *with his sword in his hand, dragging in* CELIA.

CORV.   Death of mine honour, with the city's fool!
        A juggling, tooth-drawing, prating mountebank!
        And at a public windore! where, whilst he,
        With his strain'd action, and his dole of faces,[1]
        To his drug-lecture draws your itching ears,
        A crew of old, unmarri'd, noted lechers,

---

2. *your epilogue*] i.e., the beating from Corvino.

---

1. *faces*] grimaces.

Stood leering up like satyrs: and you smile
Most graciously, and fan your favours forth,
To give your hot spectators satisfaction!
What, was your mountbank their call? their whistle?
Or were you enamour'd on his copper rings,
His saffron jewel, with the toad-stone in 't,
Or his embroid'red suit, with the cope-stitch,
Made of a hearse cloth? or his old tilt-feather?
Or his starch'd beard! Well, you shall have him, yes!
He shall come home, and minister unto you
The fricace for the mother.[2] Or, let me see,
I think you'd rather mount; would you not mount?
Why, if you'll mount, you may; yes, truly, you may!
And so you may be seen, down to the foot.
Get you a cittern,[3] Lady Vanity,
And be a dealer with the virtuous man;
Make one. I'll but protest myself a cuckold,
And save your dowry. I'm a Dutchman, I!
For if you thought me an Italian,
You would be damn'd ere you did this, you whore!
Thou 'dst tremble to imagine that the murder
Of father, mother, brother, all thy race,
Should follow, as the subject of my justice.

CEL.   Good sir, have patience.

CORV.   What couldst thou propose[4]
Less to thyself, than in this heat of wrath,
And stung with my dishonour, I should strike
This steel into thee, with as many stabs
As thou wert gaz'd upon with goatish eyes?

CEL.   Alas, sir, be appeas'd! I could not think
My being at the windore should more now
Move your impatience than at other times.

CORV.   No! not to seek and entertain a parley
With a known knave, before a multitude!
You were an actor with your handkerchief,
Which he most sweetly kist in the receipt,

2. *fricace for the mother*] massage for the womb.
3. *cittern*] a kind of guitar.
4. *propose*] expect.

	And might, no doubt, return it with a letter,

And might, no doubt, return it with a letter,
And point the place where you might meet; your sister's,
Your mother's, or your aunt's might serve the turn.

CEL.   Why, dear sir, when do I make these excuses,
Or ever stir abroad, but to the church?
And that so seldom —

CORV.   Well, it shall be less;
And thy restraint before was liberty,
To what I now decree: and therefore mark me.
First, I will have this bawdy light damm'd up;[5]
And till 't be done, some two or three yards off,
I'll chalk a line; o'er which if thou but chance
To set thy desp'rate foot, more hell, more horror,
More wild remorseless rage shall seize on thee,
Than on a conjuror that had heedless left
His circle's safety ere his devil was laid.
Then here's a lock which I will hang upon thee,
And, now I think on 't, I will keep thee backwards;
Thy lodging shall be backwards: thy walks backwards;
Thy prospect, all be backwards; and no pleasure,
That thou shalt know but backwards: nay, since you force
My honest nature, know, it is your own,
Being too open, makes me use you thus:
Since you will not contain your subtle nostrils
In a sweet room, but they must snuff the air
Of rank and sweaty passengers. (*Knock within.*) One knocks.
Away, and be not seen, pain of thy life;
Nor look toward the windore; if thou dost —
Nay, stay, hear this — let me not prosper, whore,
But I will make thee an anatomy,
Dissect thee mine own self, and read a lecture
Upon thee to the city, and in public.
Away! —   [*Exit* CELIA.]

[*Enter* SERVANT.]

        Who's there?

SER.   'T is Signior Mosca, sir.

---

5. *bawdy light dammed up*] i.e., brick up the window.

SCENE VI. — *The same*

CORVINO. *Enter* MOSCA.

CORV.   Let him come in. His master's dead; there's yet
        Some good to help the bad. — My Mosca, welcome!
        I guess your news.
MOS.   I fear you cannot, sir.
CORV.   Is 't not his death?
MOS.   Rather the contrary.
CORV.   Not his recovery?
MOS.   Yes, sir.
CORV.   I am curs'd,
        I am bewitch'd, my crosses meet to vex me.
        How? how? how? how?
MOS.   Why, sir, with Scoto's oil;
        Corbaccio and Voltore brought of it,
        Whilst I was busy in an inner room —
CORV.   Death! that damn'd mountebank! but for the law
        Now, I could kill the rascal: it cannot be
        His oil should have that virtue. Ha' not I
        Known him a common rogue, come fiddling in
        To the *osteria*,[1] with a tumbling whore,
        And, when he has done all his forc'd tricks, been glad
        Of a poor spoonful of dead wine, with flies in 't?
        It cannot be. All his ingredients
        Are a sheep's gall, a roasted bitch's marrow,
        Some few sod[2] earwigs, pounded caterpillars,
        A little capon's grease, and fasting spittle:[3]
        I know them to a dram.
MOS.   I know not, sir;
        But some on 't, there, they pour'd into his ears,

1. *osteria*] inn.
2. *sod*] boiled.
3. *fasting spittle*] spit from a hungry man.

	Some in his nostrils, and recover'd him;
	Applying but the fricace.[4]
CORV.	Pox o' that fricace!
MOS.	And since, to seem the more officious
	And flatt'ring of his health, there, they have had,
	At extreme fees, the college of physicians
	Consulting on him, how they might restore him;
	Where one would have a cataplasm[5] of spices,
	Another a flay'd ape clapp'd to his breast,
	A third would have it a dog, a fourth an oil,
	With wild cats' skins: at last, they all resolv'd
	That to preserve him, was no other means
	But some young woman must be straight sought out,
	Lusty, and full of juice, to sleep by him;
	And to this service most unhappily,
	And most unwillingly, am I now employ'd,
	Which here I thought to pre-acquaint you with,
	For your advice, since it concerns you most;
	Because I would not do that thing might cross
	Your ends, on whom I have my whole dependence, sir;
	Yet, if I do it not they may delate[6]
	My slackness to my patron, work me out
	Of his opinion; and there all your hopes,
	Ventures, or whatsoever, are all frustrate!
	I do but tell you, sir. Besides, they are all
	Now striving who shall first present him; therefore —
	I could entreat you, briefly conclude somewhat;
	Prevent 'em if you can.
CORV.	Death to my hopes,
	This is my villanous fortune! Best to hire
	Some common courtesan.
MOS.	Ay, I thought on that, sir;
	But they are all so subtle, full of art —
	And age again doting and flexible,
	So as — I cannot tell — we may, perchance,
	Light on a quean may cheat us all.

---

4. *Applying but the fricace*] All they had to do was rub it in.
5. *cataplasm*] poultice.
6. *delate*] denounce, complain of.

CORV.   'T is true.

MOS.   No, no: it must be one that has no tricks, sir,
Some simple thing, a creature made[7] unto it;
Some wench you may command. Ha' you no kinswoman?
Gods so — Think, think, think, think, think, think, think, sir.
One o' the doctors offer'd there his daughter.

CORV.   How!

MOS.   Yes, Signior Lupo, the physician.

CORV.   His daughter!

MOS.   And a virgin, sir. Why, alas,
He knows the state of 's body, what it is:
That nought can warm his blood, sir, but a fever;
Nor any incantation raise his spirit:
A long forgetfulness hath seiz'd that part.
Besides, sir, who shall know it? Some one or two —

CORV.   I pray thee give me leave. [*Walks aside.*] If any man
But I had had this luck — The thing in 't self,
I know, is nothing. — Wherefore should not I
As well command my blood and my affections
As this dull doctor? In the point of honour,
The cases are all one of wife and daughter.

MOS.   [*Aside.*] I hear him coming.[8]

CORV.   She shall do 't: 't is done.
Slight! if this doctor, who is not engag'd,
Unless 't be for his counsel, which is nothing,
Offer his daughter, what should I, that am
So deeply in? I will prevent him: Wretch!
Covetous wretch! — Mosca, I have determin'd.

MOS.   How, sir?

CORV.   We'll make all sure. The party you wot of
Shall be mine own wife, Mosca.

MOS.   Sir, the thing,
But that I would not seem to counsel you,
I should have motion'd to you, at the first:
And make your count, you have cut all their throats.
Why, 't is directly taking a possession!
And in his next fit, we may let him go.

---

7. *made unto it*] prepared for it.
8. *coming*] into the trap.

'T is but to pull the pillow from his head,
And he is throttled: it had been done before
But for your scrupulous doubts.

CORV.   Ay, a plague on 't,
My conscience fools my wit! Well, I'll be brief,
And so be thou, lest they should be before us.
Go home, prepare him, tell him with what zeal
And willingness I do it: swear it was
On the first hearing, as thou mayst do, truly,
Mine own free motion.

MOS.   Sir, I warrant you,
I'll so possess him with it, that the rest
Of his starv'd clients shall be banish'd all;
And only you receiv'd. But come not, sir,
Until I send, for I have something else
To ripen for your good, you must not know 't.

CORV.   But do not you forget to send now.

MOS.   Fear not. [*Exit.*]

SCENE VII. — *The same*

CORVINO.

CORV.   Where are you, wife? My Celia! wife!

[*Enter* CELIA.]

                              — What, blubb'ring?
Come, dry those tears. I think thou thought'st me in earnest;
Ha! by this light I talk'd so but to try thee:
Methinks, the lightness of the occasion
Should have confirm'd thee. Come, I am not jealous.

CEL.   No?

CORV.   Faith I am not, I, nor never was;
It is a poor unprofitable humour.
Do not I know, if women have a will,
They'll do 'gainst all the watches o' the world,
And that the fiercest spies are tam'd with gold?

Tut, I am confident in thee, thou shalt see 't;
And see I'll give thee cause too, to believe it.
Come kiss me. Go, and make thee ready straight,
In all thy best attire, thy choicest jewels,
Put 'em all on, and, with 'em, thy best looks:
We are invited to a solemn feast,
At old Volpone's, where it shall appear
How far I am free from jealousy or fear.

                                       [*Exeunt.*]

ACT III

SCENE I. — *A street*

Enter MOSCA.

MOS.   I fear I shall begin to grow in love
With my dear self, and my most prosp'rous parts,
They do so spring and burgeon; I can feel
A whimsy in my blood: I know not how,
Success hath made me wanton. I could skip
Out of my skin now, like a subtle snake,
I am so limber. O! your parasite
Is a most precious thing, dropt from above,
Not bred 'mongst clods and clodpoles, here on earth.
I muse, the mystery[1] was not made a science,
It is so liberally profest! Almost
All the wise world is little else, in nature,
But parasites or sub-parasites. And yet
I mean not those that have your bare town-art,
To know who's fit to feed them; have no house,
No family, no care, and therefore mould
Tales for men's ears, to bait that sense; or get
Kitchen-invention, and some stale receipts
To please the belly, and the groin; nor those,
With their court dog-tricks, that can fawn and fleer,
Make their revenue out of legs[2] and faces,
Echo my lord, and lick away a moth:
But your fine elegant rascal, that can rise

---

1. *mystery*] craft, profession.
2. *legs*] bows.

48

And stoop, almost together, like an arrow;
Shoot through the air as nimbly as a star;
Turn short as doth a swallow; and be here,
And there, and here, and yonder, all at once;
Present to any humour, all occasion;
And change a visor swifter than a thought!
This is the creature had the art born with him;
Toils not to learn it, but doth practise it
Out of most excellent nature: and such sparks
Are the true parasites, others but their zanies.

SCENE II. — *The same*

MOSCA. *Enter* BONARIO.

    Who's this? Bonario, old Corbaccio's son?
    The person I was bound to seek. Fair sir,
    You are happ'ly met.

BON.   That cannot be by thee.
MOS.   Why, sir?
BON.   Nay, pray thee know thy way, and leave me:
    I would be loth to interchange discourse
    With such a mate[1] as thou art.
MOS.   Courteous sir,
    Scorn not my poverty.
BON.   Not I, by heaven;
    But thou shalt give me leave to hate thy baseness.
MOS.   Baseness!
BON.   Ay; answer me, is not thy sloth
    Sufficient argument? thy flattery?
    Thy means of feeding?
MOS.   Heaven be good to me!
    These imputations are too common, sir,
    And easily stuck on virtue when she's poor.
    You are unequal[2] to me, and however

1. *mate*] fellow.
2. *unequal*] unfair.

Your sentence may be righteous, yet you are not,
That, ere you know me, thus proceed in censure:
St. Mark bear witness 'gainst you, 't is inhuman.

[*Weeps.*]

BON.   [*Aside.*] What! does he weep? the sign is soft and good:
I do repent me that I was so harsh.

MOS.   'T is true, that, sway'd by strong necessity,
I am enforc'd to eat my careful bread
With too much obsequy; 't is true, beside,
That I am fain to spin mine own poor raiment
Out of my mere observance, being not born
To a free fortune: but that I have done
Base offices, in rending friends asunder,
Dividing families, betraying counsels,
Whisp'ring false lies, or mining men with praises,
Train'd their credulity with perjuries,
Corrupted chastity, or am in love
With mine own tender ease, but would not rather
Prove the most rugged and laborious course,
That might redeem my present estimation,
Let me here perish, in all hope of goodness.

BON.   [*Aside.*] This cannot be a personated passion. —
I was to blame, so to mistake thy nature;
Prithee forgive me: and speak out thy business.

MOS.   Sir, it concerns you; and though I may seem
At first to make a main offence in manners,
And in my gratitude unto my master,
Yet for the pure love which I bear all right,
And hatred of the wrong, I must reveal it.
This very hour your father is in purpose
To disinherit you —

BON.   How!

MOS.   And thrust you forth,
As a mere stranger to his blood: 't is true, sir.
The work no way engageth me, but as
I claim an interest in the general state
Of goodness and true virtue, which I hear
T' abound in you; and for which mere respect,
Without a second aim, sir, I have done it.

BON.   This tale hath lost thee much of the late trust

Thou hadst with me; it is impossible.
I know not how to lend it any thought,
My father should be so unnatural.

MOS.   It is a confidence that well becomes
Your piety; and form'd, no doubt, it is
From your own simple innocence: which makes
Your wrong more monstrous and abhorr'd. But, sir,
I now will tell you more. This very minute,
It is, or will be doing; and if you
Shall be but pleas'd to go with me, I'll bring you,
I dare not say where you shall see, but where
Your ear shall be a witness of the deed;
Hear yourself written bastard, and profest
The common issue of the earth.

BON.   I 'm maz'd!

MOS.   Sir, if I do it not, draw your just sword,
And score your vengeance on my front and face;
Mark me your villain: you have too much wrong,
And I do suffer for you, sir. My heart
Weeps blood in anguish —

BON.   Lead; I follow thee.   [*Exeunt.*]

SCENE III. — *A room in Volpone's house*

Enter VOLPONE, NANO, ANDROGYNO, CASTRONE.

VOLP.   Mosca stays long, methinks. — Bring forth your sports,
And help to make the wretched time more sweet.

NAN.   "Dwarf, fool, and eunuch, well met here we be.
A question it were now, whether of us three,
Being all the known delicates of a rich man,
In pleasing him, claim the precedency can?"

CAS.   "I claim for myself."

AND.   "And so doth the fool."

NAN.   " 'T is foolish indeed: let me set you both to school.
First for your dwarf, he's little and witty,
And everything, as it is little, is pretty;

Else why do men say to a creature of my shape,
So soon as they see him, 'It's a pretty little ape'?
And why a pretty ape, but for pleasing imitation
Of greater men's actions, in a ridiculous fashion?
Beside, this feat[1] body of mine doth not crave
Half the meat, drink, and cloth, one of your bulks will have.
Admit your fool's face be the mother of laughter,
Yet, for his brain, it must always come after:
And though that do feed him, it's a pitiful case,
His body is beholding to such a bad face."

One knocks.

VOLP.   Who's there? My couch; away! look! Nano, see: [*Exeunt* AND.
          and CAS.]
          Give me my caps first — go, inquire. [*Exit* NANO.] Now, Cu-
          pid
          Send it be Mosca, and with fair return!
NAN.   [*within.*] It is the beauteous madam —
VOLP.   Would-be — is it?
NAN.   The same.
VOLP.   Now torment on me! Squire her in;
          For she will enter, or dwell here for ever:
          Nay, quickly. [*Retires to his couch.*] That my fit were past!
          I fear
          A second hell too, that my loathing this
          Will quite expel my appetite to the other:
          Would she were taking now her tedious leave.
          Lord, how it threats me what I am to suffer!

1. *feat*] neatly made.

SCENE IV. — *The same*

To him enter NANO, LADY POLITIC WOULD-BE.

LADY P.   I thank you, good sir. Pray you signify
Unto your patron I am here. — This band
Shows not my neck enough. — I trouble you, sir;
Let me request you bid one of my women
Come hither to me. In good faith, I am drest
Most favourably to-day! It is no matter:
'T is well enough.

[*Enter* 1st Waiting-woman.]

                                        Look, see these petulant things,
How they have done this!

VOLP.   [*Aside.*] I do feel the fever
Ent'ring in at mine ears; O, for a charm,
To fright it hence!

LADY P.   Come nearer: is this curl
In his right place, or this? Why is this higher
Than all the rest? You ha' not wash'd your eyes yet!
Or do they not stand even i' your head?
Where is your fellow? call her. [*Exit* 1st Woman.]

NAN.   Now, St. Mark
Deliver us! anon she'll beat her women,
Because her nose is red.

[*Re-enter* 1st *with* 2nd Woman.]

LADY P.   I pray you view
This tire,[1] forsooth: are all things apt, or no?

1ST WOM.   One hair a little here sticks out, forsooth.

LADY P.   Does 't so, forsooth! and where was your dear sight,
When it did so, forsooth! What now! bird-ey'd?[2]
And you, too? Pray you, both approach and mend it.
Now, by that light I muse you're not asham'd!

---

1. *tire*] head-dress.
2. *bird-ey'd*] sharp-sighted.

	I, that have preach'd these things so oft unto you,
	Read you the principles, argu'd all the grounds,
	Disputed every fitness, every grace,
	Call'd you to counsel of so frequent dressings —
NAN.	(*Aside.*) More carefully than of your fame or honour.
LADY P.	Made you acquainted what an ample dowry

LADY P. Made you acquainted what an ample dowry
    The knowledge of these things would be unto you,
    Able alone to get you noble husbands
    At your return: and you thus to neglect it!
    Besides, you seeing what a curious nation
    Th' Italians are, what will they say of me?
    "The English lady cannot dress herself."
    Here's a fine imputation to our country!
    Well, go your ways, and stay i' the next room.
    This fucus[3] was too coarse too; it's no matter. —
    Good sir, you'll give 'em entertainment?
                       [*Exeunt* NANO *and* Waiting-women.]

VOLP. The storm comes toward me.
LADY P. [*Goes to the couch.*] How does my Volpone?
VOLP. Troubl'd with noise, I cannot sleep; I dreamt
    That a strange fury ent'red now my house,
    And, with the dreadful tempest of her breath,
    Did cleave my roof asunder.
LADY P.   Believe me, and I
    Had the most fearful dream, could I remember 't —
VOLP. [*Aside.*] Out on my fate! I have given her the occasion
    How to torment me: she will tell me hers.
LADY P. Methought the golden mediocrity,
    Polite, and delicate —
VOLP.   O, if you do love me,
    No more: I sweat, and suffer, at the mention
    Of any dream; feel how I tremble yet.
LADY P. Alas, good soul! the passion of the heart.
    Seed-pearl were good now, boil'd with syrup of apples,
    Tincture of gold, and coral, citron-pills,
    Your elecampane[4] root, myrobalanes[5] —
VOLP. Ay me, I have ta'en a grasshopper by the wing!

---

3. *fucus*] face paint.
4. *elecampane*] horse-heal, a medicinal herb.
5. *myrobalanes*] an astringent kind of plum.

LADY P.	Burnt silk and amber. You have muscadel
	Good i' the house —
VOLP.	You will not drink, and part?
LADY P.	No, fear not that. I doubt we shall not get
	Some English saffron, half a dram would serve;
	Your sixteen cloves, a little musk, dried mints;
	Bugloss, and barley-meal —
VOLP.	[*Aside.*] She's in again!
	Before I feign'd diseases, now I have one.
LADY P.	And these appli'd with a right scarlet cloth.
VOLP.	[*Aside.*] Another flood of words! a very torrent!
LADY P.	Shall I, sir, make you a poultice?
VOLP.	No, no, no.
	I'm very well, you need prescribe no more.
LADY P.	I have a little studied physic; but now
	I'm all for music, save, i' the forenoons,
	An hour or two for painting. I would have
	A lady, indeed, to have all letters and arts,
	Be able to discourse, to write, to paint,
	But principal, as Plato holds, your music,
	And so does wise Pythagoras, I take it,
	Is your true rapture: when there is concent[6]
	In face, in voice, and clothes: and is, indeed,
	Our sex's chiefest ornament.
VOLP.	The poet
	As old in time as Plato, and as knowing,
	Says that your highest female grace is silence.
LADY P.	Which of your poets? Petrarch, or Tasso, or Dante?
	Guarini? Ariosto? Aretine?
	Cieco di Hadria? I have read them all.
VOLP.	[*Aside.*] Is everything a cause to my destruction?
LADY P.	I think I have two or three of 'em about me.
VOLP.	[*Aside.*] The sun, the sea, will sooner both stand still
	Than her eternal tongue! nothing can scape it.
LADY P.	Here's Pastor Fido —
VOLP.	[*Aside.*] Profess obstinate silence;
	That's now my safest.
LADY P.	All our English writers,
	I mean such as are happy in th' Italian,

---

6. *concent*] harmony.

Will deign to steal out of this author, mainly;
Almost as much as from Montagnié:
He has so modern and facile a vein,
Fitting the time, and catching the court-ear!
Your Petrarch is more passionate, yet he,
In days of sonnetting, trusted 'em with much:
Dante is hard, and few can understand him.
But for a desperate wit, there's Aretine;
Only his pictures are a little obscene —
You mark me not.

VOLP.   Alas, my mind's perturb'd.
LADY P. Why, in such cases, we must cure ourselves,
Make use of our philosophy —
VOLP.   Oh me!
LADY P. And as we find our passions do rebel,
Encounter them with reason, or divert 'em,
By giving scope unto some other humour
Of lesser danger: as, in politic bodies,
There's nothing more doth overwhelm the judgment,
And cloud the understanding, than too much
Settling and fixing, and, as 't were, subsiding
Upon one object. For the incorporating
Of these same outward things, into that part
Which we call mental, leaves some certain faeces
That stop the organs, and, as Plato says,
Assassinate our knowledge.
VOLP.   [*Aside.*] Now, the spirit
Of patience help me!
LADY P.   Come, in faith, I must
Visit you more a days; and make you well:
Laugh and be lusty.
VOLP. [*Aside.*] My good angel save me!
LADY P. There was but one sole man in all the world
With whom I e'er could sympathise; and he
Would lie⁷ you, often, three, four hours together
To hear me speak; and be sometime so rapt,
As he would answer me quite from the purpose,
Like you, and you are like him, just. I'll discourse,
An 't be but only, sir, to bring you asleep,

7. *Would lie you*] Would often lie.

> How we did spend our time and loves together,
> For some six years.

VOLP.   Oh, oh, oh, oh, oh, oh!

LADY P. For we were coaetanei,[8] and brought up —

VOLP. Some power, some fate, some fortune rescue me!

SCENE V. — *The same*

To them enter MOSCA.

MOS. God save you, madam!

LADY P.   Good sir.

VOLP.   Mosca! welcome,
> Welcome to my redemption.

MOS.   Why, sir?

VOLP. Oh,
> Rid me of this my torture, quickly, there;
> My madam with the everlasting voice:
> The bells, in time of pestilence, ne'er made
> Like noise, or were in that perpetual motion!
> The Cock-pit comes not near it. All my house,
> But now, steam'd like a bath with her thick breath,
> A lawyer could not have been heard; nor scarce
> Another woman, such a hail of words
> She has let fall. For hell's sake, rid her hence.

MOS. Has she presented?

VOLP.   Oh, I do not care;
> I'll take her absence upon any price,
> With any loss.

MOS.   Madam —

LADY P.   I ha' brought your patron
> A toy, a cap here, of mine own work.

MOS.   'T is well.
> I had forgot to tell you I saw your knight
> Where you would little think it. —

LADY P.   Where?

8. *coaetanei*] of the same age.

MOS.	Marry,

Where yet, if you make haste, you may apprehend him,
Rowing upon the water in a gondole,
With the most cunning courtesan of Venice.

LADY P. Is 't true?

MOS. Pursue 'em, and believe your eyes:
Leave me to make your gift.

> [*Exit* LADY P. *hastily.*]
>> I knew 't would take:
For, lightly, they that use themselves most licence,
Are still most jealous.

VOLP. Mosca, hearty thanks
For thy quick fiction, and delivery of me.
Now to my hopes, what sayst thou?

[*Re-enter* LADY P. WOULD-BE.]

LADY P. But do you hear, sir? —

VOLP. Again! I fear a paroxysm.

LADY P. Which way
Row'd they together?

MOS. Toward the Rialto.

LADY P. I pray you lend me your dwarf.

MOS. I pray you take him. [*Exit* LADY P.]
Your hopes, sir, are like happy blossoms, fair,
And promise timely fruit, if you will stay
But the maturing; keep you at your couch,
Corbaccio will arrive straight, with the will;
When he is gone, I'll tell you more. [*Exit.*]

VOLP. My blood,
My spirits are return'd; I am alive:
And, like your wanton gamester at primero,[1]
Whose thought had whisper'd to him, not go less,
Methinks I lie, and draw — for an encounter.

---

1. *not go less . . . encounter*] primero was the early form of the card game ombre; "go less,"
"draw" and "encounter" are phrases used in the game.

SCENE VI. — *The same*

Enter MOSCA, BONARIO.

MOS.   Sir, here conceal'd [*Opening a door*] you may hear all. But,
          pray you,
          Have patience, sir; [*One knocks.*] the same 's your father
          knocks:
          I am compell'd to leave you.   [*Exit.*]
BON.   Do so. — Yet
          Cannot my thought imagine this a truth.   [*Goes in.*]

SCENE VII. — *The same*

Enter MOSCA, CORVINO, CELIA. —

MOS.   Death on me! you are come too soon, what meant you?
          Did not I say I would send?
CORV.   Yes, but I fear'd
          You might forget it, and then they prevent us.
MOS.   Prevent! [*Aside.*] Did e'er man haste so for his horns?
          A courtier would not ply it so for a place.
          — Well, now there is no helping it, stay here;
          I'll presently return.
                                                          [*Exit.*]
CORV.   Where are you, Celia?
          You know not wherefore I have brought you hither?
CEL.   Not well, except you told me.
CORV.   Now I will:
          Hark hither.
                                          [*They retire to one side.*]

[*Re-enter* MOSCA.]

MOS.   (*to* BONARIO) Sir, your father hath sent word,

It will be half an hour ere he come;
And therefore, if you please to walk the while
Into that gallery — at the upper end,
There are some books to entertain the time:
And I'll take care no man shall come unto you, sir.

BON. Yes. I will stay there. — [*Aside.*] I do doubt this fellow. [*Exit.*]

MOS. [*Looking after him.*] There; he is far enough; he can hear
    nothing:
And for his father, I can keep him off.

[*Goes to* VOLPONE'S *couch, opens the curtains, and whispers to him.*]

CORV. Nay, now, there is no starting back, and therefore,
Resolve upon it: I have so decreed.
It must be done. Nor would I move 't afore,
Because I would avoid all shifts and tricks,
That might deny me.

CEL. Sir, let me beseech you,
Affect not these strange trials; if you doubt
My chastity, why, lock me up for ever;
Make me the heir of darkness. Let me live
Where I may please your fears, if not your trust.

CORV. Believe it, I have no such humour, I.
All that I speak I mean; yet I'm not mad;
Not horn-mad, you see? Go to, show yourself
Obedient, and a wife.

CEL. O heaven!

CORV. I say it,
Do so.

CEL. Was this the train?[1]

CORV. I've told you reasons;
What the physicians have set down; how much
It may concern me; what my engagements are;
My means, and the necessity of those means
For my recovery: wherefore, if you be
Loyal and mine, be won, respect my venture.

CEL. Before your honour?

CORV. Honour! tut, a breath:

---

1. *"Was this the train?"*] "Was this what you had in mind all the time?"

There's no such thing in nature; a mere term
Invented to awe fools. What is my gold
The worse for touching, clothes for being look'd on?
Why, this 's no more. An old decrepit wretch,
That has no sense, no sinew; takes his meat
With others' fingers: only knows to gape
When you do scald his gums; a voice, a shadow;
And what can this man hurt you?

CEL.   [*Aside.*] Lord! what spirit
Is this hath ent'red him?

CORV.   And for your fame,
That's such a jig; as if I would go tell it,
Cry it on the Piazza! Who shall know it
But he that cannot speak it, and this fellow,
Whose lips are i' my pocket? Save yourself,
(If you'll proclaim 't, you may,) I know no other
Should come to know it.

CEL.   Are heaven and saints then nothing?
Will they be blind or stupid?

CORV.   How!

CEL.   Good sir,
Be jealous still, emulate them; and think
What hate they burn with toward every sin.

CORV.   I grant you: if I thought it were a sin
I would not urge you. Should I offer this
To some young Frenchman, or hot Tuscan blood
That had read Aretine, conn'd all his prints,
Knew every quirk within lust's labyrinth,
And were profest critic in lechery;
And I would look upon him, and applaud him,
This were a sin: but here, 't is contrary,
A pious work, mere charity for physic,
And honest polity, to assure mine own.

CEL.   O heaven! canst thou suffer such a change?

VOLP.   Thou art mine honour, Mosca, and my pride,
My joy, my tickling, my delight! Go bring 'em.

MOS.   [*Advancing.*] Please you draw near, sir.

CORV.   Come on, what —
You will not be rebellious? By that light —

MOS.	Sir, Signior Corvino, here, is come to see you.
VOLP.	Oh!
MOS.	And hearing of the consultation had,
	So lately, for your health, is come to offer,
	Or rather, sir, to prostitute —
CORV.	Thanks, sweet Mosca.
MOS.	Freely, unask'd, or unintreated —
CORV.	Well.
MOS.	As the true fervent instance of his love,
	His own most fair and proper wife; the beauty
	Only of price in Venice —
CORV.	'T is well urg'd.
MOS.	To be your comfortress, and to preserve you.
VOLP.	Alas, I am past, already! Pray you, thank him
	For his good care and promptness; but for that,
	'T is a vain labour e'en to fight 'gainst heaven;
	Applying fire to stone — uh, uh, uh, uh!

[*Coughing.*]

	Making a dead leaf grow again. I take
	His wishes gently, though; and you may tell him
	What I have done for him: marry, my state is hopeless.
	Will him to pray for me; and to use his fortune
	With reverence when he comes to 't.
MOS.	Do you hear, sir?
	Go to him with your wife.
CORV	Heart of my father!
	Wilt thou persist thus? Come, I pray thee, come.
	Thou seest 't is nothing, Celia. By this hand
	I shall grow violent. Come, do 't, I say.
CEL.	Sir, kill me, rather: I will take down poison,
	Eat burning coals, do anything —
CORV.	Be damn'd!
	Heart, I will drag thee hence home by the hair;
	Cry thee a strumpet through the streets; rip up
	Thy mouth unto thine ears; and slit thy nose,
	Like a raw rochet![2] — Do not tempt me; come,
	Yield, I am loth — Death! I will buy some slave
	Whom I will kill, and bind thee to him alive;

2. *rochet*] a kind of fish.

	And at my windore hang you forth, devising

And at my windore hang you forth, devising
Some monstrous crime, which I, in capital letters,
Will eat into thy flesh with aquafortis,
And burning cor'sives,[3] on this stubborn breast.
Now, by the blood thou hast incens'd, I'll do it!

CEL.   Sir, what you please, you may; I am your martyr.

CORV. Be not thus obstinate, I ha' not deserv'd it:
Think who it is intreats you. Prithee, sweet; —
Good faith, thou shalt have jewels, gowns, attires,
What thou wilt think, and ask. Do but go kiss him.
Or touch him but. For my sake. At my suit —
This once. No! not! I shall remember this.
Will you disgrace me thus? Do you thirst my undoing?

MOS.   Nay, gentle lady, be advis'd.

CORV.   No, no.
She has watch'd her time. God's precious, this is scurvy,
'T is very scurvy; and you are —

MOS.   Nay, good sir.

CORV. An arrant locust — by heaven, a locust! —
Whore, crocodile, that hast thy tears prepar'd,
Expecting how thou 'lt bid 'em flow —

MOS.   Nay, pray you, sir!
She will consider.

CEL.   Would my life would serve
To satisfy —

CORV. 'Sdeath! if she would but speak to him,
And save my reputation, 't were somewhat;
But spitefully to affect my utter ruin!

MOS.   Ay, now you have put your fortune in her hands.
Why i' faith, it is her modesty, I must quit her.
If you were absent, she would be more coming;
I know it: and dare undertake for her.
What woman can before her husband? Pray you,
Let us depart and leave her here.

CORV.   Sweet Celia,
Thou mayest redeem all yet; I'll say no more:
If not, esteem yourself as lost. Nay, stay there.

                                  [*Exit with* MOSCA.]

---

3. *aquafortis . . . cor'sives*] acids and corrosives.

CEL.   O God, and his good angels! whither, whither,
               Is shame fled human breasts? that with such ease,
               Men dare put off your honours, and their own?
               Is that, which ever was a cause of life,
               Now plac'd beneath the basest circumstance,
               And modesty an exile made, for money?

VOLP.   Ay, in Corvino, and such earth-fed minds,

                                       [He leaps from his couch.]
               That never tasted the true heaven of love.
               Assure thee, Celia, he that would sell thee,
               Only for hope of gain, and that uncertain,
               He would have sold his part of Paradise
               For ready money, had he met a cope-man.[4]
               Why art thou maz'd to see me thus reviv'd?
               Rather applaud thy beauty's miracle;
               'T is thy great work, that hath, not now alone,
               But sundry times rais'd me, in several shapes,
               And, but this morning, like a mountebank,
               To see thee at thy windore: ay, before
               I would have left my practice, for thy love,
               In varying figures, I would have contended
               With the blue Proteus, or the horned flood.[5]
               Now art thou welcome.

CEL.   Sir!

VOLP.   Nay, fly me not,
               Nor let thy false imagination
               That I was bed-rid, make thee think I am so:
               Thou shalt not find it. I am now as fresh,
               As hot, as high, and in as jovial plight
               As, when, in that so celebrated scene,
               At recitation of our comedy,
               For entertainment of the great Valois,[6]
               I acted young Antinous; and attracted
               The eyes and ears of all the ladies present,
               To admire each graceful gesture, note, and footing. *[Sings.]*

---

4. *cope-man*] buyer, merchant.
5. *blue Proteus, or the horned flood*] Proteus was a sea god who could take any shape at will; horned flood refers to the river god Achelous, who fought with Hercules, first in the shape of a river, then as a snake, then as a bull — hence "horned flood."
6. *Valois*] Henry of Valois, Duke of Anjou, the newly crowned King Henry III of France, was entertained with splendid festivities when he visited Venice in 1574.

SONG[7]

Come, my Celia, let us prove
While we can, the sports of love,
Time will not be ours for ever,
He, at length, our good will sever;
Spend not then his gifts in vain:
Suns that set may rise again;
But if once we lose this light,
'T is with us perpetual night.
Why should we defer our joys?
Fame and rumour are but toys.
Cannot we delude the eyes
Of a few poor household spies?
Or his easier ears beguile,
Thus removed by our wile?
'T is no sin love's fruits to steal;
But the sweet thefts to reveal:
To be taken, to be seen,
These have crimes accounted been.

CEL.   Some serene[8] blast me, or dire lightning strike
This my offending face!

VOLP.   Why droops my Celia?
Thou hast, in place of a base husband found
A worthy lover: use thy fortune well,
With secrecy and pleasure. See, behold,
What thou art queen of; not in expectation,
As I feed others: but possess'd and crown'd.
See, here, a rope of pearl; and each more orient
Than the brave Aegyptian queen carous'd:
Dissolve and drink 'em.[9] See, a carbuncle,
May put out both the eyes of our St. Mark;
A diamond would have bought Lollia Paulina,[10]
When she came in like star-light, hid with jewels
That were the spoils of provinces; take these
And wear, and lose 'em; yet remains an earring
To purchase them again, and this whole state.

7. The opening lines of the song are taken from Catullus.
8. *serene*] mist from heaven; malignant influence.
9. *Aegyptian queen ... drink 'em*] Supposedly, Cleopatra dissolved a precious pearl in
wine, which she and Antony drank at a banquet.
10. *Lollia Paulina*] the wife of a Roman governor famed for the brilliance and costliness of
her jewels.

<blockquote>

A gem but worth a private patrimony
Is nothing; we will eat such at a meal.
The heads of parrots, tongues of nightingales,
The brains of peacocks, and of estriches,
Shall be our food, and, could we get the phoenix,
Though nature lost her kind, she were our dish.

</blockquote>

CEL.

<blockquote>

Good sir, these things might move a mind affected
With such delights; but I, whose innocence
Is all I can think wealthy, or worth th' enjoying,
And which, once lost, I have nought to lose beyond it,
Cannot be taken with these sensual baits:
If you have conscience—

</blockquote>

VOLP.

<blockquote>

                 'T is the beggar's virtue;
If thou hast wisdom, hear me, Celia.
Thy baths shall be the juice of July-flowers,
Spirit of roses, and of violets,
The milk of unicorns, and panthers' breath
Gather'd in bags, and mix'd with Cretan wines.
Our drink shall be prepared gold and amber;
Which we will take until my roof whirl round
With the vertigo: and my dwarf shall dance,
My eunuch sing, my fool make up the antic,
Whilst we, in changed shapes, act Ovid's tales,
Thou, like Europa now, and I like Jove,
Then I like Mars, and thou like Erycine:
So of the rest, till we have quite run through,
And wearied all the fables of the gods.
Then will I have thee in more modern forms,
Attired like some sprightly dame of France,
Brave Tuscan lady, or proud Spanish beauty;
Sometimes unto the Persian sophy's[11] wife;
Or the grand signior's mistress; and for change,
To one of our most artful courtesans,
Or some quick Negro, or cold Russian;
And I will meet thee in as many shapes:
Where we may so transfuse our wand'ring souls
Out at our lips, and score up sums of pleasures,

</blockquote>

                                                               [Sings.]

11. *Persian sophy*] the Shah of Persia.

> That the curious shall not know
> How to tell them as they flow;
> And the envious, when they find
> What their number is, be pin'd.

CEL.   If you have ears that will be pierc'd — or eyes
That can be open'd — a heart that may be touch'd —
Or any part that yet sounds man about you —
If you have touch of holy saints — or heaven —
Do me the grace to let me scape: — if not,
Be bountiful and kill me. You do know,
I am a creature, hither ill betray'd,
By one whose shame I would forget it were:
If you will deign me neither of these graces,
Yet feed your wrath, sir, rather than your lust,
(It is a vice comes nearer manliness,)
And punish that unhappy crime of nature,
Which you miscall my beauty: flay my face,
Or poison it with ointments for seducing
Your blood to this rebellion. Rub these hands
With what may cause an eating leprosy,
E'en to my bones and marrow: anything
That may disfavour me, save in my honour —
And I will kneel to you, pray for you, pay down
A thousand hourly vows, sir, for your health;
Report, and think you virtuous —

VOLP.   Think me cold,
Frozen, and impotent, and so report me?
That I had Nestor's hernia,[12] thou wouldst think.
I do degenerate, and abuse my nation,
To play with opportunity thus long;
I should have done the act, and then have parley'd.
Yield, or I'll force thee.   *[Seizes her.]*

CEL.   O! just God!
VOLP.   In vain —
BON.   (*leaps out from where* MOSCA *had placed him.*) Forbear, foul
ravisher! libidinous swine!
Free the forc'd lady, or thou diest, impostor.

---

12. *Nestor's hernia*] from Juvenal's sixth satire; senile impotence.

But that I'm loth to snatch thy punishment
Out of the hand of justice, thou shouldst yet
Be made the timely sacrifice of vengeance,
Before this altar and this dross, thy idol. —
Lady, let's quit the place, it is the den
Of villany; fear nought, you have a guard:
And he ere long shall meet his just reward.

                              [*Exeunt* Bon. *and* Cel.]

Volp. Fall on me, roof, and bury me in ruin!
Become my grave, that wert my shelter! O!
I am unmask'd, unspirited, undone,
Betray'd to beggary, to infamy —

Scene VIII. — *The same*

Volpone. *Enter* Mosca, *wounded and bleeding*.

Mos.   Where shall I run, most wretched shame of men,
To beat out my unlucky brains?
Volp.   Here, here.
What! dost thou bleed?
Mos.   O, that his well-driv'n sword
Had been so courteous to have cleft me down
Unto the navel, ere I liv'd to see
My life, my hopes, my spirits, my patron, all
Thus desperately engaged by my error!
Volp. Woe on thy fortune!
Mos.   And my follies, sir.
Volp. Thou hast made me miserable.
Mos.   And myself, sir.
Who would have thought he would have heark'ned so?
Volp. What shall we do?
Mos.   I know not; if my heart
Could expiate the mischance, I'd pluck it out.
Will you be pleas'd to hang me, or cut my throat?
And I'll requite you, sir. Let 's die like Romans,[1]

---

1. *die like Romans*] i.e., by suicide.

        Since we have liv'd like Grecians.

They knock without.

VOLP.   Hark! who's there?
I hear some footing; officers, the saffi,[2]
Come to apprehend us! I do feel the brand
Hissing already at my forehead; now
Mine ears are boring.

MOS.   To your couch, sir, you,
Make that place good, however. [VOLPONE *lies down as before.*] Guilty men
Suspect what they deserve still. Signior Corbaccio!

SCENE IX. — *The same*

To them enter CORBACCIO.

CORB.   Why, how now, Mosca?
MOS.   O, undone, amaz'd, sir.
Your son, I know not by what accident,
Acquainted with your purpose to my patron,
Touching your will, and making him your heir,
Ent'red our house with violence, his sword drawn,
Sought for you, called you wretch, unnatural,
Vow'd he would kill you.

CORB.   Me!
MOS.   Yes, and my patron.
CORB.   This act shall disinherit him indeed:
Here is the will.

MOS.   'T is well, sir.
CORB.   Right and well:
Be you as careful now for me.

[*Enter* VOLTORE *behind.*]

MOS.   My life, sir,
Is not more tender'd; I am only yours.

    2. *saffi*] bailiff's attendants.

CORB.   How does he? Will he die shortly, think'st thou?
MOS.   I fear
        He'll outlast May.
CORB.   To-day?
MOS.   No, last out May, sir.
CORB.   Couldst thou not gi' him a dram?
MOS.   O, by no means, sir.
CORB.   Nay, I'll not bid you.
VOLT.   [*coming forward.*] This is a knave, I see.
MOS.   [*Aside, seeing* VOLT.] How! Signior Voltore! did he hear me?
VOLT.   Parasite!
MOS.   Who's that? — O, sir, most timely welcome —
VOLT.   Scarce,
        To the discovery of your tricks, I fear.
        You are his, *only*? And mine also, are you not?
MOS.   Who? I, sir!
VOLT.   You, sir. What device is this
        About a will?
MOS.   A plot for you, sir.
VOLT.   Come,
        Put not your foists[1] upon me; I shall scent 'em.
MOS.   Did you not hear it?
VOLT.   Yes, I hear Corbaccio
        Hath made your patron there his heir.
MOS.   'T is true,
        By my device, drawn to it by my plot,
        With hope —
VOLT.   Your patron should reciprocate?
        And you have promis'd?
MOS.   For your good I did, sir.
        Nay, more, I told his son, brought, hid him here,
        Where he might hear his father pass the deed;
        Being persuaded to it by this thought, sir,
        That the unnaturalness, first, of the act,
        And then his father's oft disclaiming in him,
        (Which I did mean t' help on), would sure enrage him
        To do some violence upon his parent,
        On which the law should take sufficient hold,
        And you be stated in a double hope.

---

1. *foists*] tricks, deceits, but also bad smells.

	Truth be my comfort, and my conscience,
	My only aim was to dig you a fortune
	Out of these two rotten sepulchres —
VOLT.	I cry thee mercy, Mosca.
MOS.	—Worth your patience,
	And your great merit, sir. And see the change!
VOLT.	Why, what success?
MOS.	Most hapless! you must help, sir.
	Whilst we expected th' old raven, in comes
	Corvino's wife, sent hither by her husband —
VOLT.	What, with a present?
MOS.	No, sir, on visitation;
	(I'll tell you how anon;) and staying long,
	The youth he grows impatient, rushes forth,
	Seizeth the lady, wounds me, makes her swear
	(Or he would murder her, that was his vow)
	T' affirm my patron to have done her rape:
	Which how unlike it is, you see! and hence,
	With that pretext he's gone, t' accuse his father,
	Defame my patron, defeat you —
VOLT.	Where 's her husband?
	Let him be sent for straight.
MOS.	Sir, I'll go fetch him.
VOLT.	Bring him to the Scrutineo.[2]
MOS.	Sir, I will.
VOLT.	This must be stopt.
MOS.	O you do nobly, sir.
	Alas, 't was labour'd all, sir, for your good;
	Nor was there want of counsel in the plot:
	But Fortune can, at any time, o'erthrow
	The projects of a hundred learned clerks, sir.
CORB.	[listening.] What 's that?
VOLT.	Wilt please you, sir, to go along?
	[Exit CORBACCIO, followed by VOLTORE.]
MOS.	Patron, go in, and pray for our success.
VOLP.	[rising from his couch.] Need makes devotion: heaven your
	labour bless!
	[Exeunt.]

2. *Scrutineo*] Senate House, or court of law.

ACT IV

SCENE I. — *A street*

Enter SIR POLITIC WOULD-BE, PEREGRINE.

SIR P. I told you, sir, it was a plot; you see
What observation is! You mention'd[1] me
For some instructions: I will tell you, sir,
(Since we are met here in this height of Venice,)
Some few particulars I have set down,
Only for this meridian, fit to be known
Of your crude traveller; and they are these.
I will not touch, sir, at your phrase, or clothes,
For they are old.

PER.   Sir, I have better.

SIR P.   Pardon,
I meant, as they are themes.

PER.   .   O, sir, proceed:
I'll slander you no more of wit, good sir.

SIR P. First, for your garb,[2] it must be grave and serious,
Very reserv'd and lockt; not tell a secret
On any terms, not to your father; scarce
A fable, but with caution: make sure choice
Both of your company and discourse; beware
You never speak a truth —

PER.   How!

SIR P.   Not to strangers,
For those be they you must converse with most;

1. *mention'd*] asked.
2. *garb*] bearing, demeanor.

72

	Others I would not know, sir, but at distance
	So as I still might be a saver in them:
	You shall have tricks else past upon you hourly.
	And then, for your religion, profess none,
	But wonder at the diversity of all;
	And, for your part, protest, were there no other
	But simply the laws o' th' land, you could content you.
	Nic. Machiavel and Monsieur Bodin,[3] both
	Were of this mind. Then must you learn the use
	And handling of your silver fork at meals,
	The metal of your glass; (these are main matters
	With your Italian;) and to know the hour
	When you must eat your melons and your figs.
PER.	Is that a point of state too?
SIR P.	Here it is:
	For your Venetian, if he see a man
	Preposterous in the least, he has him straight;
	He has; he strips him. I'll acquaint you, sir.
	I now have liv'd here 't is some fourteen months:
	Within the first week of my landing here,
	All took me for a citizen of Venice,
	I knew the forms so well —
PER.	[Aside.] And nothing else.
SIR P.	I had read Contarene,[4] took me a house,
	Dealt with my Jews to furnish it with movables —
	Well, if I could but find one man, one man
	To mine own heart, whom I durst trust, I would —
PER.	What, what, sir?
SIR P.	Make him rich; make him a fortune:
	He should not think again. I would command it.
PER.	As how?
SIR P.	With certain projects that I have;
	Which I may not discover.[5]
PER.	[Aside.] If I had

---

3. *Nic. Machiavel . . . Bodin*] Niccolò Machiavelli (1469–1527), the Italian statesman, politician and philosopher, and Jean Bodin, a French political philosopher, who advocated religious tolerance.

4. *Contarene*] Contarini, author of a book on Venetian government.

5. *discover*] disclose, reveal.

But one to wager with, I would lay odds now,
He tells me instantly.

SIR P.   One is, and that
I care not greatly who knows, to serve the state
Of Venice with red herrings for three years,
And at a certain rate, from Rotterdam,
Where I have correspondence. There 's a letter,
Sent me from one o' th' states, and to that purpose:
He cannot write his name, but that's his mark.

PER.   He is a chandler?

SIR P.   No, a cheesemonger.
There are some others too with whom I treat
About the same negotiation;
And I will undertake it: for 't is thus.
I'll do 't with ease, I have cast it all. Your hoy[6]
Carries but three men in her, and a boy;
And she shall make me three returns a year:
So if there come but one of three, I save;
If two, I can defalk:[7] — but this is now,
If my main project fail.

PER.   Then you have others?

SIR P.   I should be loth to draw the subtle air
Of such a place, without my thousand aims.
I'll not dissemble, sir: where'er I come,
I love to be considerative; and 't is true,
I have at my free hours thought upon
Some certain goods unto the state of Venice,
Which I do call my Cautions; and, sir, which
I mean, in hope of pension, to propound
To the Great Council, then unto the Forty,
So to the Ten.[8] My means are made already —

PER.   By whom?

SIR P.   Sir, one that though his place be obscure,
Yet he can sway, and they will hear him. He 's
A *commandadore*.

PER.   What! a common serjeant?

SIR P.   Sir, such as they are, put it in their mouths,

6. *hoy*] a small passenger sloop.
7. *defalk*] cut off, reduce.
8. *Great Council . . . the Ten*] increasingly lofty legislative bodies of the Venetian government.

	What they should say, sometimes; as well as greater:

What they should say, sometimes; as well as greater:
I think I have my notes to show you —

[Searching his pockets.]

PER.   Good sir.

SIR P.   But you shall swear unto me, on your gentry,
Not to anticipate —

PER.   I, sir!

SIR P.   Nor reveal
A circumstance — My paper is not with me.

PER.   O, but you can remember, sir.

SIR P.   My first is
Concerning tinder-boxes. You must know,
No family is here without its box.
Now, sir, it being so portable a thing,
Put case, that you or I were ill affected
Unto the state, sir; with it in our pockets,
Might not I go into the Arsenal,
Or you come out again, and none the wiser?

PER.   Except yourself, sir.

SIR P.   Go to, then. I therefore
Advertise to the state, how fit it were
That none but such as were known patriots,
Sound lovers of their country, should be suffer'd
T' enjoy them in their houses; and even those
Seal'd at some office, and at such a bigness
As might not lurk in pockets.

PER.   Admirable!

SIR P.   My next is, how t' inquire, and be resolv'd
By present demonstration, whether a ship,
Newly arriv'd from Soria,[9] or from
Any suspected part of all the Levant,[10]
Be guilty of the plague: and where they use
To lie out forty, fifty days, sometimes,
About the Lazaretto, for their trial;
I'll save that charge and loss unto the merchant,
And in an hour clear the doubt.

PER.   Indeed, sir!

SIR P.   Or — I will lose my labour.

---

9. *Soria*] Syria.
10. *Levant*] Middle East.

PER.　　　　　　　　　My faith, that's much.

SIR P.　　Nay, sir, conceive me. It will cost me in onions,
　　　　　Some thirty livres —

PER.　　　　　　　　　　　　Which is one pound sterling.

SIR P.　　Beside my waterworks: for this I do, sir.
　　　　　First, I bring in your ship 'twixt two brick walls;
　　　　　But those the state shall venture. On the one
　　　　　I strain me a fair tarpauling, and in that
　　　　　I stick my onions, cut in halves; the other
　　　　　Is full of loopholes, out of which I thrust
　　　　　The noses of my bellows; and those bellows
　　　　　I keep, with waterworks, in perpetual motion,
　　　　　Which is the easiest matter of a hundred.
　　　　　Now, sir, your onion, which doth naturally
　　　　　Attract th' infection, and your bellows blowing
　　　　　The air upon him, will show instantly,
　　　　　By his chang'd colour, if there be contagion;
　　　　　Or else remain as fair as at the first.
　　　　　Now it is known, 't is nothing.

PER.　　　　　　　　　　　　　　You are right, sir.

SIR P.　　I would I had my note.

PER.　　　　　　　　Faith, so would I:
　　　　　But you ha' done well for once, sir.

SIR P.　　　　　　　　　　　　　Were I false,
　　　　　Or would be made so, I could show you reasons
　　　　　How I could sell this state now to the Turk,
　　　　　Spite of their galleys, or their —
　　　　　　　　　　　　　　　　[*Examining his papers.*]

PER.　　　　　　　　　　　Pray you, Sir Pol.

SIR P.　　I have 'em not about me.

PER.　　　　　　　　　　That I fear'd.
　　　　　They are there, sir?

SIR P.　　　　　　　　　No, this is my diary,
　　　　　Wherein I note my actions of the day.

PER.　　Pray you let 's see, sir. What is here? *Notandum*,[11]　　[*Reads.*]
　　　　　"A rat had gnawn my spur-leathers; notwithstanding,
　　　　　I put on new, and did go forth; but first
　　　　　I threw three beans over the threshold. Item,

　11.　Notandum] take special note.

I went and bought two toothpicks, whereof one
I burst immediately, in a discourse
With a Dutch merchant, 'bout *ragion' del stato*.[12]
From him I went and paid a *moccinigo*
For piecing my silk stockings; by the way
I cheapen'd[13] sprats; and at St. Mark's I urin'd."
'Faith these are politic notes!

SIR P.   Sir, I do slip
No action of my life, but thus I quote[14] it.

PER.   Believe me, it is wise!
SIR P.   Nay, sir, read forth.

SCENE II. — *The same*

Enter, at a distance, LADY POLITIC WOULD-BE, NANO, 2 *Waiting-women.*

LADY P. Where should this loose knight be, trow? Sure he's hous'd.
NAN.   Why, then he's fast.
LADY P.   Ay, he plays both[1] with me.
I pray you stay. This heat will do more harm
To my complexion than his heart is worth.
(I do not care to hinder, but to take him.)
How it comes off!   [*Rubbing her cheeks.*]
1ST WOM. My master's yonder.
LADY P.   Where?
2ND WOM. With a young gentleman.
LADY P.   That same's the party:
In man's apparel! Pray you, sir, jog my knight:
I will be tender to his reputation,
However he demerit.

12. ragion' del stato] "reason of state," politics.
13. *cheapen'd*] bargained for.
14. *quote*] note.

1. *he plays both*] both "fast and loose."

SIR P.   [*seeing her.*] My lady!
PER.   Where?
SIR P.   'T is she indeed, sir; you shall know her. She is,
          Were she not mine, a lady of that merit,
          For fashion and behaviour; and for beauty
          I durst compare —
PER.   It seems you are not jealous,
          That dare commend her.
SIR P.   Nay, and for discourse —
PER.   Being your wife, she cannot miss that.
SIR P.   [*introducing Per.*]   Madam,
          Here is a gentleman, pray you, use him fairly;
          He seems a youth, but he is —
LADY P.   None.
SIR P.   Yes one
          Has put his face as soon into the world —
LADY P.   You mean, as early? But to-day?
SIR P.   How's this?
LADY P.   Why, in this habit, sir; you apprehend me.
          Well, Master Would-be, this doth not become you;
          I had thought the odour, sir, of your good name
          Had been more precious to you; that you would not
          Have done this dire massacre on your honour;
          One of your gravity, and rank besides!
          But knights, I see, care little for the oath
          They make to ladies; chiefly their own ladies.
SIR P.   Now, by my spurs, the symbol of my knighthood —
PER.   [*Aside.*] Lord, how his brain is humbl'd for an oath!
SIR P.   I reach² you not.
LADY P.   Right, sir, your polity
          May bear it through thus. Sir, a word with you.
                                              [*To* PER.]

          I would be loth to contest publicly
          With any gentlewoman, or to seem
          Froward, or violent, as the courtier says;
          It comes too near rusticity in a lady,
          Which I would shun by all means: and however

---

2. *reach*] understand.

        I may deserve from Master Would-be, yet
        T' have one fair gentlewoman thus be made
        The unkind instrument to wrong another,
        And one she knows not, ay, and to perséver;
        In my poor judgment, is not warranted
        From being a solecism in our sex,
        If not in manners.

PER.   How is this!

SIR P.   Sweet madam,
        Come nearer to your aim.

LADY P.   Marry, and will, sir.
        Since you provoke me with your impudence,
        And laughter of your light land-syren here,
        Your Sporus,[3] your hermaphrodite —

PER.   What 's here?
        Poetic fury and historic storms!

SIR P.   The gentleman, believe it, is of worth
        And of our nation.

LADY P.   Ay, your Whitefriars nation.[4]
        Come, I blush for you, Master Would-be, I;
        And am asham'd you should ha' no more forehead
        Than thus to be the patron, or St. George,
        To a lewd harlot, a base fricatrice,[5]
        A female devil, in a male outside.

SIR P.   Nay,
        An you be such a one, I must bid adieu
        To your delights. The case appears too liquid.

                                           [*Exit.*]

LADY P. Ay, you may carry 't clear, with you state-face!
        But for your carnival concupiscence,
        Who here is fled for liberty of conscience,
        From furious persecution of the marshal,
        Her will I disc'ple.[6]

PER.   This is fine, i' faith!
        And do you use this often? Is this part

---

3. *Sporus*] one of Nero's favorite catamites, whom he dressed in drag and married.
4. *Whitefriars nation*] a disreputable part of London, inhabited by prostitutes.
5. *fricatrice*] prostitute.
6. *disc'ple*] discipline.

Of your wit's exercise, 'gainst you have occasion?
Madam —

LADY P.   Go to, sir.

PER.   Do you hear me, lady?
Why, if your knight have set you to beg shirts,
Or to invite me home, you might have done it
A nearer way by far.

LADY P.   This cannot work you
Out of my snare.

PER.   Why, am I in it, then?
Indeed your husband told me you were fair,
And so you are; only your nose inclines,
That side that 's next the sun, to the queen-apple.[7]

LADY P.   This cannot be endur'd by any patience.

SCENE III. — *The same*

To them enter MOSCA.

MOS.   What is the matter, madam?

LADY P.   If the senate
Right not my quest in this, I will protest 'em
To all the world no aristocracy.

MOS.   What is the injury, lady?

LADY P.   Why, the callet[1]
You told me of, here I have ta'en disguis'd.

MOS.   Who? this! what means your ladyship? The creature
I mention'd to you is apprehended now,
Before the senate; you shall see her —

LADY P.   Where?

MOS.   I'll bring you to her. This young gentleman,
I saw him land this morning at the port.

LADY P.   Is 't possible! how has my judgment wander'd?

---

7. *your nose ... queen-apple*] her nose is red.

---

1. *callet*] prostitute.

PER.   Sir, I must, blushing, say to you, I have err'd;

And plead your pardon.

PER.   What, more changes yet!

LADY P.   I hope you ha' not the malice to remember

A gentlewoman's passion. If you stay

In Venice here, please you to use me, sir —

MOS.   Will you go, madam?

LADY P.   Pray you, sir, use me; in faith,

The more you see me the more I shall conceive

You have forgot our quarrel.

[*Exeunt* LADY WOULD-BE, MOSCA, NANO, *and* Waiting-women.]

PER.   This is rare!

Sir Politic Would-be? No, Sir Politic Bawd,

To bring me thus acquainted with his wife!

Well, wise Sir Pol, since you have practis'd thus

Upon my freshman-ship, I'll try your salt-head,[2]

What proof it is against a counter-plot.

                                           [*Exit.*]

SCENE IV. — *The Scrutineo*

Enter VOLTORE, CORBACCIO, CORVINO, MOSCA.

VOLT.   Well, now you know the carriage of the business,

Your constancy is all that is requir'd

Unto the safety of it.

MOS.   Is the lie

Safely convey'd amongst us? Is that sure?

Knows every man his burden?

CORV.   Yes.

MOS.   Then shrink not.

CORV.   But knows the advocate the truth?

MOS.   O, sir,

By no means; I devis'd a formal tale,

That salv'd your reputation. But be valiant, sir.

_____

2. *salt-head*] salaciousness, lasciviousness.

CORV.   I fear no one but him that this his pleading
        Should make him stand for a co-heir —
MOS.   Co-halter!
        Hang him; we will but use his tongue, his noise,
        As we do croaker's[1] here.
CORV.   Ay, what shall he do?
MOS.   When we ha' done, you mean?
CORV.   Yes.
MOS.   Why, we'll think;
        Sell him for mummia:[2] he's half dust already. —
        Do you not smile, (*to* VOLTORE) to see this buffalo,[3]
        How he doth sport it with his head? [*Aside.*] I should,
        If all were well and past. — Sir, (*to* CORBACCIO) only you
        Are he that shall enjoy the crop of all,
        And these not know for whom they toil.
CORB.   Ay, peace.
MOS.   (*turning to* CORVINO.) But you shall eat it. [*Aside.*] Much! —
           Worshipful sir, (*to* VOLTORE)
        Mercury sit upon your thund'ring tongue,
        Or the French Hercules, and make your language
        As conquering as his club, to beat along,
        As with a tempest, flat, our adversaries;
        But much more yours, sir.
VOLT.   Here they come, ha' done.
MOS.   I have another witness, if you need, sir,
        I can produce.
VOLT.   Who is it?
MOS.   Sir, I have her.

---

1. *croaker's*] Corbaccio's.
2. *mummia*] a medicine; supposedly made from the oozing from mummies.
3. *buffalo*] an allusion to a cuckold's horns.

SCENE V. — *The same*

Enter 4 Avocatori, *and take their seats*, BONARIO, CELIA, Notario, Commandadori, Saffi, *and other* Officers of Justice.

1ST AVOC.   The like of this the senate never heard of.
2ND AVOC.   'T will come most strange to them when we report it.
4TH AVOC.   The gentlewoman has been ever held
       Of unreproved name.
3RD AVOC.   So has the youth.
4TH AVOC.   The more unnatural part that of his father.
2ND AVOC.   More of the husband.
1ST AVOC.   I not know to give
       His act a name, it is so monstrous!
4TH AVOC.   But the impostor, he's a thing created.
       T' exceed example!
1ST AVOC.   And all after-times!
2ND AVOC.   I never heard a true voluptuary
       Describ'd but him.
3RD AVOC.   Appear yet those were cited?
NOT.   All but the old magnifico, Volpone.
1ST AVOC.   Why is not he here?
MOS.   Please your fatherhoods,
       Here is his advocate: himself's so weak,
       So feeble —
4TH AVOC.   Who are you?
BON.   His parasite,
       His knave, his pander. I beseech the court
       He may be forc'd to come, that your grave eyes
       May bear strong witness of his strange impostures.
VOLT.   Upon my faith and credit with your virtues.
       He is not able to endure the air.
2ND AVOC.   Bring him.
3RD AVOC.   We will see him.
4TH AVOC.   Fetch him.
VOLT.   Your fatherhoods' fit pleasures be obey'd;

                           [*Exeunt* Officers.]

> But sure, the sight will rather move your pities
> Than indignation. May it please the court,
> In the mean time, he may be heard in me.
> I know this place most void of prejudice,
> And therefore crave it, since we have no reason
> To fear our truth should hurt our cause.

3RD AVOC.   Speak free.

VOLT.   Then know, most honour'd fathers, I must now
> Discover to your strangely abus'd ears,
> The most prodigious and most frontless piece
> Of solid impudence, and treachery,
> That ever vicious nature yet brought forth
> To shame the state of Venice. This lewd woman,
> That wants no artificial looks or tears
> To help the vizor she has now put on,
> Hath long been known a close adulteress
> To that lascivious youth there; not suspected,
> I say, but known, and taken in the act
> With him; and by this man, the easy husband,
> Pardon'd; whose timeless bounty makes him now
> Stand here, the most unhappy, innocent person,
> That ever man's own goodness made accus'd.
> For these not knowing how to owe a gift
> Of that dear grace, but with their shame; being plac'd
> So above all powers of their gratitude,
> Began to hate the benefit; and in place
> Of thanks, devise t' extirp the memory
> Of such an act: wherein I pray your fatherhoods
> To observe the malice, yea, the rage of creatures
> Discover'd in their evils: and what heart
> Such take, ev'n from their crimes: — but that anon
> Will more appear. — This gentleman, the father,
> Hearing of this foul fact, with many others,
> Which daily struck at his too tender ears,
> And griev'd in nothing more than that he could not
> Preserve himself a parent (his son's ills
> Growing to that strange flood), at last decreed
> To disinherit him.

1ST AVOC.   These be strange turns!

2ND AVOC.   The young man's fame was ever fair and honest.

VOLT.   So much more full of danger is his vice,
           That can beguile so, under shade of virtue.
           But, as I said, my honour'd sires, his father
           Having this settled purpose, by what means
           To him betray'd, we know not, and this day
           Appointed for the deed; that parricide,
           I cannot style him better, by confederacy
           Preparing this his paramour to be there,
           Ent'red Volpone's house (who was the man,
           Your fatherhoods must understand, design'd
           For the inheritance), there sought his father: —
           But with what purpose sought he him, my lords?
           I tremble to pronounce it, that a son
           Unto a father, and to such a father,
           Should have so foul, felonious intent!
           It was to murder him: when being prevented
           By his more happy absence, what then did he?
           Not check his wicked thoughts; no, now new deeds;
           (Mischief doth never end where it begins)
           An act of horror, fathers! He dragg'd forth
           The aged gentleman that had there lain bedrid
           Three years and more, out of his innocent couch,
           Naked upon the floor; there left him; wounded
           His servant in the face; and with this strumpet,
           The stale[1] to his forg'd practice, who was glad
           To be so active, — (I shall here desire
           Your fatherhoods to note but my collections,
           As most remarkable, —) thought at once to stop
           His father's ends, discredit his free choice
           In the old gentleman, redeem themselves,
           By laying infamy upon this man,
           To whom, with blushing, they should owe their lives.

1ST AVOC.   What proofs have you of this?

BON.   Most honour'd fathers,
           I humbly crave there be no credit given
           To this man's mercenary tongue.

2ND AVOC.   Forbear.

BON.   His soul moves in his fee.

---

1. *The stale*] The decoy.

3RD AVOC.   O, sir.
BON.   This fellow,
For six sols[2] more would plead against his Maker.
1ST AVOC.   You do forget yourself.
VOLT.   Nay, nay, grave fathers,
Let him have scope: can any man imagine
That he will spare his accuser, that would not
Have spar'd his parent?
1ST AVOC.   Well, produce your proofs.
CEL.   I would I could forget I were a creature.
VOLT.   Signior Corbaccio!

                          [CORBACCIO *comes forward.*]

4TH AVOC.   What is he?
VOLT.   The father.
2ND AVOC. Has he had an oath?
NOT.   Yes.
CORB.   What must I do now?
NOT.   Your testimony's crav'd.
CORB.   Speak to the knave?
I'll ha' my mouth first stopt with earth; my heart
Abhors his knowledge: I disclaim in[3] him.
1ST AVOC.   But for what cause?
CORB.   The mere portent of nature!
He is an utter stranger to my loins.
BON.   Have they made you to this?
CORB.   I will not hear thee,
Monster of men, swine, goat, wolf, parricide!
Speak not, thou viper.
BON.   Sir, I will sit down,
And rather wish my innocence should suffer
Than I resist the authority of a father.
VOLT.   Signior Corvino!

                        [CORVINO *comes forward.*]

2ND AVOC.   This is strange.
1ST AVOC.   Who's this?
NOT.   The husband.
4TH AVOC.   Is he sworn?

2. *six sols*] three pence.
3. *disclaim in him*] disown him.

NOT.   He is.
3RD AVOC.   Speak then.
CORV.   This woman, please your fatherhoods, is a whore,
          Of most hot exercise, more than a partridge,
          Upon record —
1ST AVOC.   No more.
CORV.   Neighs like a jennet.[4]
NOT.   Preserve the honour of the court.
CORV.   I shall,
          And modesty of your most reverend ears.
          And yet I hope that I may say, these eyes
          Have seen her glu'd unto that piece of cedar,
          That fine well timber'd gallant: and that here
          The letters may be read, thorough the horn,[5]
          That make the story perfect.
MOS.   Excellent! sir.
CORV.   [*Aside to* MOSCA.] There is no shame in this now, is there?
MOS.   None.
CORV.   Or if I said, I hop'd that she were onward
          To her damnation, if there be a hell
          Greater than whore and woman, a good Catholic
          May make the doubt.
3RD AVOC.   His grief hath made him frantic.
1ST AVOC. Remove him hence.
2ND AVOC.   Look to the woman.

                                   [CELIA *swoons*.]
CORV.   Rare!
          Prettily feign'd again!
4TH AVOC.   Stand from about her.
1ST AVOC. Give her the air.
3RD AVOC.   What can you say?   [*To* MOSCA.]
MOS.   My wound,
          May it please your wisdoms, speaks for me, receiv'd
          In aid of my good patron, when he mist
          His sought-for father, when that well-taught dame
          Had her cue giv'n her to cry out, "A rape!"

---

4. *jennet*] mare in heat.
5. *the horn*] of the cuckold.

BON.   O most laid[6] impudence! Fathers —
3RD AVOC.   Sir, be silent;
            You had your hearing free, so must they theirs.
2ND AVOC.   I do begin to doubt th' imposture here.
4TH AVOC.   This woman has too many moods.
VOLT.   Grave fathers,
            She is a creature of a most profest
            And prostituted lewdness.
CORV.   Most impetuous,
            Unsatisfi'd, grave fathers!
VOLT.   May her feignings
            Not take your wisdoms: but this day she baited
            A stranger, a grave knight, with her loose eyes,
            And more lascivious kisses. This man saw 'em
            Together on the water, in a gondola.
MOS.   Here is the lady herself, that saw them too,
            Without; who then had in the open streets
            Pursu'd them, but for saving her knight's honour.
1ST AVOC.   Produce that lady.
2ND AVOC.   Let her come.   [*Exit* MOSCA.]
4TH AVOC.   These things,
            They strike with wonder.
3RD AVOC.   I am turn'd a stone.

SCENE VI. — *The same*

To them re-enter MOSCA *with* LADY WOULD-BE.

MOS.   Be resolute, madam.
LADY P.   Ay, this same is she.
                                          [*Pointing to* CELIA.]
            Out, thou chameleon harlot! now thine eyes
            Vie tears with the hyena. Dar'st thou look
            Upon my wronged face? I cry your pardons,

---

    6. *laid*] well-contrived.

   I fear I have forgettingly transgrest
   Against the dignity of the court—
2ND AVOC.   No, madam.
LADY P. And been exorbitant—
2ND AVOC.   You have not, lady.
4TH AVOC. These proofs are strong.
LADY P.   Surely, I had no purpose
   To scandalize your honours, or my sex's.
3RD AVOC. We do believe it.
LADY P.   Surely you may believe it.
2ND AVOC. Madam, we do.
LADY P.   Indeed you may; my breeding
   Is not so coarse—
4TH AVOC.   We know it.
LADY P.   To offend
   With pertinacy—
3RD AVOC.   Lady—
LADY P.   Such a presence!
   No surely.
1ST AVOC. We will think it.
LADY P.   You may think it.
1ST AVOC. Let her o'ercome. What witnesses have you,
   To make good your report?
BON.   Our consciences.
CEL. And heaven, that never fails the innocent.
1ST AVOC. These are no testimonies.
BON.   Not in your courts,
   Where multitude and clamour overcomes.
1ST AVOC. Nay, then you do wax insolent.

VOLPONE [*brought in, as impotent*].

VOLT.   Here, here,
   The testimony comes that will convince,
   And put to utter dumbness their bold tongues!
   See here, grave fathers, here's the ravisher,
   The rider on men's wives, the great impostor,
   The grand voluptuary! Do you not think
   These limbs should affect venery? or these eyes
   Covet a concubine? Pray you mark these hands;

Are they not fit to stroke a lady's breasts?
Perhaps he doth dissemble!

BON.   So he does.
VOLT.   Would you ha' him tortur'd?
BON.   I would have him prov'd.
VOLT.   Best try him then with goads, or burning irons;
Put him to the strappado:[1] I have heard
The rack hath cur'd the gout; faith, give it him,
And help him of a malady; be courteous.
I'll undertake, before these honour'd fathers,
He shall have yet as many left diseases,
As she has known adulterers, or thou strumpets.
O, my most equal hearers, if these deeds,
Acts of this bold and most exorbitant strain,
May pass with suff'rance, what one citizen
But owes the forfeit of his life, yea, fame,
To him that dares traduce him? Which of you
Are safe, my honour'd fathers? I would ask,
With leave of your grave fatherhoods, if their plot
Have any face or colour like to truth?
Or if, unto the dullest nostril here,
It smell not rank, and most abhorred slander?
I crave your care of this good gentleman,
Whose life is much endanger'd by their fable;
And as for them, I will conclude with this,
That vicious persons, when they're hot, and flesh'd
In impious acts, their constancy[2] abounds:
Damn'd deeds are done with greatest confidence.
1ST AVOC.   Take 'em to custody, and sever them.
2ND AVOC.   'T is pity two such prodigies should live.
1ST AVOC.   Let the old gentleman be return'd with care.

[*Exeunt* Officers *with* VOLPONE.]

I'm sorry our credulity wrong'd him.
4TH AVOC.   These are two creatures!

---

1. *strappado*] a form of torture in which a man's hands were tied behind his back and he was
   hoisted by his wrists on a gallows, the usual result being the dislocation of his shoulders.
2. *constancy*] boldness.

3RD AVOC.   I've an earthquake in me.
2ND AVOC. Their shame, ev'n in their cradles, fled their faces.
4TH AVOC. You have done a worthy service to the state, sir,
          In their discovery.   [*To* VOLT.]
1ST AVOC.   You shall hear, ere night,
          What punishment the court decrees upon 'em.
          [*Exeunt* Avocat., Not., *and* Officers *with* BONARIO *and*
             CELIA.]
VOLT.   We thank your fatherhoods. How like you it?
MOS.   Rare.
          I'd ha' your tongue, sir, tipt with gold for this;
          I'd ha' you be the heir to the whole city;
          The earth I'd have want men ere you want living:
          They're bound to erect your statue in St. Mark's.
          Signior Corvino, I would have you go
          And show yourself that you have conquer'd.
CORV.   Yes.
MOS.   It was much better that you should profess
          Yourself a cuckold thus, than that the other
          Should have been prov'd.
CORV.   Nay, I consider'd that:
          Now it is her fault.
MOS.   Then it had been yours.
CORV.   True; I do doubt this advocate still.
MOS.   I' faith.
          You need not, I dare ease you of that care.
CORV.   I trust thee, Mosca.   [*Exit.*]
MOS.   As your own soul, sir.
CORB.   Mosca!
MOS.   Now for your business, sir.
CORB.   How! ha' you business?
MOS.   Yes, yours, sir,
CORB.   O, none else?
MOS.   None else, not I.
CORB.   Be careful then.
MOS.   Rest you with both your eyes, sir.
CORB.   Dispatch it.
MOS.   Instantly.
CORB.   And look that all,

   Whatever, be put in, jewels, plate, moneys,
   Household stuff, bedding, curtains.

MOS.   Curtain-rings, sir:
   Only the advocate's fee must be deducted.

CORB. I'll pay him now; you'll be too prodigal.

MOS. Sir, I must tender it.

CORB.   Two chequins is well.

MOS. No, six, sir.

CORB.   'T is too much.

MOS.   He talk'd a great while;
   You must consider that, sir.

CORB.   ·   Well, there's three —

MOS. I'll give it him.

CORB.   Do so, and there's for thee.   [*Exit.*]

MOS. [*Aside.*] Bountiful bones! What horrid strange offence
   Did he commit 'gainst nature, in his youth,
   Worthy this age? — You see, sir, [*to* VOLT] how I work
   Unto your ends; take you no notice.

VOLT.   No,
   I'll leave you.

MOS.   All is yours, the devil and all,
   Good advocate! — Madam, I'll bring you home.

LADY P. No, I'll go see your patron.

MOS.   That you shall not:
   I'll tell you why. My purpose is to urge
   My patron to reform his will, and for
   The zeal you 've shown to-day, whereas before
   You were but third or fourth, you shall be now
   Put in the first; which would appear as begg'd
   If you were present. Therefore —

LADY P.   You shall sway me.   [*Exeunt.*]

ACT V

SCENE I. — *A room in Volpone's house*

Enter VOLPONE.

VOLP. Well, I am here, and all this brunt is past.
I ne'er was in dislike with my disguise
Till this fled moment: here 't was good, in private;
But in your public, — *cavè*[1] whilst I breathe.
'Fore God, my left leg 'gan to have the cramp.
And I apprehended straight some power had struck me
With a dead palsy. Well! I must be merry,
And shake it off. A many of these fears
Would put me into some villanous disease,
Should they come thick upon me: I'll prevent 'em.
Give me a bowl of lusty wine, to fright
This humour from my heart. (*Drinks.*) Hum, hum, hum!
'T is almost gone already; I shall conquer.
Any device now of rare ingenious knavery,
That would possess me with a violent laughter,
Would make me up again. (*Drinks again.*) So, so, so, so!
This heat is life; 't is blood by this time: — Mosca!

---

1. cavè] Latin for "beware," "watch out."

SCENE II. — *The same*

VOLPONE. *Enter* MOSCA.

MOS.　　How now, sir? Does the day look clear again?
　　　　Are we recover'd, and wrought out of error,
　　　　Into our way, to see our path before us?
　　　　Is our trade free once more?
VOLP.　　　　　　　　　　　　　Exquisite Mosca!
MOS.　　Was it not carri'd learnedly?
VOLP.　　　　　　　　　　　And stoutly:
　　　　Good wits are greatest in extremities.
MOS.　　It were folly beyond thought to trust
　　　　Any grand act unto a cowardly spirit.
　　　　You are not taken with it enough, methinks.
VOLP.　　O, more than if I had enjoy'd the wench:
　　　　The pleasure of all woman-kind 's not like it.
MOS.　　Why, now you speak, sir. We must here be fix'd;
　　　　Here we must rest; this is our masterpiece;
　　　　We cannot think to go beyond this.
VOLP.　　　　　　　　　　　　　　　True,
　　　　Thou hast play'd thy prize, my precious Mosca.
MOS.　　　　　　　　　　　　　Nay, sir,
　　　　To gull the court —
VOLP.　　　　　　　　And quite divert the torrent
　　　　Upon the innocent.
MOS.　　　　　　　　　Yes, and to make
　　　　So rare a music out of discords —
VOLP.　　　　　　　　　　　　Right.
　　　　That yet to me 's the strangest, how thou 'st borne it!
　　　　That these, being so divided 'mongst themselves,
　　　　Should not scent somewhat, or in me or thee,
　　　　Or doubt their own side.
MOS.　　　　　　　　　True, they will not see 't.
　　　　Too much light blinds 'em, I think. Each of 'em
　　　　Is so possest and stuft with his own hopes
　　　　That anything unto the contrary,

	Never so true, or never so apparent,
	Never so palpable, they will resist it —
VOLP.	Like a temptation of the devil.
MOS.	Right, sir.

Merchants may talk of trade, and your great signiors
Of land that yields well; but if Italy
Have any glebe[1] more fruitful than these fellows,
I am deceiv'd. Did not your advocate rare?

VOLP. O — "My most honour'd fathers, my grave fathers,
Under correction of your fatherhoods,
What face of truth is here? If these strange deeds
May pass, most honour'd fathers" — I had much ado
To forbear laughing.

MOS.   It seem'd to me, you sweat, sir.

VOLP. In troth, I did a little.

MOS.   But confess, sir,
Were you not daunted?

VOLP.   In good faith, I was
A little in a mist, but not dejected;
Never but still myself.

MOS.   I think it, sir.
Now, so truth help me, I must needs say this, sir,
And out of conscience for your advocate,
He has taken pains, in faith, sir, and deserv'd,
In my poor judgment, I speak it under favour,
Not to contrary you, sir, very richly —
Well — to be cozen'd.

VOLP.   Troth, and I think so too,
By that I heard him in the latter end.

MOS. O, but before, sir: had you heard him first
Draw it to certain heads, then aggravate,
Then use his vehement figures — I look'd still
When he would shift a shirt;[2] and doing this
Out of pure love, no hope of gain —

VOLP.   'T is right.
I cannot answer him, Mosca, as I would,
Not yet; but for thy sake, at thy entreaty,

1. *glebe*] soil.
2. *shift a shirt*] change his shirt (because he had sweated so much over his speech).

	I will begin, even now — to vex 'em all,
	This very instant.
MOS.	Good sir.
VOLP.	Call the dwarf
	And eunuch forth.
MOS.	Castrone, Nano!

[*Enter* CASTRONE *and* NANO.]

NANO.	Here.
VOLP.	Shall we have a jig now?
MOS.	What you please, sir.
VOLP.	Go,
	Straight give out about the streets, you two,
	That I am dead; do it with constancy,
	Sadly,[3] do you hear? Impute it to the grief
	Of this late slander.

[*Exeunt* CAST. *and* NANO.]

MOS.	What do you mean, sir?
VOLP.	O,
	I shall have instantly my Vulture, Crow,
	Raven, come flying hither, on the news,
	To peck for carrion, my she-wolf, and all,
	Greedy, and full of expectation —
MOS.	And then to have it ravish'd from their mouths!
VOLP.	'T is true. I will ha' thee put on a gown,
	And take upon thee, as thou wert mine heir;
	Show 'em a will. Open that chest, and reach
	Forth one of those that has the blanks; I'll straight
	Put in thy name.
MOS.	It will be rare, sir.

[*Gives him a paper.*]

VOLP.	Ay,
	When they e'en gape, and find themselves deluded —
MOS.	Yes.
VOLP.	And thou use them scurvily!
	Get on thy gown.
MOS.	[*putting on a gown.*] But what, sir, if they ask
	After the body?
VOLP.	Say, it was corrupted.

3. *Sadly*] Seriously.

MOS.	I'll say it stunk, sir; and was fain to have it
	Coffin'd up instantly, and sent away.
VOLP.	Anything; what thou wilt. Hold, here's my will.
	Get thee a cap, a count-book, pen and ink,
	Papers afore thee; sit as thou wert taking
	An inventory of parcels. I'll get up
	Behind the curtain, on a stool, and hearken:
	Sometime peep over, see how they do look,
	With what degrees their blood doth leave their faces.
	O, 't will afford me a rare meal of laughter!
MOS.	[*putting on a cap, and setting out the table, &c.*] Your advocate
	will turn stark dull upon it.
VOLP.	It will take off his oratory's edge.
MOS.	But your clarissimo, old roundback, he
	Will crump you like a hog-louse, with the touch.[4]
VOLP.	And what Corvino?
MOS.	O, sir, look for him,
	To-morrow morning, with a rope and dagger,
	To visit all the streets; he must run mad,
	My lady too, that came into the court,
	To bear false witness for your worship —
VOLP.	Yes,
	And kiss'd me 'fore the fathers, when my face
	Flow'd all with oils —
MOS.	And sweat, sir. Why, your gold
	Is such another med'cine, it dries up
	All those offensive savours: it transforms
	The most deformed, and restores them lovely,
	As 't were the strange poetical girdle.[5] Jove
	Could not invent t' himself a shroud more subtle
	To pass Acrisius'[6] guards. It is the thing
	Makes all the world her grace, her youth, her beauty.
VOLP.	I think she loves me.
MOS.	Who? The lady, sir?
	She's jealous of you.
VOLP.	Dost thou say so?

[*Knocking within.*]

---

4. *Will crump ... touch*] There was a kind of louse that would curl (crump) up when
touched.

5. *poetical girdle*] The girdle of Venus made any wearer irresistibly beautiful.

6. *Acrisius*] the father of Danaë, who locked her up in a tower.

MOS.   Hark.
    There's some already.
VOLP.   Look.
MOS.   It is the Vulture;
    He has the quickest scent.
VOLP.   I'll to my place,
    Thou to thy posture.   [*Goes behind the curtain.*]
MOS.   I am set.
VOLP.   But, Mosca,
    Play the artificer now, torture 'em rarely.

SCENE III. — *The same*

MOSCA. *Enter* VOLTORE.

VOLT.   How now, my Mosca?
MOS.   [*writing*]. "Turkey carpets, nine —"
VOLT.   Taking an inventory! that is well.
MOS.   "Two suits of bedding, tissue —"
VOLT.   Where's the will?
    Let me read that the while.

[*Enter* Servants *with* CORBACCIO *in a chair.*]

CORB.   So, set me down,
    And get you home.   [*Exeunt* Servants.]
VOLT.   Is he come now, to trouble us?
MOS.   "Of cloth of gold, two more —"
CORB.   Is it done, Mosca?
MOS.   "Of several velvets, eight —"
VOLT.   I like his care.
CORB.   Dost thou not hear?

[*Enter* CORVINO.]

CORV.   Ha! is the hour come, Mosca?
VOLP.   Ay, now they muster.
                  [*Peeps from behind a traverse.*]
CORV.   What does the advocate here,
    Or this Corbaccio?

CORB.   What do these here?

[*Enter* LADY POL. WOULD-BE.]

LADY P.   Mosca!
          Is his thread spun?
MOS.   "Eight chests of linen —"
VOLP.   O,
          My fine Dame Would-be, too!
CORV.   Mosca, the will,
          That I may show it these, and rid 'em hence.
MOS.   "Six chests of diaper, four of damask." — There.
                    [*Gives them the will carelessly, over his shoulder.*]
CORB.   Is that the will?
MOS.   "Down-beds, and bolsters —"
VOLP.   Rare!
          Be busy still. Now they begin to flutter:
          They never think of me. Look, see, see, see!
          How their swift eyes run over the long deed,
          Unto the name, and to the legacies,
          What is bequeath'd them there —
MOS.   "Ten suits of hangings —"
VOLP.   Ay, in their garters, Mosca. Now their hopes
          Are at the gasp.
VOLT.   Mosca the heir.
CORB.   What's that?
VOLP.   My advocate is dumb; look to my merchant,
          He 's heard of some strange storm, a ship is lost,
          He faints; my lady will swoon. Old glazen-eyes,
          He hath not reach'd his despair yet.
CORB.   All these
          Are out of hope; I am, sure, the man.
                                        [*Takes the will.*]
CORV.   But, Mosca —
MOS.   "Two cabinets —"
CORV.   Is this in earnest?
MOS.   "One
          Of ebony —"
CORV.   Or do you but delude me?
MOS.   "The other, mother of pearl." — I'm very busy,

	Good faith, it is a fortune thrown upon me —
	"Item, one salt of agate" — not my seeking.
LADY P.	Do you hear, sir?
MOS.	"A perfum'd box" — Pray you forbear,
	You see I'm troubl'd — "made of an onyx — "
LADY P.	How!
MOS.	To-morrow or next day, I shall be at leisure
	To talk with you all.
CORV.	Is this my large hope's issue?
LADY P.	Sir, I must have a fairer answer.
MOS.	Madam!

Marry, and shall: pray you, fairly quit my house.
Nay, raise no tempest with your looks; but hark you,
Remember what your ladyship off'red me
To put you in an heir; go to, think on it:
And what you said e'en your best madams did
For maintenance; and why not you? Enough.
Go home, and use the poor Sir Pol, your knight, well,
For fear I tell some riddles; go, be melancholic.

[Exit LADY WOULD-BE.]

VOLP.	O, my fine devil!
CORV.	Mosca, pray you a word.
MOS.	Lord! will not you take your dispatch hence yet?

Methinks, of all, you should have been th' example.
Why should you stay here? With what thought, what promise?
Hear you; do you not know, I know you an ass,
And that you would most fain have been a wittol[1]
If fortune would have let you? that you are
A declar'd cuckold, on good terms? This pearl,
You'll say, was yours? right: this diamond?
I'll not deny 't, but thank you. Much here else?
It may be so. Why, think that these good works
May help to hide your bad. I'll not betray you;
Although you be but extraordinary,
And have it only in title, it sufficeth:
Go home, be melancholy too, or mad.   [*Exit* CORVINO.]

| VOLP. | Rare Mosca! how his villany becomes him! |
| VOLT. | Certain he doth delude all these for me. |

---

1. *wittol*] a pimp for his own wife.

CORB.   Mosca the heir!
VOLP.   O, his four eyes have found it.
CORB.   I am cozen'd, cheated, by a parasiteslave;
        Harlot,[2] th' hast gull'd me.
MOS.   Yes, sir. Stop your mouth,
        Or I shall draw the only tooth is left.
        Are not you he, that filthy covetous wretch,
        With the three legs, that here, in hope of prey,
        Have, any time this three years, snuff'd about,
        With your most grov'ling nose, and would have hir'd
        Me to the pois'ning of my patron, sir?
        Are not you he that have to-day in court
        Profess'd the disinheriting of your son?
        Perjur'd yourself? Go home, and die, and stink;
        ·If you but croak a syllable, all comes out:
        Away, and call your porters! [*Exit* CORBACCIO.] Go, go, stink.
VOLP.   Excellent varlet!
VOLT.   Now, my faithful Mosca,
        I find thy constancy—
MOS.   Sir!
VOLT.   Sincere.
MOS.   [*writing.*]   "A table
        Of porphyry"—I marle[3] you'll be thus troublesome.
VOLT.   Nay, leave off now, they are gone.
MOS.   Why, who are you?
        What! who did send for you? O, cry you mercy,
        Reverend sir! Good faith, I am griev'd for you,
        That any chance of mine should thus defeat
        Your (I must needs say) most deserving travails:
        But I protest, sir, it was cast upon me,
        And I could almost wish to be without it,
        But that the will o' the dead must be observ'd.
        Marry, my joy is that you need it not;
        You have a gift, sir (thank your education),
        Will never let you want, while there are men,
        And malice, to breed causes.[4] Would I had

---

2. *Harlot*] frequently used of both sexes, here meaning "scoundrel."
3. *marle*] marvel.
4. *causes*] lawsuits.

But half the like, for all my fortune, sir!
If I have any suits, as I do hope,
Things being so easy and direct, I shall not,
I will make bold with your obstreperous aid,
Conceive me — for your fee, sir. In mean time,
You that have so much law, I know ha' the conscience
Not to be covetous of what is mine.
Good sir, I thank you for my plate; 't will help
To set up a young man. Good faith, you look
As you were costive; best go home and purge, sir.

[*Exit* VOLTORE.]

VOLP. [*comes from behind the curtain.*] Bid him eat lettuce[5] well. My
    witty mischief,
    Let me embrace thee. O that I could now
    Transform thee to a Venus! — Mosca, go,
    Straight take my habit of clarissimo,[6]
    And walk the streets; be seen, torment 'em more:
    We must pursue, as well as plot. Who would
    Have lost this feast?

MOS.   I doubt it will lose them.

VOLP. O, my recovery shall recover all.
    That I could now but think on some disguise
    To meet 'em in, and ask 'em questions:
    How I would vex 'em still at every turn!

MOS. Sir, I can fit you.

VOLP.   Canst thou?

MOS.   Yes, I know
    One o' the commandadori, sir, so like you;
    Him will I straight make drunk, and bring you his habit.

VOLP. A rare disguise, and answering thy brain!
    O, I will be a sharp disease unto 'em.

MOS. Sir, you must look for curses —

VOLP.   Till they burst;
    The Fox fares ever best when he is curst.

[*Exeunt.*]

5. *lettuce*] thought to have a soporific effect.
6. *clarissimo*] patrician.

SCENE IV. — A hall in Sir Politic's house

Enter PEREGRINE disguised and 3 Mercatori.

PER.   Am I enough disguis'd?
1ST MER.   I warrant you.
PER.   All my ambition is to fright him only.
2ND MER.   If you could ship him away, 't were excellent.
3RD MER.   To Zant, or to Aleppo![1]
PER.   Yes, and ha' his
           Adventures put i' th' Book of Voyages,
           And his gull'd story regist'red for truth.
           Well, gentlemen, when I am in a while,
           And that you think us warm in our discourse,
           Know your approaches.
1ST MER.   Trust it to our care.
                                        [Exeunt Merchants.]

[Enter Waiting-woman.]

PER.   Save you, fair lady! Is Sir Pol within?
WOM.   I do not know, sir.
PER.   Pray you say unto him
           Here is a merchant, upon earnest business,
           Desires to speak with him.
WOM.   -   I will see, sir.   [Exit.]
PER.   Pray you.
           I see the family is all female here.

[Re-enter Waiting-woman.]

WOM.   He says, sir, he has weighty affairs of state,
           That now require him whole; some other time
           You may possess him.
PER.   Pray you say again,
           If those require him whole, these will exact him,

1. Zant, Aleppo] Zakynthos (Zant) is an Ionian island; Aleppo is in Syria.

      Whereof I bring him tidings. [*Exit* Woman.] What might be
      His grave affair of state now! How to make
      Bolognian sausages here in Venice, sparing
      One o' th' ingredients?

[*Re-enter* Waiting-woman.]

WOM.   Sir, he says, he knows
      By your word "tidings," that you are no statesman,
      And therefore wills you stay.
PER.   Sweet, pray you return him;
      I have not read so many proclamations,
      And studied them for words, as he has done —
      But — here he deigns to come.   [*Exit* Woman.]

[*Enter* SIR POLITIC.]

SIR P.   Sir, I must crave
      Your courteous pardon. There hath chanc'd today
      Unkind disaster 'twixt my lady and me;
      And I was penning my apology,
      To give her satisfaction, as you came now.
PER.   Sir, I am griev'd I bring you worse disaster:
      The gentleman you met at th' port to-day,
      That told you he was newly arriv'd —
SIR P.   Ay, was
      A fugitive punk?
PER.   No, sir, a spy set on you:
      And he has made relation to the senate,
      That you profest to him to have a plot
      To sell the State of Venice to the Turk.
SIR P.   O me!
PER.   For which warrants are sign'd by this time
      To apprehend you, and to search your study
      For papers —
SIR P.   Alas, sir, I have none, but notes
      Drawn out of play-books —
PER.   All the better, sir.
SIR P.   And some essays. What shall I do?
PER.   Sir, best
      Convey yourself into a sugar-chest;

           Or, if you could lie round, a frail[2] were rare;
           And I could send you aboard.
Sir P.   Sir, I but talk'd so,
           For discourse sake merely.   [*They knock without.*]
Per.   Hark! they are there.
Sir P.   I am a wretch, a wretch!
Per.   What will you do, sir?
           Have you ne'er a currant-butt[3] to leap into?
           They'll put you to the rack; you must be sudden.
Sir P.   Sir, I have an engine[4] —
3rd Mer.   [*within.*]   Sir Politic Would-be!
2nd Mer.   [*within.*] Where is he?
Sir P.   That I've thought upon before time.
Per.   What is it?
Sir P.   I shall ne'er endure the torture.
           Marry, it is, sir, of a tortoise-shell,
           Fitted for these extremities: pray you, sir, help me.
           Here I've a place, sir, to put back my legs,
           Please you to lay it on, sir, [*Lies down while* Per. *places the
               shell upon him.*] — with this cap,
           And my black gloves. I'll lie, sir, like a tortoise,
           Till they are gone.
Per.   And call you this an engine?
Sir P.   Mine own device. — Good sir, bid my wife's women
           To burn my papers.   [*Exit* Per.]

The three Merchants *rush in.*

1st Mer.   Where is he hid?
3rd Mer.   We must,
           And will sure find him.
2nd Mer.   Which is his study?

[*Re-enter* Peregrine.]

1st Mer.   What
           Are you, sir?
Per.   I'm a merchant, that came here
           To look upon this tortoise.

   2. *frail*] rush basket.
   3. *currant-butt*] cask for holding currants.
   4. *engine*] contrivance.

3RD MER.   How!
1ST MER.   St. Mark!
       What beast is this?
PER.   It is a fish.
2ND MER.   Come out here!
PER.   Nay, you may strike him, sir, and tread upon him;
       He'll bear a cart.
1ST MER.   What, to run over him?
PER.   Yes, sir.
3RD MER.   Let's jump upon him.
2ND MER.   Can he not go?
PER.   He creeps, sir.
1ST MER.   Let's see him creep.
PER.   No, good sir, you will hurt him.
2ND MER.   Heart, I will see him creep, or prick his guts.
3RD MER.   Come out here!
PER.   Pray you, sir, creep a little.
1ST MER.   Forth.
2ND MER.   Yet further.
PER.   Good sir! — Creep.
2ND MER.   We'll see his legs.
       [*They pull off the shell and discover him.*]
3RD MER.   Gods so, he has garters!
1ST MER.   Ay, and gloves!
2ND MER.   Is this
       Your fearful tortoise?
PER.   [*discovering himself.*] Now, Sir Pol, we're even;
       For your next project I shall be prepar'd:
       I am sorry for the funeral of your notes, sir.
1ST MER.   'T were a rare motion[5] to be seen in Fleet-street.
2ND MER.   Ay, in the Term.
1ST MER.   Or Smithfield, in the fair.
3RD MER.   Methinks 't is but a melancholic sight.
PER.   Farewell, most politic tortoise!
             [*Exeunt* PER. *and* Merchants.]

[*Re-enter* Waiting-woman.]

SIR P.   Where's my lady?
       Knows she of this?

   5. *motion*] show.

WOM.	I know not, sir.
SIR P.	Enquire.—

O, I shall be the fable of all feasts,
The freight of the gazetti,[6] ship-boys' tale;
And, which is worst, even talk for ordinaries.

WOM. My lady's come most melancholic home,
And says, sir, she will straight to sea, for physic.

SIR P. And I, to shun this place and clime for ever,
Creeping with house on back, and think it well
To shrink my poor head in my politic shell.

[*Exeunt.*]

SCENE V.—*A room in Volpone's house*

Enter MOSCA *in the habit of a clarissimo, and* VOLPONE *in that of a commandadore.*

VOLP. Am I then like him?
MOS.   O, sir, you are he;
No man can sever you.
VOLP.   Good.
MOS.   But what am I?
VOLP. 'Fore heaven, a brave clarissimo; thou becom'st it!
Pity thou wert not born one.
MOS. [*Aside.*]   If I hold
My made one, 't will be well.
VOLP.   I'll go and see
What news first at the court.   [*Exit.*]
MOS.   Do so. My Fox
Is out of his hole, and ere he shall re-enter,
I'll make him languish in his borrow'd case,[1]
Except he come to composition with me.—
Androgyno, Castrone, Nano!

6. *The freight of the gazetti*] The theme of the newspapers.

1. *his borrow'd case*] his disguise.

[*Enter* ANDROGYNO, CASTRONE, *and* NANO.]

ALL.   Here.
MOS.   Go, recreate yourselves abroad; go, sport. —   [*Exeunt.*]
        So, now I have the keys, and am possest.
        Since he will needs be dead afore his time,
        I'll bury him, or gain by 'm: I'm his heir,
        And so will keep me, till he share at least.
        To cozen him of all, were but a cheat
        Well plac'd; no man would construe it a sin:
        Let his sport pay for 't. This is call'd the Fox-trap.   [*Exit.*]

SCENE VI. — *A street*

Enter CORBACCIO, CORVINO.

CORB.   They say the court is set.
CORV.   We must maintain
        Our first tale good, for both our reputations.
CORB.   Why, mine's no tale: my son would there have kill'd me.
CORV.   That's true, I had forgot: — mine is, I'm sure.
        But for your will, sir.
CORB.   Ay, I'll come upon him
        For that hereafter, now his patron's dead.

[*Enter* VOLPONE.]

VOLP.   Signior Corvino! and Corbaccio! sir,
        Much joy unto you.
CORV.   Of what?
VOLP.   The sudden good
        Dropt down upon you —
CORB.   Where?
VOLP.   And none knows how,
        From old Volpone, sir.
CORB.   Out, arrant knave!
VOLP.   Let not your too much wealth, sir, make you furious.
CORB.   Away, thou varlet.
VOLP.   Why, sir?
CORB.   Dost thou mock me?

VOLP.	You mock the world, sir; did you not change wills?
CORB.	Out, harlot!
VOLP.	O! belike you are the man,

Signior Corvino? Faith, you carry it well;
You grow not mad withal; I love your spirit:
You are not over-leaven'd with your fortune.
You should ha' some would swell now, like a wine-fat,
With such an autumn. — Did he gi' you all, sir?

CORB.	Avoid, you rascal!
VOLP.	Troth, your wife has shown

Herself a very woman; but you are well,
You need not care, you have a good estate,
To bear it out, sir, better by this chance:
Except Corbaccio have a share.

CORB.	Hence, varlet.
VOLP.	You will not be acknown, sir; why, 't is wise.

Thus do all gamesters, at all games, dissemble:
No man will seem to win. [*Exeunt* CORVINO *and* CORBAC-
CIO.] Here comes my vulture,
Heaving his beak up i' the air, and snuffing.

SCENE VII. — *The same*

VOLPONE. *Enter* VOLTORE.

VOLT.	Outstript thus, by a parasite! a slave,

Would run on errands, and make legs for crumbs!
Well, what I'll do —

VOLP.	The court stays for your worship.

I e'en rejoice, sir, at your worship's happiness,
And that it fell into so learned hands,
That understand the fing'ring —

VOLT.	What do you mean?
VOLP.	I mean to be a suitor to your worship,

For the small tenement, out of reparations,[1]
That, at the end of your long row of houses,

---

1. *out of reparations*] out of repair.

	By the Piscaria: it was, in Volpone's time,
	Your predecessor, ere he grew diseas'd,
	A handsome, pretty, custom'd² bawdy-house
	As any was in Venice, none disprais'd;
	But fell with him: his body and that house
	Decay'd together.
VOLT.	Come, sir, leave your prating.
VOLP.	Why, if your worship give me but your hand
	That I may ha' the refusal, I have done.
	'T is a mere toy to you, sir; candle-rents;³
	As your learn'd worship knows —
VOLT.	What do I know?
VOLP.	Marry, no end of your wealth, sir; God decrease it!
VOLT.	Mistaking knave! what, mock'st thou my misfortune? [*Exit.*]
VOLP.	His blessing on your heart, sir; would 't were more! —
	Now to my first again, at the next corner.

                                                      [*Exit.*]

SCENE VIII. — *The Scrutineo*

Enter CORBACCIO *and* CORVINO; — (MOSCA *passant.*)

CORB.	See, in our habit!¹ see the impudent varlet!
CORV.	That I could shoot mine eyes at him, like gun-stones!

[*Enter* VOLPONE.]

VOLP.	But is this true, sir, of the parasite?
CORB.	Again, t' afflict us! monster!
VOLP.	In good faith, sir,
	I'm heartily griev'd, a beard of your grave length
	Should be so over-reach'd. I never brook'd
	That parasite's hair; methought his nose should cozen:²

2. *custom'd*] well-frequented.
3. *candle-rents*] trivial things (to a rich man).

———————

1. *in our habit*] dressed like us.
2. *cozen*] swindle.

There still was somewhat in his look, did promise
The bane of a clarissimo.

CORB.   Knave —

VOLP.   Methinks
Yet you, that are so traded i' the world,
A witty merchant, the fine bird, Corvino,
That have such moral emblems on your name,
Should not have sung your shame, and dropt your cheese,
To let the Fox laugh at your emptiness.

CORV.   Sirrah, you think the privilege of the place,
And your red saucy cap, that seems to me
Nail'd to your jolt-head with those two chequins,
Can warrant your abuses; come you hither:
You shall perceive, sir, I dare beat you; approach.

VOLP.   No haste, sir, I do know your valour well,
Since you durst publish what you are, sir.

CORV.   Tarry,
I'd speak with you.

VOLP.   Sir, sir, another time —

CORV.   Nay, now.

VOLP.   O lord, sir! I were a wise man,
Would stand the fury of a distracted cuckold.
                              — [MOSCA *walks by them.*]

CORB.   What, come again!

VOLP.   Upon 'em, Mosca; save me.

CORB.   The air's infected where he breathes.

CORV.   Let's fly him.
                              [*Exeunt* CORV. *and* CORB.]

VOLP.   Excellent basilisk! turn upon the vulture.

SCENE IX. — *The same*

MOSCA, VOLPONE. [*Enter*] VOLTORE.

VOLT.   Well, flesh-fly, it is summer with you now;
Your winter will come on.

MOS.   Good advocate,
Prithee not rail, nor threaten out of place thus;

Thou 'lt make a solecism, as madam says.
Get you a biggin[1] more; your brain breaks loose.　　　[*Exit.*]
VOLT.　Well sir.
VOLP.　Would you ha' me beat the insolent slave,
　　　Throw dirt upon his first good clothes?
VOLT.　　　　　　　　　　　　　　This same
　　　Is doubtless some familiar.
VOLP.　　　　　　　　　　　Sir, the court,
　　　In troth, stays for you. I am mad, a mule
　　　That never read Justinian, should get up,
　　　And ride an advocate. Had you no quirk
　　　To avoid gullage, sir, by such a creature?
　　　I hope you do but jest; he has not done 't:
　　　This 's but confederacy to blind the rest.
　　　You are the heir?
VOLT.　　　　　　　　A strange, officious,
　　　Troublesome knave! thou dost torment me.
VOLP.　　　　　　　　　　　　　I know —
　　　It cannot be, sir, that you should be cozen'd;
　　　'T is not within the wit of man to do it;
　　　You are so wise, so prudent; and 't is fit
　　　That wealth and wisdom still should go together.　[*Exeunt.*]

SCENE X. — *The same*

Enter 4 Avocatori, Notario, BONARIO, CELIA, CORBACCIO, CORVINO,
Commandadori, [Saffi, *etc.*]

1ST AVOC.　Are all the parties here?
NOT.　　　　　　　　　All but th' advocate.
2ND AVOC.　And here he comes.

[*Enter* VOLTORE *and* VOLPONE.]

1ST AVOC.　Then bring them forth to sentence.
VOLT.　　O, my most honour'd fathers, let your mercy
　　　Once win upon your justice, to forgive —
　　　I am distracted —

1. *biggin*] barrister's cap.

VOLP.   (*Aside.*) What will he do now?
VOLT.   .   O,
           I know not which t' address myself to first;
           Whether your fatherhoods, or these innocents —
CORV.   (*Aside.*) Will he betray himself?
VOLT.   Whom equally
           I have abus'd, out of most covetous ends —
CORV.   The man is mad!
CORB.   What's that?
CORV.   He is possest.
VOLT.   For which, now struck in conscience, here I prostrate
           Myself at your offended feet, for pardon.
1ST, 2ND AVOC.   Arise.
CEL.   O heaven, how just thou art!
VOLP.   I'm caught
           I' mine own noose —
CORV.   [*to* CORBACCIO.] Be constant, sir; nought now
           Can help but impudence.
1ST AVOC.   Speak forward.
COM.   Silence!
VOLT.   It is not passion in me, reverend fathers,
           But only conscience, conscience, my good sires,
           That makes me now tell truth. That parasite,
           That knave, hath been the instrument of all.
1ST AVOC.   Where is that knave? Fetch him.
VOLP.   I go.   /   [*Exit.*]
CORV.   Grave fathers,
           This man 's distracted; he confest it now:
           For, hoping to be old Volpone's heir,
           Who now is dead —
3RD AVOC.   How!
2ND AVOC.   Is Volpone dead?
CORV.   Dead since, grave fathers.
BON.   O sure vengeance!
1ST AVOC.   Stay,
           Then he was no deceiver?
VOLT.   O no, none:
           This parasite, grave fathers.
CORV.   He does speak
           Out of mere envy, 'cause the servant 's made
           The thing he gap'd for. Please your fatherhoods,

This is the truth, though I'll not justify
The other, but he may be some-deal faulty.

VOLT.　Ay, to your hopes, as well as mine, Corvino:
But I'll use modesty.[1] Pleaseth your wisdoms,
To view these certain notes, and but confer[2] them;
And as I hope favour, they shall speak clear truth.

CORV.　The devil has ent'red him!

BON.　　　　　　　　　　Or bides in you.

4TH AVOC.　We have done ill, by a public officer
To send for him, if he be heir.

2ND AVOC.　　　　　　　　　For whom?

4TH AVOC.　Him that they call the parasite.

3RD AVOC.　　　　　　　　'T is true,
He is a man of great estate, now left.

4TH AVOC.　Go you, and learn his name, and say the court
Entreats his presence here, but to the clearing
Of some few doubts.　　　　　[*Exit* Notary.]

2ND AVOC.　　　　　　　This same 's a labyrinth!

1ST AVOC.　Stand you unto your first report?

CORV.　　　　　　　　　My state,
My life, my fame —

BON.　　　　　　　Where is 't?

CORV.　　　　　　　　　Are at the stake.

1ST AVOC.　Is yours so too?

CORB.　　　　　The advocate 's a knave,
And has a forked tongue —

2ND AVOC.　　　　　　　Speak to the point.

CORB.　So is the parasite too.

1ST AVOC.　　　　　　This is confusion.

VOLT.　I do beseech your fatherhoods, read but those —
　　　　　　　　　　　　[*Giving them papers.*]

CORV.　And credit nothing the false spirit hath writ:
It cannot be but he's possest, grave fathers.
　　　　　　　　　　　　[*The scene closes.*]

1. *modesty*] moderation.
2. *confer*] compare.

SCENE XI. — A *street*

Enter VOLPONE.

VOLP.   To make a snare for mine own neck! and run
        My head into it, wilfully! with laughter!
        When I had newly scap'd, was free and clear,
        Out of mere wantonness! O, the dull devil
        Was in this brain of mine when I devis'd it,
        And Mosca gave it second; he must now
        Help to sear up this vein, or we bleed dead.

[*Enter* NANO, ANDROGYNO, *and* CASTRONE.]

        How now! Who let you loose? Whither go you now?
        What, to buy gingerbread, or to drown kitlings?
NAN.   Sir, Master Mosca call'd us out of doors,
        And bid us all go play, and took the keys.
AND.   Yes.
VOLP.   Did Master Mosca take the keys? Why, so!
        I'm farther in. These are my fine conceits!
        I must be merry, with a mischief to me!
        What a vile wretch was I, that could not bear
        My fortune soberly? I must ha' my crochets,[1]
        And my conundrums! Well, go you, and seek him:
        His meaning may be truer than my fear.
        Bid him, he straight come to me to the court;
        Thither will I, and, if 't be possible,
        Unscrew my advocate, upon new hopes:
        When I provok'd him, then I lost myself.

                                                   [*Exeunt.*]

1. *crochets*] perverse conceits, odd fancies.

Scene XII. — *The Scrutineo*

Avocatori, Bonario, Celia, Corbaccio, Corvino, Commandadori,
Saffi, *etc., as before.*

1st Avoc.   These things can ne'er be reconcil'd.
           He here   *[showing the papers]*
           Professeth that the gentleman was wrong'd,
           And that the gentlewoman was brought thither,
           Forc'd by her husband, and there left.
Volt.   Most true.
Cel.   How ready is heaven to those that pray!
1st Avoc.   But that
           Volpone would have ravish'd her, he holds
           Utterly false, knowing his impotence.
Corv.   Grave fathers, he's possest; again, I say,
           Possest: nay, if there be possession, and
           Obsession, he has both.
3rd Avoc.   Here comes our officer.

[*Enter* Volpone.]

Volp.   The parasite will straight be here, grave fathers.
4th Avoc. You might invent some other name, sir varlet.
3rd Avoc. Did not the notary meet him?
Volp.   Not that I know.
4th Avoc. His coming will clear all.
2nd Avoc.   Yet it is misty.
Volt.   May 't please your fatherhoods —
Volp.   (*whispers* Volt.)   Sir, the parasite
           Will'd me to tell you that his master lives;
           That you are still the man; your hopes the same;
           And this was only a jest —
Volt.   How?
Volp.   Sir, to try
           If you were firm, and how you stood affected.
Volt.   Art sure he lives?
Volp.   Do I live, sir?

VOLT.   O me!
  I was too violent.
VOLP.   Sir, you may redeem it.
  They said you were possest; fall down, and seem so:
  I'll help to make it good. (VOLTORE *falls*.) God bless the
   man! —
  Stop your wind hard, and swell — See, see, see, see!
  He vomits crooked pins! His eyes are set,
  Like a dead hare's hung in a poulter's shop!
  His mouth's running away! Do you see, signior?
  Now it is in his belly.
CORV.   Ay, the devil!
VOLP. Now in his throat.
CORV.   Ay, I perceive it plain.
VOLP. 'T will out, 't will out! stand clear. See where it flies,
  In shape of a blue toad, with a bat's wings!
  Do you not see it, sir?
CORB.   What? I think I do.
CORV. 'T is too manifest.
VOLP.   Look! he comes t' himself!
VOLT. Where am I?
VOLP. Take good heart, the worst is past, sir.
  You're dispossest.
1ST AVOC.   What accident is this!
2ND AVOC. Sudden and full of wonder!
3RD AVOC.   If he were
  Possest, as it appears, all this is nothing.
CORV. He has been often subject to these fits.
1ST AVOC. Show him that writing: — do you know it, sir?
VOLP. (*whispers* VOLT.) Deny it, sir, forswear it; know it not.
VOLT. Yes, I do know it well, it is my hand;
  But all that it contains is false.
BON.   O practice![1]
2ND AVOC. What maze is this!
1ST AVOC.   Is he not guilty then,
  Whom you there name the parsite?
VOLT.   Grave fathers,
  No more than his good patron, old Volpone.

---

1. *practice*] conspiracy.

4TH AVOC. Why, he is dead.
VOLT.   O no, my honour'd fathers,
        He lives —
1ST AVOC. How! lives?
VOLT.   Lives.
2ND AVOC.   This is subtler yet!
3RD AVOC. You said he was dead.
VOLT.   Never.
3RD AVOC.   You said so.
CORV.   I heard so.
4TH AVOC. Here comes the gentleman; make him way.

[*Enter* MOSCA.]

3RD AVOC.   A stool,
4TH AVOC. [*Aside.*] A proper man; and were Volpone dead,
        A fit match for my daughter.
3RD AVOC.   Give him way.
VOLP.   [*Aside to* MOS.] Mosca, I was a'most lost; the advocate
        Had betray'd all; but now it is recover'd;
        All's on the hinge again — Say I am living.
MOS.   What busy knave is this! — Most reverend fathers,
        I sooner had attended your grave pleasures,
        But that my order for the funeral
        Of my dear patron did require me —
VOLP.   [*Aside.*]   Mosca!
MOS.   Whom I intend to bury like a gentleman.
VOLP.   [*Aside.*] Ay, quick, and cozen me of all.
2ND AVOC.   Still stranger!
        More intricate!
1ST AVOC.   And come about again!
4TH AVOC. [*Aside.*] It is a match, my daughter is bestow'd.
MOS.   [*Aside to* VOLP.] Will you gi' me half?
VOLP.   First I'll be hang'd.
MOS.   I know
        Your voice is good, cry not so loud.
1ST AVOC.   Demand
        The advocate. — Sir, did you not affirm
        Volpone was alive?
VOLP.   Yes, and he is;

    This gent'man told me so. — [*Aside to* MOS.] Thou shalt have
      half.

MOS.   Whose drunkard is this same? Speak, some that know him:
      I never saw his face. — [*Aside to* VOLP.] I cannot now
      Afford it you so cheap.

VOLP.   No!

1ST AVOC.   What say you?

VOLT.   The officer told me.

VOLP.   I did, grave fathers,
      And will maintain he lives, with mine own life,
      And that this creature [*points to* MOS.] told me. [*Aside.*] — I
        was born
      With all good stars my enemies.

MOS.   Most grave fathers,
      If such an insolence as this must pass
      Upon me, I am silent: 't was not this
      For which you sent, I hope.

2ND AVOC.   Take him away.

VOLP.   Mosca!

3RD AVOC.   Let him be whipt.

VOLP.   Wilt thou betray me?
      Cozen me?

3RD AVOC.   And taught to bear himself
      Toward a person of his rank.

4TH AVOC.   Away.

                    [*The* Officers *seize* VOLPONE.]

MOS.   I humbly thank your fatherhoods.

VOLP.   Soft, soft: [*Aside.*] Whipt!
      And lose all that I have! If I confess,
      It cannot be much more.

4TH AVOC.   Sir, are you married?

VOLP.   They 'll be alli'd anon; I must be resolute;
      The Fox shall here uncase.

                        Puts off his disguise.

MOS.   Patron!

VOLP.   Nay, now
      My ruin shall not come alone; your match
      I'll hinder sure: my substance shall not glue you,
      Nor screw you into a family.

Mos.	Why, patron!
Volp.	I am Volpone, and this is my knave;

                                                 [Pointing to Mosca.*]*

This [*to* Volt.], his own knave; this [*to* Corb.], avarice's fool;

This [*to* Corv.], a chimera of wittol, fool, and knave:
And, reverend fathers, since we all can hope
Nought but a sentence, let 's not now despair it.
You hear me brief.

Corv.	May it please your fatherhoods —
Com.	Silence.
1st Avoc.	The knot is now undone by miracle.
2nd Avoc.	Nothing can be more clear.
3rd Avoc.	Or can more prove

These innocent.

1st Avoc.	Give 'em their liberty.
Bon.	Heaven could not long let such gross crimes be hid.
2nd Avoc.	If this be held the highway to get riches,

           May I be poor!

3rd Avoc.	This 's not the gain, but torment.
1st Avoc.	These possess wealth, as sick men possess fevers,

           Which trulier may be said to possess them.

2nd Avoc.	Disrobe that parasite.
Corv. Mos.	Most honour'd fathers —
1st Avoc.	Can you plead aught to stay the course of justice?

           If you can, speak.

Corv. Volt.	We beg favour.
Cel.	And mercy.
1st Avoc.	You hurt your innocence, suing for the guilty.

           Stand forth; and first the parasite. You appear
           T' have been the chiefest minister, if not plotter,
           In all these lewd impostures, and now, lastly,
           Have with your impudence abus'd the court,
           And habit of a gentleman of Venice,
           Being a fellow of no birth or blood:
           For which our sentence is, first, thou be whipt;
           Then live perpetual prisoner in our galleys.

Volp.	I thank you for him.
Mos.	Bane to thy wolfish nature!

1ST AVOC.   Deliver him to the saffi. [MOSCA *is carried out.*] Thou,
              Volpone,
              By blood and rank a gentleman, canst not fall
              Under like censure; but our judgment on thee
              Is, that thy substance all be straight confiscate
              To the hospital of the Incurabili:
              And since the most was gotten by imposture,
              By feigning lame, gout, palsy, and such diseases,
              Thou art to lie in prison, cramp'd with irons,
              Till thou be'st sick and lame indeed. Remove him.
                                    [He is taken from the Bar.]

VOLP.   This is called mortifying of a Fox.

1ST AVOC.   Thou, Voltore, to take away the scandal
              Thou hast giv'n all worthy men of thy profession,
              Art banish'd from their fellowship, and our state.
              Corbaccio! — bring him near. We here possess
              Thy son of all thy state, and confine thee
              To the monastery of San Spirito;
              Where, since thou knew'st not how to live well here,
              Thou shalt be learn'd to die well.

CORB.   Ha! what said he?

COM.   You shall know anon, sir.

1ST AVOC.   Thou, Corvino, shalt
              Be straight embark'd from thine own house, and row'd
              Round about Venice, through the Grand Canal,
              Wearing a cap, with fair long ass's ears,
              Instead of horns! and so to mount, a paper
              Pinn'd on thy breast, to the Berlina.[2]

CORV.   Yes,
              And have mine eyes beat out with stinking fish,
              Bruis'd fruit, and rotten eggs — 't is well. I'm glad
              I shall not see my shame yet.

1ST AVOC.   And to expiate
              Thy wrongs done to thy wife, thou art to send her
              Home to her father, with her dowry trebled:
              And these are all your judgments.

ALL.   Honour'd fathers —

---

  2. *Berlina*] pillory.

1ST AVOC.   Which may not be revok'd. Now you begin,
                When crimes are done and past, and to be punish'd,
                To think what your crimes are. Away with them!
                Let all that see these vices thus rewarded,
                Take heart, and love to study 'em. Mischiefs feed
                Like beasts, till they be fat, and then they bleed. [*Exeunt.*]

VOLPONE [*comes forward*].

        "The seasoning of a play is the applause.
        Now, though the Fox be punish'd by the laws,
        He yet doth hope, there is no suff'ring due,
        For any fact[3] which he hath done 'gainst you;
        If there be, censure him; here he doubtful stands:
        If not, fare jovially, and clap your hands."

                                        [*Exit.*]

3. *fact*] deed.

The Alchemist

DRAMATIS PERSONAE

SUBTLE, *the Alchemist.*
FACE, *the House-keeper.*
DOL COMMON, *their colleague.*
DAPPER, *a [Lawyer's] clerk.*
DRUGGER, *a Tobacco-man.*
LOVEWIT, *Master of the House.*
[SIR] EPICURE MAMMON, *a Knight.*
[PERTINAX] SURLY, *a Gamester.*
TRIBULATION [WHOLESOME], *a Pastor of Amsterdam.*
ANANIAS, *a Deacon there.*
KASTRILL, *the angry boy.*
DAME PLIANT, *his sister, a Widow.*
Neighbours.
Officers, Mutes.

SCENE.—*London.*

TO THE READER

IF thou beest more, thou art an understander, and then I trust thee. If thou art one that tak'st up, and but a pretender, beware at what hands thou receiv'st thy commodity; for thou wert never more fair in the way to be coz'ned than in this age in poetry, especially in plays: wherein now the concupiscence of jigs and dances so reigneth, as to run away from nature and be afraid of her is the only point of art that tickles the spectators. But how out of purpose and place do I name art, when the professors are grown so obstinate contemners of it, and presumers on their own naturals,[1] as they are deriders of all diligence that way, and, by simple mocking at the terms when they understand not the things, think to get off wittily with their ignorance! Nay, they are esteem'd the more learned and sufficient for this by the multitude, through their excellent vice[2] of judgment. For they commend writers as they do fencers or wrastlers; who, if they come in robustiously and put for it with a great deal of violence, are receiv'd for the braver fellows; when many times their own rudeness is the cause of their disgrace, and a little touch of their adversary gives all that boisterous force the foil.[3] I deny not but that these men who always seek to do more than enough may some time happen on some thing that is good and great; but very seldom: and when it comes, it doth not recompence the rest of their ill. It sticks out, perhaps, and is more eminent, because all is sordid and vile about it; as lights are more discern'd in a thick darkness than a faint shadow. I speak not this out of a hope to do good on any man against his will; for I know, if it were put to the question of theirs and mine, the worse would find more suffrages, because the most favour common errors. But I give thee this warning, that there is a great difference between those that (to gain the opinion of copie[4]) utter[5] all they can, however

1. *naturals*] natural gifts.
2. *vice*] surpassing defect.
3. *foil*] defeat.
4. *copie*] *copia*, copiousness.
5. *utter*] publish.

unfitly, and those that use election and a mean. For it is only the disease of the unskillful to think rude things greater than polish'd, or scatter'd more numerous than compos'd.

ARGUMENT

T HE sickness hot, a master quit, for fear,
H is house in town, and left one servant there.
E ase him corrupted, and gave means to know
A Cheater and his punk;[1] who now brought low,
L eaving their narrow practice, were become
C oz'ners[2] at large; and only wanting some
H ouse to set up, and with him they here contract,
E ach for a share, and all begin to act.
M uch company they draw, and much abuse,
 I n casting figures, telling fortunes, news,
S elling of flies,[3] flat bawdry, with the stone,[4]
T ill it, and they, and all in fume[5] are gone.

1. *punk*] mistress.
2. *coz'ners*] swindlers.
3. *flies*] familiar spirits.
4. *stone*] philosophers' stone.
5. *fume*] smoke.

PROLOGUE

FORTUNE, that favours fools, these two short hours
   We wish away, both for your sakes and ours,
Judging spectators; and desire in place,
   To th' author justice, to ourselves but grace.
Our scene is London, 'cause we would make known,
   No country's mirth is better than our own.
No clime breeds better matter for your whore,
   Bawd, squire, impostor, many persons more,
Whose manners, now call'd humours, feed the stage;
   And which have still been subject for the rage
Or spleen of comic writers. Though this pen
   Did never aim to grieve, but better men;
Howe'er the age he lives in doth endure
   The vices that she breeds, above their cure.
But when the wholesome remedies are sweet,
   And, in their working gain and profit meet,
He hopes to find no spirit so much diseas'd,
   But will with such fair correctives be pleas'd.
For here he doth not fear who can apply.
   If there be any that will sit so nigh
Unto the stream, to look what it doth run,
   They shall find things, they 'd think, or wish, were done;
They are so natural follies, but so shown,
   As even the doers may see, and yet not own.

ACT I

SCENE I.—*A room in Lovewit's house*

[*Enter*] FACE, [*in a captain's uniform, with his sword drawn, and*] SUBTLE [*with a vial, quarrelling, and followed by*] DOL COMMON.

FACE.   Believe 't, I will.
SUB.   Thy worst. I fart at thee.
DOL.   Ha' you your wits? Why, gentlemen! for love——
FACE.   Sirrah, I 'll strip you——
SUB.   What to do? Lick figs
Out at my——
FACE.   Rogue, rogue!—out of all your sleights.[1]
DOL.   Nay, look ye, sovereign, general, are you madmen?
SUB.   O, let the wild sheep loose. I 'll gum your silks
With good strong water, an you come.
DOL.   Will you have
The neighbours hear you? Will you betray all?
Hark! I hear somebody.
FACE.   Sirrah——
SUB.   I shall mar
All that the tailor has made, if you approach.
FACE.   You most notorious whelp, you insolent slave,
Dare you do this?
SUB.   Yes, faith; yes, faith.
FACE.   Why, who
Am I, my mongrel, who am I?
SUB.   I 'll tell you,
Since you know not yourself.
FACE.   Speak lower, rogue.
SUB.   Yes. You were once (time 's not long past) the good,

1. *sleights*] drop your tricks.

133

	Honest, plain, livery-three-pound-thrum,[2] that kept
	Your master's worship's house here in the Friars,
	For the vacations——
FACE.	Will you be so loud?
SUB.	Since, by my means, translated suburb-captain.
FACE.	By your means, doctor dog!
SUB.	Within man 's memory,
	All this I speak of.
FACE.	Why, I pray you, have I
	Been countenanc'd by you, or you by me?
	Do but collect, sir, where I met you first.
SUB.	I do not hear well.
FACE.	Not of this, I think it.
	But I shall put you in mind, sir;—at Pie-corner,
	Taking your meal of steam in, from cooks' stalls,
	Where, like the father of hunger, you did walk
	Piteously costive, with your pinch'd-horn-nose,
	And your complexion of the Roman wash,[3]
	Stuck full of black and melancholic worms,
	Like powder-corns shot at the artillery-yard.
SUB.	I wish you could advance your voice a little.
FACE.	When you went pinn'd up in the several rags
	You had rak'd and pick'd from dunghills, before day;
	Your feet in mouldy slippers, for your kibes;[4]
	A felt of rug,[5] and a thin threaden cloak,
	That scarce would cover your no-buttocks——
SUB.	So, sir!
FACE.	When all your alchemy, and your algebra,
	Your minerals, vegetals, and animals,
	Your conjuring, coz'ning; and your dozen of trades,
	Could not relieve your corpse with so much linen
	Would make you tinder, but to see a fire;
	I ga' you count'nance, credit for your coals,
	Your stills, your glasses, your materials;
	Built you a furnace, drew you customers,
	Advanc'd all your black arts; lent you, beside,
	A house to practise in——
SUB.	Your master's house!

2. *livery-three-pound-thrum*] poorly paid servant.
3. *complexion of the Roman wash*] i.e., sallow.
4. *kibes*] chilblains.
5. *felt of rug*] a hat of coarse material.

FACE.   Where you have studied the more thriving skill
          Of bawdry, since.
SUB.   Yes, in your master's house.
          You and the rats here kept possession.
          Make it not strange. I know you were one could keep
          The buttery-hatch still lock'd, and save the chippings,
          Sell the dole beer to aqua-vitae men,
          The which, together with your Christmas vails[6]
          At post-and-pair,[7] your letting out of counters,
          Made you a pretty stock, some twenty marks,
          And gave you credit to converse with cobwebs,
          Here, since your mistress' death hath broke up house.
FACE.   You might talk softlier, rascal.
SUB.   No, you scarab,
          I 'll thunder you in pieces. I will teach you
          How to beware to tempt a Fury again
          That carries tempest in his hand and voice.
FACE.   The place has made you valiant.
SUB.   No, your clothes.
          Thou vermin, have I ta'en thee out of dung,
          So poor, so wretched, when no living thing
          Would keep thee company, but a spider or worse?
          Rais'd thee from brooms, and dust, and wat'ring-pots,
          Sublim'd thee, and exalted thee, and fix'd thee
          In the third region, call'd our state of grace?
          Wrought thee to spirit, to quintessence, with pains
          Would twice have won me the philosopher's work?
          Put thee in words and fashion? made thee fit
          For more than ordinary fellowships?
          Giv'n thee thy oaths, thy quarrelling dimensions?
          Thy rules to cheat at horse-race, cock-pit, cards,
          Dice, or whatever gallant tincture else?
          Made thee a second in mine own great art?
          And have I this for thanks! Do you rebel?
          Do you fly out i' the projection?
          Would you be gone now?
DOL.   Gentlemen, what mean you?
          Will you mar all?
SUB.   Slave, thou hadst had no name——
DOL.   Will you undo yourselves with civil war?

6. *vails*] tips.
7. *post-and-pair*] a game of cards.

SUB.   Never been known, past *equi clibanum*,
          The heat of horse-dung, under ground, in cellars,
          Or an ale-house darker than deaf John 's; been lost
          To all mankind, but laundresses and tapsters,
          Had not I been.
DOL.   Do you know who hears you, sovereign?
FACE.   Sirrah——
DOL.   Nay, general, I thought you were civil.
FACE.   I shall turn desperate, if you grow thus loud,
SUB.   And hang thyself, I care not.
FACE.   Hang thee, collier,
          And all thy pots and pans, in picture I will,
          Since thou hast mov'd me——
DOL.   [*Aside.*] O, this 'll o'erthrow all.
FACE.   Write thee up bawd in Paul's; have all thy tricks
          Of coz'ning with a hollow coal, dust, scrapings.
          Searching for things lost, with a sieve and shears,
          Erecting figures in your rows of houses,[8]
          And taking in of shadows with a glass,
          Told in red letters; and a face cut for thee,
          Worse than Gamaliel Ratsey's.[9]
DOL.   Are you sound?
          Ha' you your senses, masters?
FACE.   I will have
          A book, but rarely reckoning thy impostures,
          Shall prove a true philosopher's stone to printers.
SUB.   Away, you trencher-rascal!
FACE.   Out, you dog-leech!
          The vomit of all prisons——
DOL.   Will you be
          Your own destructions, gentlemen?
FACE.   Still spew'd out
          For lying too heavy o' the basket.[10]
SUB.   Cheater!
FACE.   Bawd!
SUB.   Cow-herd!
FACE.   Conjurer!
SUB.   Cutpurse!
FACE.   Witch!

8. *rows of houses*] astrological tricks.
9. A notorious highwayman.
10. *For . . . basket*] eating more than his share of rations.

DOL.   O me!
      We are ruin'd, lost! Ha' you no more regard
      To your reputations? Where 's your judgment? 'Slight,
      Have yet some care of me, o' your republic——
FACE.   Away, this brach![11] I 'll bring thee, rogue, within
      The statute of sorcery, tricesimo tertio
      Of Harry the Eighth: ay, and perhaps thy neck
      Within a noose, for laund'ring gold and barbing it.
DOL.   You 'll bring your head within a cocks-comb, will you?

[*She catcheth out* FACE *his sword, and breaks* SUBTLE's *glass.*]

      And you, sir, with your menstrue![12]—Gather it up.
      'Sdeath, you abominable pair of stinkards,
      Leave off your barking, and grow one again,
      Or, by the light that shines, I 'll cut your throats.
      I 'll not be made a prey unto the marshal
      For ne'er a snarling dog-bolt[13] o' you both.
      Ha' you together cozen'd all this while,
      And all the world, and shall it now be said,
      You 've made most courteous shift to cozen yourselves?
      [*To* FACE.] You will accuse him! You will "bring him in
      Within the statute!" Who shall take your word?
      A whoreson, upstart, apocryphal captain,
      Whom not a Puritan in Blackfriars will trust
      So much as for a feather: and you, too, [*to* SUBTLE]
      Will give the cause, forsooth! You will insult,
      And claim a primacy in the divisions!
      You must be chief! As if you, only, had
      The powder to project[14] with, and the work
      Were not begun out of equality!
      The venture tripartite! All things in common!
      Without priority! 'Sdeath! you perpetual curs,
      Fall to your couples again, and cozen kindly,
      And heartily, and lovingly, as you should,
      And lose not the beginning of a term,
      Or, by this hand, I shall grow factious too,
      And take my part, and quit you.
FACE.   'T is his fault;
      He ever murmurs, and objects his pains,

11. *brach*] bitch.
12. *menstrue*] a liquid which dissolves solids.
13. *dog-bolt*] a contemptible fellow.
14. *project*] transmute metals.

	And says, the weight of all lies upon him.
SUB.	Why, so it does,
DOL.	How does it? Do not we
	Sustain our parts?
SUB.	Yes, but they are not equal.
DOL.	Why, if your part exceed to-day, I hope
	Ours may to-morrow match it.
SUB.	Ay, they *may*.
DOL.	May, murmuring mastiff! Ay, and do. Death on me!
	Help me to throttle him. [*Seizes* SUBTLE *by the throat.*]
SUB.	Dorothy! Mistress Dorothy!
	'Ods precious, I 'll do anything. What do you mean?
DOL.	Because o' your fermentation and cibation?[15]
SUB.	Not I, by heaven——
DOL.	Your Sol and Luna——help me. [*To* FACE.]
SUB.	Would I were hang'd then! I 'll conform myself.
DOL.	Will you, sir? Do so then, and quickly: swear.
SUB.	What should I swear?
DOL.	To leave your faction,[16] sir,
	And labour kindly in the common work.
SUB.	Let me not breathe if I meant aught beside.
	I only us'd those speeches as a spur
	To him.
DOL.	I hope we need no spurs, sir. Do we?
FACE.	'Slid, prove to-day who shall shark best.
SUB.	Agreed.
DOL.	Yes, and work close and friendly.
SUB.	'Slight, the knot
	Shall grow the stronger for this breach, with me.

[*They shake hands.*]

DOL.	Why, so, my good baboons! Shall we go make
	A sort of sober, scurvy, precise neighbours,
	That scarce have smil'd twice sin' the king came in,[17]
	A feast of laughter at our follies? Rascals,
	Would run themselves from breath, to see me ride,
	Or you t' have but a hole to thrust your heads in,
	For which you should pay ear-rent?[18] No, agree.
	And may Don Provost ride a feasting long,

15. *fermentation and cibation*] alchemical terms.
16. *faction*] quarreling.
17. Seven years before.
18. *ear-rent*] have your ears cut off

	In his old velvet jerkin and stain'd scarfs,
	My noble sovereign, and worthy general,
	Ere we contribute a new crewel garter
	To his most worsted worship.
SUB.	Royal Dol!
	Spoken like Claridiana, and thyself.
FACE.	For which at supper, thou shalt sit in triumph,
	And not be styl'd Dol Common, but Dol Proper,
	Dol Singular: the longest cut at night,
	Shall draw thee for his Dol Particular.

[*Bell rings without.*]

SUB.	Who's that? One rings. To the window.
	Dol: [*Exit* DOL.]—Pray heav'n,
	The master do not trouble us this quarter.
FACE.	O, fear not him. While there dies one a week
	O' the plague, he's safe from thinking toward London.
	Beside, he's busy at his hop-yards now;
	I had a letter from him. If he do,
	He 'll send such word, for airing o' the house,
	As you shall have sufficient time to quit it:
	Though we break up a fortnight, 't is no matter.

[*Re-enter* DOL.]

SUB.	Who is it, Dol?
DOL.	A fine young quodling.[19]
FACE.	O,
	My lawyer's clerk, I lighted on last night,
	In Holborn, at the Dagger. He would have
	(I told you of him) a familiar,
	To rifle with at horses, and win cups.
DOL.	O, let him in.
SUB.	Stay. Who shall do 't?
FACE.	Get you
	Your robes on; I will meet him, as going out.
DOL.	And what shall I do?
FACE.	Not be seen; away! [*Exit* DOL.]
	Seem you very reserv'd.
SUB.	Enough. [*Exit.*]
FACE.	[*aloud and retiring.*] God be wi' you, sir,
	I pray you let him know that I was here:
	His name is Dapper. I would gladly have staid, but——

19. *quodling*] green apple, a youth.

SCENE II.—*The same*

FACE.

DAP. [*within.*] Captain, I am here.
FACE. Who 's that?—He 's come, I think, doctor.

[*Enter* DAPPER.]

Good faith, sir, I was going away.
DAP. In truth,
I am very sorry, captain.
FACE. But I thought
Sure I should meet you.
DAP. Ay, I am very glad.
I had a scurvy writ or two to make,
And I had lent my watch last night to one
That dines to-day at the sheriff's, and so was robb'd
Of my pass-time.[1]

[*Re-enter* SUBTLE *in his velvet cap and gown.*]

Is this the cunning-man?
FACE. This is his worship.
DAP. Is he a doctor?
FACE. Yes.
DAP. And ha' you broke with him, captain?
FACE. Ay.
DAP. And how?
FACE. Faith, he does make the matter, sir, so dainty,
I know not what to say.
DAP. Not so, good captain.
FACE. Would I were fairly rid on 't, believe me.
DAP. Nay, now you grieve me, sir. Why should you wish so?
I dare assure you, I 'll not be ungrateful.
FACE. I cannot think you will, sir. But the law
Is such a thing——and then he says, Read's[2] matter
Falling so lately——
DAP. Read! he was an ass,
And dealt, sir, with a fool.
FACE. It was a clerk, sir.
DAP. A clerk!

1. *pass-time*] watch.
2. A magician recently convicted.

FACE.   Nay, hear me, sir. You know the law
          Better, I think——

DAP.   I should, sir, and the danger:
          You know, I show'd the statute to you.

FACE.   You did so.

DAP.   And will I tell then! By this hand of flesh,
          Would it might never write good courthand more,
          If I discover. What do you think of me,
          That I am a chiaus?[3]

FACE.   What 's that?

DAP.   The Turk was here.
          As one would say, do you think I am a Turk?

FACE.   I 'll tell the doctor so.

DAP.   Do, good sweet captain.

FACE.   Come, noble doctor, pray thee let 's prevail;
          This is the gentleman, and he is no chiaus.

SUB.   Captain, I have return'd you all my answer.
          I would do much, sir, for your love——But this
          I neither may, nor can.

FACE.   Tut, do not say so.
          You deal now with a noble fellow, doctor,
          One that will thank you richly; and he 's no chiaus:
          Let that, sir, move you.

SUB.   Pray you, forbear——

FACE.   He has
          Four angels here.

SUB.   You do me wrong, good sir.

FACE.   Doctor, wherein? To tempt you with these spirits?

SUB.   To tempt my art and love, sir, to my peril.
          'Fore heav'n, I scarce can think you are my friend,
          That so would draw me to apparent danger.

FACE.   I draw you! A horse draw you, and a halter,
          You, and your flies together——

DAP.   Nay, good captain.

FACE.   That know no difference of men.

SUB.   Good words, sir.

FACE.   Good deeds, sir, doctor dogs'-meat. 'Slight, I bring you
          No cheating Clim o' the Cloughs[4] or Claribels,[5]
          That look as big as five-and-fifty, and flush;
          And spit out secrets like hot custard——

3. *chiaus*] a Turkish interpreter, like the one who had recently cheated some merchants.
4. An outlaw hero.
5. Probably a hero of romance. The name occurs in Spenser.

DAP.   Captain!

FACE.   Nor any melancholic underscribe,
         Shall tell the vicar; but a special gentle,
         That is the heir to forty marks a year,
         Consorts with the small poets of the time,
         Is the sole hope of his old grandmother;
         That knows the law, and writes you six fair hands,
         Is a fine clerk, and has his ciph'ring perfect.
         Will take his oath o' the Greek Xenophon,
         If need be, in his pocket; and can court
         His mistress out of Ovid.

DAP.   Nay, dear captain——

FACE.   Did you not tell me so?

DAP.   Yes; but I 'd ha' you
         Use master doctor with some more respect.

FACE.   Hang him, proud stag, with his broad velvet head!—
         But for your sake, I 'd choke ere I would change
         An article of breath with such a puck-fist!
         Come, let 's be gone.   [*Going.*]

SUB.   Pray you le' me speak with you.

DAP.   His worship calls you, captain.

FACE.   I am sorry
         I e'er embark'd myself in such a business.

DAP.   Nay, good sir; he did call you.

FACE.   Will he take then?

SUB.   First, hear me——

FACE.   Not a syllable, 'less you take.

SUB.   Pray ye, sir——

FACE.   Upon no terms but an *assumpsit*.[6]

SUB.   Your humour must be law.   [*He takes the money.*]

FACE.   Why now, sir, talk.
         Now I dare hear you with mine honour. Speak.
         So may this gentleman too.

SUB.   Why, sir——
                                   [*Offering to whisper* FACE.]

FACE.   No whisp'ring.

SUB.   'Fore heav'n, you do not apprehend the loss
         You do yourself in this.

FACE.   Wherein? for what?

SUB.   Marry, to be so importunate for one
         That, when he has it, will undo you all:

6. *assumpsit*] that he has undertaken the affair.

          He 'll win up all the money i' the town.

FACE.   How?

SUB.   Yes, and blow up gamester after gamester,
          As they do crackers in a puppet-play.
          If I do give him a familiar,
          Give you him all you play for; never set[7] him:
          For he will have it.

FACE.   You 're mistaken, doctor.
          Why, he does ask one but for cups and horses,
          A rifling fly; none o' your great familiars.

DAP.   Yes, captain, I would have it for all games.

SUB.   I told you so.

FACE.   [taking DAP. aside.] 'Slight, that is a new business!
          I understood you, a tame bird, to fly
          Twice in a term, or so, on Friday nights,
          When you had left the office; for a nag
          Of forty or fifty shillings.

DAP.   Ay, 't is true, sir;
          But I do think, now, I shall leave the law,
          And therefore——

FACE.   Why, this changes quite the case.
          Do you think that I dare move him?

DAP.   If you please, sir;
          All 's one to him, I see.

FACE.   What! for that money?
          I cannot with my conscience; nor should you
          Make the request, methinks.

DAP.   No, sir, I mean
          To add consideration.

FACE.   Why, then, sir,
          I 'll try. [Goes to SUBTLE.] Say that it were for all games,
            doctor?

SUB.   I say then, not a mouth shall eat for him
          At any ordinary,[8] but o' the score,[9]
          That is a gaming mouth, conceive me.

FACE.   Indeed!

SUB.   He 'll draw you all the treasure of the realm,
          If it be set him.

---

7. *set*] stake against.
8. *ordinary*] table d'hôte restaurant.
9. *score*] The gamblers (who frequented ordinaries) will be so impoverished through his winnings that they will have to eat on credit.

FACE.	Speak you this from art?
SUB.	Ay, sir, and reason too, the ground of art.
	He is o' the only best complexion,
	The queen of Fairy loves.
FACE.	What! Is he?
SUB.	Peace.
	He 'll overhear you. Sir, should she but see him——
FACE.	What?
SUB.	Do not you tell him.
FACE.	Will he win at cards too?
SUB.	The spirits of dead Holland, living Isaac,
	You 'd swear, were in him; such a vigorous luck
	As cannot be resisted. 'Slight, he 'll put
	Six o' your gallants to a cloak, indeed.
FACE.	A strange success, that some man shall be born to!
SUB.	He hears you, man——
DAP.	Sir, I 'll not be ingrateful.
FACE.	Faith, I have a confidence in his good nature:
	You hear, he says he will not be ingrateful.
SUB.	Why, as you please; my venture follows yours.
FACE.	Troth, do it, doctor; think him trusty, and make him.
	He may make us both happy in an hour;
	Win some five thousand pound, and send us two on 't.
DAP.	Believe it, and I will, sir.
FACE.	And you shall, sir.
	You have heard all? [FACE *takes him aside.*]
DAP.	No, what was 't? Nothing, I, sir.
FACE.	Nothing?
DAP.	A little, sir.
FACE.	Well, a rare star
	Reign'd at your birth.
DAP.	At mine, sir! No.
FACE.	The doctor
	Swears that you are——
SUB.	Nay, captain, you 'll tell all now.
FACE.	Allied to the queen of Fairy.
DAP.	Who! That I am?
	Believe it, no such matter——
FACE.	Yes, and that
	You were born with a caul o' your head.
DAP.	Who says so?
FACE.	Come
	You know it well enough, though you dissemble it.

DAP.	I' fac,[10] I do not; you are mistaken.
FACE.	How!
	Swear by your fac, and in a thing so known
	Unto the doctor? How shall we, sir, trust you
	I' the other matter? Can we ever think,
	When you have won five or six thousand pound,
	You 'll send us shares in 't, by this rate?
DAP.	By Jove, sir,
	I 'll win ten thousand pound, and send you half.
	I' fac 's no oath.
SUB.	No, no, he did but jest.
FACE.	Go to. Go thank the doctor. He 's your friend,
	To take it so.
DAP.	I thank his worship.
FACE.	So!
	Another angel.
DAP.	Must I?
FACE.	Must you! 'Slight,
	What else is thanks? Will you be trivial? — Doctor,
	[DAPPER *gives him the money*.]
	When must he come for his familiar?
DAP.	Shall I not ha' it with me?
SUB.	O, good sir!
	There must a world of ceremonies pass;
	You must be bath'd and fumigated first:
	Besides, the queen of Fairy does not rise
	Till it be noon.
FACE.	Not if she danc'd to-night.
SUB.	And she must bless it.
FACE.	Did you never see
	Her royal grace yet?
DAP.	Whom?
FACE.	Your aunt of Fairy?
SUB.	Not since she kist him in the cradle, captain;
	I can resolve you that.
FACE.	Well, see her grace,
	Whate'er it cost you, for a thing that I know.
	It will be somewhat hard to compass; but
	However, see her. You are made, believe it,
	If you can see her. Her grace is a lone woman,
	And very rich; and if she take a fancy,

10. *fac*] faith.

	She will do strange things. See her, at any hand.
	'Slid, she may hap to leave you all she has!
	It is the doctor's fear.
DAP.	How will 't be done, then?
FACE.	Let me alone, take you no thought. Do you
	But say to me, "Captain, I 'll see her grace."
DAP.	"Captain, I 'll see her grace."
FACE.	Enough. [*One knocks without.*]
SUB.	Who 's there?
	Anon. — [*Aside to* FACE.] Conduct him forth by the back way.
	Sir, against one o'clock prepare yourself;
	Till when you must be fasting; only take
	Three drops of vinegar in at your nose,
	Two at your mouth, and one at either ear;
	Then bathe your fingers' ends and wash your eyes,
	To sharpen your five senses, and cry *hum*
	Thrice, and then *buz* as often; and then come. [*Exit.*]
FACE.	Can you remember this?
DAP.	I warrant you.
FACE.	Well then, away. It is but your bestowing
	Some twenty nobles 'mong her grace's servants,
	And put on a clean shirt. You do not know
	What grace her grace may do you in clean linen.
	[*Exeunt* FACE *and* DAPPER.]

SCENE III. — *The same*

SUB.	[*within.*] Come in! Good wives, I pray you forbear me now;
	Troth, I can do you no good till afternoon. —

[*Enter* SUBTLE, *followed by* DRUGGER.]

SUB.	What is your name, say you? Abel Drugger?
DRUG.	Yes, sir.
SUB.	A seller of tobacco?
DRUG.	Yes, sir.
SUB.	Umph!
	Free of the grocers?
DRUG.	Ay, an 't please you.
SUB.	Well——
	Your business, Abel?
DRUG.	This, an 't please your worship;

I am a young beginner, and am building
Of a new shop, an 't like your worship, just
At corner of a street: — Here is the plot[1] on 't——
And I would know by art, sir, of your worship,
Which way I should make my door, by necromancy,
And where my shelves; and which should be for boxes,
And which for pots. I would be glad to thrive, sir:
And I was wish'd to your worship by a gentleman,
One Captain Face, that says you know men's planets,
And their good angels, and their bad.

SUB.   I do,
If I do see 'em——

[*Enter* FACE.]

FACE.   What! my honest Abel?
Thou art well met here.

DRUG.   Troth, sir, I was speaking,
Just as your worship came here, of your worship.
I pray you speak for me to master doctor.

FACE.   He shall do anything. Doctor, do you hear?
This is my friend, Abel, an honest fellow;
He lets me have good tobacco, and he does not
Sophisticate it with sack-lees or oil,
Nor washes it in muscadel and grains,
Nor buries it in gravel, under ground,
Wrapp'd up in greasy leather, or piss'd clouts:
But keeps it in fine lily pots, that, open'd,
Smell like conserve of roses, or French beans.
He has his maple block,[2] his silver tongs,
Winchester pipes, and fire of juniper:[3]
A neat, spruce, honest fellow, and no goldsmith.[4]

SUB.   He 's a fortunate fellow, that I am sure on.
FACE.   Already, sir, ha' you found it? Lo thee, Abel!
SUB.   And in right way toward riches——
FACE.   Sir!
SUB.   This summer.
He will be of the clothing of his company,
And next spring call'd to the scarlet; spend what he can.

1. *plot*] plan.
2. *maple block*] On which tobacco was shredded.
3. *fire of juniper*] The coals of which were used to light pipes.
4. *goldsmith*] usurer.

FACE. What, and so little beard?
SUB.   Sir, you must think,
       He may have a receipt to make hair come:
       But he 'll be wise, preserve his youth, and fine for 't;
       His fortune looks for him another way.
FACE. 'Slid, doctor, how canst thou know this so soon?
       I am amus'd at that.
SUB.   By a rule, captain,
       In metoposcopy,⁵ which I do work by;
       A certain star i' the forehead, which you see not.
       Your chestnut or your olive-colour'd face
       Does never fail: and your long ear doth promise.
       I knew 't, by certain spots, too, in his teeth,
       And on the nail of his mercurial finger.
FACE. Which finger 's that?
SUB.   His little finger. Look.
       You were born upon a Wednesday?
DRUG.   Yes, indeed, sir.
SUB.   The thumb, in chiromancy, we give Venus;
       The forefinger to Jove; the midst to Saturn;
       The ring to Sol; the least to Mercury,
       Who was the lord, sir, of his horoscope,
       His house of life being Libra; which forshow'd
       He should be a merchant, and should trade with balance
FACE. Why, this is strange! Is it not, honest Nab?
SUB.   There is a ship now coming from Ormus,
       That shall yield him such a commodity
       Of drugs——This is the west, and this the south?
                                    [*Pointing to the plan.*]
DRUG. Yes, sir.
SUB.   And those are your two sides?
DRUG.   Ay, sir.
SUB.   Make me your door then, south; your broad side, west:
       And on the east side of your shop, aloft,
       Write Mathlai, Tarmiel, and Baraborat;
       Upon the north part, Rael, Velel, Thiel.
       They are the names of those Mercurial spirits
       That do fright flies from boxes.
DRUG.   Yes, sir.
SUB.   And
       Beneath your threshold, bury me a loadstone

5. *metoposcopy*] a branch of physiognomy.

To draw in gallants that wear spurs: the rest,
They 'll seem to follow.

FACE.   That 's a secret, Nab!

SUB.   And, on your stall, a puppet, with a vice
And a court-fucus,[6] to call city-dames:
You shall deal much with minerals.

DRUG.   Sir, I have.
At home, already——

SUB.   Ay, I know, you 've arsenic,
Vitriol, sal-tartar, argaile, alkali,
Cinoper: I know all. — This fellow, captain,
Will come, in time, to be a great distiller,
And give a say — I will not say directly,
But very fair — at the philosopher's stone.

FACE.   Why, how now, Abel! is this true?

DRUG.   [*Aside to* FACE.]   Good captain,
What must I give?

FACE.   Nay, I 'll not counsel thee.
Thou hear'st what wealth (he says, spend what thou canst),
Thou 'rt like to come to.

DRUG.   I would gi' him a crown.

FACE.   A crown! and toward such a fortune? Heart,
Thou shalt rather gi' him thy shop. No gold about thee?

DRUG.   Yes, I have a portague,[7] I ha' kept this half-year.

FACE.   Out on thee, Nab! 'Slight, there was such an offer—
Shalt keep 't no longer, I 'll gi' it him for thee. Doctor,
Nab prays your worship to drink this, and swears
He will appear more grateful, as your skill
Does raise him in the world.

DRUG.   I would entreat
Another favour of his worship.

FACE.   What is 't, Nab?

DRUG.   But to look over, sir, my almanac,
And cross out my ill-days, that I may neither
Bargain, nor trust upon them.

FACE.   That he shall, Nab:
Leave it, it shall be done, 'gainst afternoon.

SUB.   And a direction for his shelves.

FACE.   Now, Nab,
Art thou well pleas'd, Nab?

6. *court-fucus*] paint for the face.
7. *portague*] A gold coin worth about three pounds, twelve shillings.

DRUG.   'Thank, sir, both your worships.
FACE.   Away.   [*Exit* DRUGGER.]
             Why, now, you smoaky persecutor of nature!
             Now do you see, that something 's to be done,
             Beside your beech-coal, and your cor'sive waters,
             Your crosslets, crucibles, and cucurbites?[8]
             You must have stuff brought home to you, to work on:
             And yet you think, I am at no expense
             In searching out these veins, then following 'em,
             Then trying 'em out. 'Fore God, my intelligence
             Costs me more money than my share oft comes to,
             In these rare works.
SUB.   You 're pleasant, sir. — How now!

SCENE IV. — *The same*

FACE, SUBTLE. [*Enter*] DOL.

SUB.   What says my dainty Dolkin?
DOL.   Yonder fish-wife
             Will not away. And there 's your giantess,
             The bawd of Lambeth.
SUB.   Heart, I cannot speak with 'em.
DOL.   Not afore night, I have told 'em in a voice,
             Thorough the trunk, like one of your familiars.
             But I have spied Sir Epicure Mammon——
SUB.   Where?
DOL.   Coming along, at far end of the lane,
             Slow of his feet, but earnest of his tongue
             To one that 's with him.
SUB.   Face, go you and shift.
             Dol, you must presently make ready too.   [*Exit* FACE.]
DOL.   Why, what 's the matter?
SUB.   O, I did look for him
             With the sun's rising: marvel he could sleep!
             This is the day I am to perfect for him
             The magisterium, our great work, the stone;
             And yield it, made, into his hands; of which
             He has, this month, talk'd as he were possess'd.

---

8. *cucurbites*] glass retort, shaped like a gourd.

And now he 's dealing pieces on 't away.
Methinks I see him ent'ring ordinaries,
Dispensing for the pox, and plaguy houses,
Reaching his dose, walking Moorfields for lepers,
And off'ring citizens' wives pomander[1]-bracelets,
As his preservative, made of the elixir;
Searching the 'spital, to make old bawds young;
And the highways, for beggars to make rich.
I see no end of his labours. He will make
Nature asham'd of her long sleep; when art,
Who 's but a step-dame, shall do more than she,
In her best love to mankind, ever could.
If his dream last, he 'll turn the age to gold.   [*Exeunt.*]

---

1. *pomander*] A ball of perfume carried against infection.

ACT II

SCENE I.—*An outer room in Lovewit's house*

[*Enter*] SIR EPICURE MAMMON *and* SURLY.

MAM.   Come on, sir. Now you set your foot on shore
      In *Novo Orbe*; here 's the rich Peru:
      And there within, sir, are the golden mines,
      Great Solomon's Ophir! He was sailing to 't
      Three years, but we have reach'd it in ten months.
      This is the day wherein, to all my friends,
      I will pronounce the happy word, BE RICH;
      THIS DAY YOU SHALL BE SPECTATISSIMI.[1]
      You shall no more deal with the hollow die,
      Or the frail card; no more be at charge of keeping
      The livery-punk[2] for the young heir, that must
      Seal, at all hours, in his shirt: no more,
      If he deny, ha' him beaten to 't, as he is
      That brings him the commodity; no more
      Shall thirst of satin, or the covetous hunger
      Of velvet-entrails for a rude-spun cloak,
      To be display'd at Madam Augusta's, make
      The sons of Sword and Hazard fall before
      The golden calf, and on their knees, whole nights,
      Commit idolatry with wine and trumpets:
      Or go a feasting after drum and ensign.
      No more of this. You shall start up young viceroys,
      And have your punks and punkettes, my Surly.
      And unto thee I speak it first, BE RICH.
      Where is my Subtle there? Within, ho!

1. *spectatissimi*] most gazed at.
2. *livery-punk*] Female accomplice in swindling heirs out of property.

                                  [FACE. *within.*] Sir,

MAM.   He 'll come to you by and by.

MAM.   That is his fire-drake,
His Lungs, his Zephyrus, he that puffs his coals,
Till he firk[3] nature up, in her own centre.
You are not faithful, sir. This night I 'll change
All that is metal in my house to gold:
And, early in the morning, will I send
To all the plumbers and the pewterers,
And buy their tin and lead up; and to Lothbury
For all the copper.

SUR.   What, and turn that, too?

MAM.   Yes, and I 'll purchase Devonshire and Cornwall,
And make them perfect Indies! You admire now?

SUR.   No, faith.

MAM.   But when you see th' effects of the Great Med'cine,
Of which one part projected on a hundred
Of Mercury, or Venus, or the Moon,
Shall turn it to as many of the Sun;[4]
Nay, to a thousand, so *ad infinitum:*
You will believe me.

SUR.   Yes, when I see 't, I will.
But if my eyes do cozen me so, and I
Giving 'em no occasion, sure I 'll have
A whore, shall piss 'em out next day.

MAM.   Ha! why?
Do you think I fable with you? I assure you,
He that has once the flower of the sun,
The perfect ruby, which we call elixir,
Not only can do that, but by its virtue,
Can confer honour, love, respect, long life;
Give safety, valour, yea, and victory,
To whom he will. In eight and twenty days,
I 'll make an old man of fourscore, a child.

SUR.   No doubt; he 's that already.

MAM.   Nay, I mean,
Restore his years, renew him, like an eagle,
To the fifth age; make him get sons and daughters,
Young giants; as our philosophers have done,
The ancient patriarchs, afore the flood,

3. *firk*] stir, rouse.
4. *Shall . . . Sun*] Turn mercury, copper, or silver into gold.

	But taking, once a week, on a knife's point,
	The quantity of a grain of mustard of it;
	Become stout Marses, and beget young Cupids.
SUR.	The decay'd vestals of Pickt-hatch[5] would thank you,
	That keep the fire alive there.

MAM.   'T is the secret
Of nature naturiz'd 'gainst all infections,
Cures all diseases coming of all causes;
A month's grief in a day, a year's in twelve;
And, of what age soever, in a month.
Past all the doses of your drugging doctors.
I 'll undertake, withal, to fright the plague
Out o' the kingdom in three months.

SUR.   And I 'll
Be bound, the players shall sing your praises then,
Without their poets.

MAM.   Sir, I 'll do 't. Meantime,
I 'll give away so much unto my man,
Shall serve th' whole city with preservative
Weekly; each house his dose, and at the rate——

SUR.   As he that built the Water-work does with water?

MAM.   You are incredulous.

SUR.   Faith, I have a humour,
I would not willingly be gull'd.[6] Your stone
Cannot transmute me.

MAM.   Pertinax Surly,
Will you believe antiquity? Records?
I 'll show you a book where Moses, and his sister,
And Solomon have written of the art;
Ay, and a treatise penn'd by Adam——

SUR.   How!

MAM.   Of the philosopher's stone, and in High Dutch.

SUR.   Did Adam write, sir, in High Dutch?

MAM.   He did;
Which proves it was the primitive tongue.

SUR.   What paper?

MAM.   On cedar board.

SUR.   O that, indeed, they say,
Will last 'gainst worms.

MAM.   'T is like your Irish wood

5. *Pickt-hatch*] a disreputable locality.
6. *gull'd*] fooled.

'Gainst cobwebs. I have a piece of Jason's fleece too,
Which was no other than a book of alchemy,
Writ in large sheepskin, a good fat ram-vellum.
Such was Pythagoras' thigh, Pandora's tub,
And all that fable of Medea's charms,
The manner of our work; the bulls, our furnace,
Still breathing fire; our argent-vive,[7] the dragon:
The dragon's teeth, mercury sublimate,
That keeps the whiteness, hardness, and the biting;
And they are gather'd into Jason's helm,
Th' alembic, and then sow'd in Mars his field,
And thence sublim'd so often, till they're fix'd.
Both this, th' Hesperian garden, Cadmus' story,
Jove's shower, the boon of Midas, Argus' eyes,
Boccace his Demogorgon, thousands more,
All abstract riddles of our stone. — How now!

SCENE II. — *The same*

MAMMON, SURLY. [*Enter*] FACE, [*as a Servant.*]

MAM.   Do we succeed? Is our day come? And holds it?
FACE.   The evening will set red upon you, sir;
          You have colour for it, crimson: the red ferment
          Has done his office; three hours hence prepare you
          To see projection.
MAM.   Pertinax, my Surly.
          Again I say to thee, aloud, BE RICH.
          This day thou shalt have ingots; and to-morrow
          Give lords th' affront. — Is it, my Zephyrus, right?
          Blushes the bolt's-head?[1]
FACE.   Like a wench with child, sir,
          That were but now discover'd to her master.
MAM.   Excellent witty Lungs! — My only care is
          Where to get stuff enough now, to project on;
          This town will not half serve me.
FACE.   No, sir? Buy
          The covering off o' churches.

---

7. *argent-vive*] quicksilver.

---

1. *bolt's-head*] a kind of flask.

MAM.   That's true.
FACE.   Yes.
        Let 'em stand bare, as do their auditory;
        Or cap 'em new with shingles.
MAM.   No, good thatch:
        Thatch will lie light upo' the rafters, Lungs.
        Lungs, I will manumit thee from the furnace;
        I will restore thee thy complexion, Puff,
        Lost in the embers; and repair this brain,
        Hurt wi' the fume o' the metals.
FACE.   I have blown, sir,
        Hard, for your worship; thrown by many a coal,
        When 't was not beech; weigh'd those I put in, just
        To keep your heat still even. These blear'd eyes
        Have wak'd to read your several colours, sir,
        Of the pale citron, the green lion, the crow,
        The peacock's tail, the plumed swan.
MAM.   And lastly,
        Thou hast descried the flower, the *sanguis agni*?
FACE.   Yes, sir.
MAM.   Where 's master?
FACE.   At 's prayers, sir, he;
        Good man, he 's doing his devotions
        For the success.
MAM.   Lungs, I will set a period
        To all thy labours; thou shalt be the master
        Of my seraglio.
FACE.   Good, sir.
MAM.   But do you hear?
        I 'll geld you, Lungs.
FACE.   Yes, sir.
MAM.   For I do mean
        To have a list of wives and concubines
        Equal with Solomon, who had the stone
        Alike with me; and I will make me a back
        With the elixir, that shall be as tough
        As Hercules, to encounter fifty a night. —
        Thou 'rt sure thou saw 'st it blood?
FACE.   Both blood and spirit, sir.
MAM.   I will have all my beds blown up, not stuft;
        Down is too hard: and then, mine oval room
        Fill 'd with such pictures as Tiberius took
        From Elephantis, and dull Aretine

But coldly imitated. Then, my glasses
Cut in more subtle angles, to disperse
And multiply the figures, as I walk
Naked between my succubae.[2] My mists
I 'll have of perfume, vapour'd 'bout the room,
To lose our selves in; and my baths, like pits
To fall into; from whence we will come forth,
And roll us dry in gossamer and roses.—
Is it arrived at ruby?——Where I spy
A wealthy citizen, or [a] rich lawyer,
Have a sublim'd pure wife, unto that fellow
I 'll send a thousand pound to be my cuckold.

FACE.   And I shall carry it?

MAM.   No. I 'll ha' no bawds
But fathers and mothers: they will do it best,
Best of all others. And my flatterers
Shall be the pure and gravest of divines,
That I can get for money. My mere fools,
Eloquent burgesses, and then my poets
The same that writ so subtly of the fart,
Whom I will entertain still for that subject.
The few that would give out themselves to be
Court and town-stallions, and, cach-where, bely
Ladies who are known most innocent, for them,—
Those will I beg, to make me eunuchs of:
And they shall fan me with ten estrich tails
A-piece, made in a plume to gather wind.
We will be brave, Puff, now we ha' the med'cine.
My meat shall all come in, in Indian shells,
Dishes of agate set in gold, and studded
With emeralds, sapphires, hyacinths, and rubies.
The tongues of carps, dormice, and camels' heels,
Boil 'd i' the spirit of sol, and dissolv'd pearl
(Apicius' diet, 'gainst the epilepsy):
And I will eat these broths with spoons of amber,
Headed with diamond and carbuncle.
My foot-boy shall eat pheasants, calver'd salmons,
Knots, godwits, lampreys: I myself will have
The beards of barbel[3] serv'd, instead of salads;
Oil'd mushrooms; and the swelling unctuous paps

2. *succubae*] mistresses.
3. *barbel*] a fish.

Of a fat pregnant sow, newly cut off,
Drest with an exquisite and poignant sauce;
For which, I 'll say unto my cook, *There 's gold;*
Go forth, and be a knight.

FACE. Sir, I 'll go look
A little, how it heightens. [*Exit.*]

MAM. Do.—My shirts
I 'll have of taffeta-sarsnet, soft and light
As cobwebs; and for all my other raiment,
It shall be such as might provoke the Persian,
Were he to teach the world riot anew.
My gloves of fishes and birds' skins, perfum'd
With gums of paradise, and Eastern air——

SUR. And do you think to have the stone with this?

MAM. No, I do think t' have all this with the stone.

SUR. Why, I have heard he must be *homo frugi*,[4]
A pious, holy, and religious man,
One free from mortal sin, a very virgin.

MAN. That makes it, sir; he is so. But I buy it;
My venture brings it me. He, honest wretch,
A notable, superstitious, good soul,
Has worn his knees bare, and his slippers bald,
With prayer and fasting for it: and, sir, let him
Do it alone, for me, still. Here he comes.
Not a profane word afore him; 't is poison.—

SCENE III.—*The same*

MAMMON, SURLY. [*Enter*] SUBTLE.

MAM. Good morrow, father.

SUB. Gentle son, good morrow,
And to your friend there. What is he is with you?

MAM. An heretic, that I did bring along,
In hope, sir, to convert him.

SUB. Son, I doubt
You 're covetous, that thus you meet your time
I' the just point, prevent[1] your day at morning.

4. *homo frugi*] a virtuous man.

1. *prevent*] anticipate.

This argues something worthy of a fear
Of importune and carnal appetite.
Take heed you do not cause the blessing leave you,
With your ungovern'd haste. I should be sorry
To see my labours, now e'en at perfection,
Got by long watching and large patience,
Not prosper where my love and zeal hath plac'd 'em.
Which (heaven I call to witness, with yourself,
To whom I have pour'd my thoughts) in all my ends,
Have look'd no way, but unto public good,
To pious uses, and dear charity,
Now grown a prodigy with men. Wherein
If you, my son, should now prevaricate,
And to your own particular lusts employ
So great and catholic a bliss, be sure
A curse will follow, yea, and overtake
Your subtle and most secret ways.

MAM.   I know, sir;
You shall not need to fear me; I but come
To ha' you confute this gentleman.

SUR.   Who is,
Indeed, sir, somewhat costive of belief
Toward your stone; would not be gull'd.

SUB.   Well, son,
All that I can convince him in, is this,
The work is done, bright Sol is in his robe.
We have a med'cine of the triple soul,
The glorified spirit. Thanks be to heaven,
And make us worthy of it!—Ulen Spiegel![2]

FACE. [*within.*] Anon, sir.

SUB.   Look well to the register.
And let your heat still lessen by degrees,
To the aludels.[3]

FACE. [*within.*] Yes, sir.

SUB.   Did you look
O' the bolt's head yet?

FACE. [*within.*] Which? On D, sir?

SUB.   Ay;
What 's the complexion?

FACE. [*within.*] Whitish.

2. The hero of a well-known German jest-book.
3. *aludels*] a pear-shaped vessel, open at both ends.

SUB.   Infuse vinegar,
           To draw his volatile substance and his tincture:
           And let the water in glass E be filt'red,
           And put into the gripe's egg.[4] Lute[5] him well;
           And leave him clos'd *in balneo.*[6]
FACE.   [*within.*]   I will, sir.
SUR.   What a brave language here is! next to canting.
SUB.   I have another work you never saw, son,
           That three days since past the philosopher's wheel,
           In the lent heat of Athanor; and 's become
           Sulphur o' Nature.
MAM.   But 't is for me?
SUB.   What need you?
           You have enough, in that is, perfect.
MAM.   O, but——
SUB.   Why, this is covetise!
MAM.   No, I assure you,
           I shall employ it all in pious uses,
           Founding of colleges and grammar schools,
           Marrying young virgins, building hospitals,
           And, now and then, a church.

[*Re-enter* FACE.]

SUB.   How now!
FACE.   Sir, please you,
           Shall I not change the filter?
SUB.   Marry, yes;
           And bring me the complexion of glass B.
                                           [*Exit* FACE.]

MAM.   Ha' you another?
SUB.   Yes, son; were I assur'd
           Your piety were firm, we would not want
           The means to glorify it: but I hope the best.
           I mean to tinct C in sand-heat to-morrow,
           And give him imbibition.
MAM.   Of white oil?
SUB.   No, sir, of red. F is come over the helm too,
           I thank my maker, in S. Mary's bath.
           And shows *lac virginis.* Blessed be heaven!
           I sent you of his faeces there calcin'd:

4. *gripe's egg*] an egg-shaped vessel. *Gripe* is griffin.
5. *Lute*] Seal with clay.
6. *in balneo*] a dish of warm water.

          Out of that calx, I ha' won the salt of mercury.

MAM.   By pouring on your rectified water?

SUB.   Yes, and reverberating in Athanor.

[*Re-enter* FACE.]

          How now! what colour says it?

FACE.   The ground black, sir.

MAM.   That 's your crow's head?

SUR.   Your cock's comb's, is it not?

SUB.   No, 't is not perfect. Would it were the crow!
That work wants something.

SUR.   [*Aside.*]   O, I look'd for this,
The hay 's a pitching.

SUB.   Are you sure you loos'd 'em
In their own menstrue?

FACE.   Yes, sir, and then married 'em,
And put 'em in a bolt's-head nipp'd to digestion,
According as you bade me, when I set
The liquor of Mars to circulation
In the same heat.

SUB.   The process then was right.

FACE.   Yes, by the token, sir, the retort brake,
And what was sav'd was put into the pellican,
And sign'd with Hermes' seal.

SUB.   I think 't was so.
We should have a new amalgama.

SUR.   [*Aside.*]   O, this ferret
Is rank as any polecat.

SUB.   But I care not;
Let him e'en die; we have enough beside,
In embrion. He has his white shirt on?

FACE.   Yes, sir,
He 's ripe for inceration, he stands warm,
In his ash-fire. I would not you should let
Any die now, if I might counsel, sir,
For luck's sake to the rest: it is not good.

MAM.   He says right.

SUR.   [*Aside.*]   Ay, are you bolted?

FACE.   Nay, I know 't sir,
I 've seen th' ill fortune. What is some three ounces
Of fresh materials?

MAM.   Is 't no more?

FACE.   No more, sir,

	Of gold, t' amalgam with some six of mercury.
MAM.	Away, here 's money. What will serve?
FACE.	Ask him, sir.
MAM.	How much?
SUB.	Give him nine pound: you may gi' him ten.
SUR.	Yes, twenty, and be cozen'd, do.
MAM.	There 't is. [*Gives* FACE *the money.*]
SUB.	This needs not; but that you will have it so,
	To see conclusions of all: for two
	Of our inferior works are at fixation,
	A third is in ascension. Go your ways.
	Ha' you set the oil of Luna in kemia?
FACE.	Yes, sir.
SUB.	And the philosopher's vinegar?
FACE.	Ay. [*Exit.*]
SUR.	We shall have a salad!
MAM.	When do you make projection?
SUB.	Son, be not hasty, I exalt our med'cine,
	By hanging him *in balneo vaporoso,*
	And giving him solution; then congeal him;
	And then dissolve him; then again congeal him;
	For look, how oft I iterate the work,
	So many times I add unto his virtue.
	As, if at first one ounce convert a hundred,
	After his second loose, he 'll turn a thousand;
	His third solution, ten; his fourth, a hundred;
	After his fifth, a thousand thousand ounces
	Of any imperfect metal, into pure
	Silver or gold, in all examinations,
	As good as any of the natural mine.
	Get you your stuff here against afternoon,
	Your brass, your pewter, and your andirons.
MAM.	Not those of iron?
SUB.	Yes, you may bring them too;
	We 'll change all metals.
SUR.	I believe you in that.
MAM.	Then I may send my spits?
SUB.	Yes, and your racks.
SUR.	And dripping-pans, and pot-hangers, and hooks?
	Shall he not?
SUB.	If he please.
SUR.	—To be an ass.
SUB.	How, sir!

MAM. This gent'man you must bear withal.
      I told you he had no faith.
SUR.   And little hope, sir;
      But much less charity, should I gull myself.
SUB. Why, what have you observ'd, sir, in our art,
      Seems so impossible?
SUR.   But your whole work, no more.
      That you should hatch gold in a furnace, sir,
      As they do eggs in Egypt!
SUB.   Sir, do you
      Believe that eggs are hatch'd so?
SUR.   If I should?
SUB. Why, I think that the greater miracle.
      No egg but differs from a chicken more
      Than metals in themselves.
SUR.   That cannot be.
      The egg 's ordain'd by nature to that end,
      And is a chicken *in potentia*.
SUB. The same we say of lead and other metals,
      Which would be gold if they had time.
MAM.   And that
      Our art doth further.
SUB.   Ay, for 't were absurd
      To think that nature in the earth bred gold
      Perfect i' the instant: something went before.
      There must be remote matter.
SUR.   Ay, what is that?
SUB. Marry, we say——
MAM.   Ay, now it heats: stand, father,
      Pound him to dust.
SUB.   It is, of the one part,
      A humid exhalation, which we call
      Materia liquida, or the unctuous water;
      On th' other part, a certain crass and viscous
      Portion of earth; both which, concorporate,
      Do make the elementary matter of gold;
      Which is not yet *propria materia*,
      But common to all metals and all stones;
      For, where it is forsaken of that moisture,
      And hath more dryness, it becomes a stone:
      Where it retains more of the humid fatness,
      It turns to sulphur, or to quicksilver,
      Who are the parents of all other metals.

Nor can this remote matter suddenly
Progress so from extreme unto extreme,
As to grow gold, and leap o'er all the means.
Nature doth first beget th' imperfect, then
Proceeds she to the perfect. Of that airy
And oily water, mercury is engend'red;
Sulphur o' the fat and earthy part; the one,
Which is the last, supplying the place of male,
The other of the female, in all metals.
Some do believe hermaphrodeity,
That both do act and suffer. But these two
Make the rest ductile, malleable, extensive.
And even in gold they are; for we do find
Seeds of them by our fire, and gold in them;
And can produce the species of each metal
More perfect thence, than nature doth in earth.
Beside, who doth not see in daily practice
Art can beget bees, hornets, beetles, wasps,
Out of the carcases and dung of creatures;
Yea, scorpions of an herb, being rightly plac'd?
And these are living creatures, far more perfect
And excellent than metals.

MAM.   Well said, father!
Nay, if he take you in hand, sir, with an argument,
He 'll bray you in a mortar.

SUR.   Pray you, sir, stay.
Rather than I 'll be bray'd, sir, I 'll believe
That Alchemy is a pretty kind of game,
Somewhat like tricks o' the cards, to cheat a man
With charming.

SUB.   Sir?

SUR.   What else are all your terms,
Whereon no one o' your writers 'grees with other?
Of your elixir, your *lac virginis*,
Your stone, your med'cine, and your chrysosperm,
Your sal, your sulphur, and your mercury,
Your oil of height, your tree of life, your blood,
Your marchesite, your tutie, your magnesia,
Your toad, your crow, your dragon, and your panther;
Your sun, your moon, your firmament, your adrop,
Your lato, azoch, zernich, chibrit, heautarit,
And then your red man, and your white woman,
With all your broths, your menstrues, and materials

Of piss and egg-shells, women's terms, man's blood,
Hair o' the head, burnt clouts, chalk, merds, and clay,
Powder of bones, scalings of iron, glass,
And worlds of other strange ingredients,
Would burst a man to name?

SUB.   And all these, nam'd,
Intending but one thing; which art our writers
Us'd to obscure their art.

MAM.   Sir, so I told him—
Because the simple idiot should not learn it,
And make it vulgar.

SUB.   Was not all the knowledge
Of the Aegyptians writ in mystic symbols?
Speak not the scriptures oft in parables?
Are not the choicest fables of the poets,
That were the fountains and first springs of wisdom,
Wrapt in perplexed allegories?

MAM.   I urg'd that,
And clear'd to him, that Sisyphus was damn'd
To roll the ceaseless stone, only because
He would have made ours common. [DOL *is seen at the
    door.*]—Who is this?

SUB.   God's precious!—What do you mean? Go in, good lady.
Let me entreat you. [DOL *retires.*]—Where's this varlet?

[*Re-enter* FACE.]

FACE.   Sir.
SUB.   You very knave! do you use me thus?
FACE.   Wherein, sir?
SUB.   Go in and see, you traitor. Go!
                                        [*Exit* FACE.]
MAM.   Who is it, sir?
SUB.   Nothing, sir; nothing.
MAM.   What's the matter, good sir?
I have not seen you thus distemp'red: who is 't?
SUB.   All arts have still had, sir, their adversaries;
But ours the most ignorant.—

[FACE *returns.*]   What now?

FACE.   'T was not my fault, sir; she would speak with you.
SUB.   Would she, sir! Follow me.   [*Exit.*]
MAM.   [*stopping him.*] Stay, Lungs.
FACE.   I dare not, sir.

MAM.   How! pray thee, stay.
FACE.   She 's mad, sir, and sent hither—
MAM.   Stay, man; what is she?
FACE.   A lord's sister, sir.
          He 'll be mad too.—
MAM.   I warrant thee.—Why sent hither?
FACE.   Sir, to be cur'd.
SUB.   [*within.*] Why, rascal!
FACE.   Lo you!—Here, sir!   [*Exit.*]
MAM.   'Fore God, a Bradamante, a brave piece.
SUR.   Heart, this is a bawdy-house! I 'll be burnt else.
MAM.   O, by this light, no: do not wrong him. He 's
          Too scrupulous that way: it is his vice.
          No, he 's a rare physician, do him right,
          An excellent Paracelsian, and has done
          Strange cures with mineral physic. He deals all
          With spirits, he; he will not hear a word
          Of Galen; or his tedious recipes.—

[FACE *again.*]

                                   How now, Lungs!
FACE.   Softly, sir; speak softly. I meant
          To ha' told your worship all. This must not hear.
MAM.   No, he will not be gull'd; let him alone.
FACE.   You 're very right, sir; she is a most rare scholar,
          And is gone mad with studying Broughton's[7] works.
          If you but name a word touching the Hebrew,
          She falls into her fit, and will discourse
          So learnedly of genealogies,
          As you would run mad too, to hear her, sir.
MAM.   How might one do t' have conference with her, Lungs?
FACE.   O, divers have run mad upon the conference.
          I do not know, sir: I am sent in haste
          To fetch a vial.
SUR.   Be not gull'd, Sir Mammon.
MAM.   Wherein? Pray ye, be patient.
SUR.   Yes, as you are,
          And trust confederate knaves and bawds and whores.
MAM.   You are too foul, believe it.—Come here, Ulen,
          One word.
FACE.   I dare not, in good faith.   [*Going.*]

7. A learned eccentric of the time.

MAM.   Stay, knave.
FACE.   He 's extreme angry that you saw her, sir.
MAM.   Drink that. [*Gives him money.*] What is she when she 's out
              of her fit?
FACE.   O, the most affablest creature, sir! so merry!
              So pleasant! She 'll mount you up, like quicksilver,
              Over the helm; and circulate like oil,
              A very vegetal: discourse of state,
              Of mathematics, bawdry, anything——
MAM.   Is she no way accessible? no means,
              No trick to give a man a taste of her——wit——
              Or so?

[SUB. *within.*] Ulen!

FACE.   I 'll come to you again, sir.   [*Exit.*]
MAM.   Surly, I did not think one o' your breeding
              Would traduce personages of worth.
SUR.   Sir Epicure,
              Your friend to use; yet still loth to be gull'd:
              I do not like your philosophical bawds.
              Their stone is lechery enough to pay for,
              Without this bait.
MAM.   Heart, you abuse yourself.
              I know the lady, and her friends, and means,
              The original of this disaster. Her brother
              Has told me all.
SUR.   And yet you ne'er saw her
              Till now!
MAM.   O yes, but I forgot. I have, believe it,
              One o' the treacherous'st memories, I do think,
              Of all mankind.
SUR.   What call you her brother?
MAM.   My lord——
              He wi' not have his name known, now I think on 't.
SUR.   A very treacherous memory!
MAM.   O' my faith——
SUR.   Tut, if you ha' it not about you, pass it
              Till we meet next.
MAM.   Nay, by this hand, 't is true.
              He 's one I honour, and my noble friend;
              And I respect his house.
SUR.   Heart! can it be
              That a grave sir, a rich, that has no need,

A wise sir, too, at other times, should thus,
With his own oaths, and arguments, make hard means
To gull himself? An this be your elixir,
Your *lapis mineralis*, and your lunary,
Give me your honest trick yet at primero,
Or gleek,[8] and take your *lutum sapientis*,
Your *menstruum simplex!* I 'll have gold before you,
And with less danger of the quicksilver,
Or the hot sulphur.

[*Re-enter* FACE.]

FACE. Here 's one from Captain Face, sir. [*To* SURLY.]
Desires you meet him i' the Temple-church,
Some half-hour hence, and upon earnest business.
Sir, [*whispers* MAMMON] if you please to quit us now, and
come
Again within two hours, you shall have
My master busy examining o' the works;
And I will steal you in unto the party,
That you may see her converse. — Sir, shall I say
You 'll meet the captain's worship?

SUR.   Sir, I will. — [*Walks aside.*]
But, by attorney, and to a second purpose.
Now, I am sure it is a bawdy-house;
I 'll swear it, were the marshal here to thank me:
The naming this commander doth confirm it.
Don Face! why, he 's the most authentic dealer
I' these commodities, the superintendent
To all the quainter traffickers in town!
He is the visitor, and does appoint
Who lies with whom, and at what hour; what price;
Which gown, and in what smock; what fall;[9] what tire.[10]
Him will I prove, by a third person, to find
The subtleties of this dark labyrinth:
Which if I do discover, dear Sir Mammon,
You 'll give your poor friend leave, though no philosopher,
To laugh; for you that are, 't is thought, shall weep.

FACE. Sir, he does pray you 'll not forget.
SUR.   I will not, sir.
Sir Epicure, I shall leave you.   [*Exit.*]

8. *gleek*] games at cards.
9. *fall*] a collar, or a veil.
10. *tire*] a head-dress.

Mam.	I follow you straight.
Face.	But do so, good sir, to avoid suspicion.
	This gent'man has a parlous head.
Mam.	But wilt thou, Ulen,
	Be constant to thy promise?
Face.	As my life, sir.
Mam.	And wilt thou insinuate what I am, and praise me,
	And say I am a noble fellow?
Face.	O, what else, sir?
	And that you 'll make her royal with the stone,
	An empress; and yourself King of Bantam.
Mam.	Wilt thou do this?
Face.	Will I, sir!
Mam.	Lungs, my Lungs!
	I love thee.
Face.	Send your stuff, sir, that my master
	May busy himself about projection.
Mam.	Thou 'st witch'd me, rogue: take, go. [*Gives him money.*]
Face.	Your jack, and all, sir.
Mam.	Thou art a villain — I will send my jack,
	And the weights too. Slave, I could bite thine ear.
	Away, thou dost not care for me.
Face.	Not I, sir!
Mam.	Come, I was born to make thee, my good weasel,
	Set thee on a bench, and ha' thee twirl a chain
	With the best lord's vermin of 'em all.
Face.	Away, sir.
Mam.	A count, nay, a count palatine——
Face.	Good sir, go.
Mam.	Shall not advance thee better: no, nor faster. [*Exit.*]

Scene IV. — *The same*

Face. [*Re-enter*] Subtle *and* Dol.

Sub.	Has he bit? has he bit?
Face.	And swallow'd, too, my Subtle.
	I ha' given him line, and now he plays, i' faith.
Sub.	And shall we twitch him?
Face.	Thorough both the gills.
	A wench is a rare bait, with which a man

No sooner 's taken, but he straight firks mad.

SUB.   Dol, my Lord What's-hum's sister, you must now
Bear yourself *statelich*.

DOL.   O, let me alone,
I 'll not forget my race, I warrant you.
I 'll keep my distance, laugh and talk aloud;
Have all the tricks of a proud scurvy lady,
And be as rude 's her woman.

FACE.   Well said, sanguine![1]

SUB.   But will he send his andirons?

FACE.   His jack too.
And 's iron shoeing-horn; I ha' spoke to him. Well,
I must not lose my wary gamester yonder.

SUB.   O, Monsieur Caution, that will not be gull'd?

FACE.   Ay,
If I can strike a fine hook into him, now! —
The Temple-church, there I have cast mine angle.
Well, pray for me. I 'll about it.

[*One knocks.*]

SUB.   What, more gudgeons![2]
Dol, scout, scout! [DOL *goes to the window.*] Stay, Face, you
    must go to the door;
'Pray God it be my anabaptist — Who is 't, Dol?

DOL.   I know him not: he looks like a gold-end-man.[3]

SUB.   Gods so! 't is he, he said he would send — what call you him?
The sanctified elder, that should deal
For Mammon's jack and andirons. Let him in.
Stay, help me off, first, with my gown. [*Exit* FACE *with the
    gown.*] Away,
Madam, to your withdrawing chamber. Now,
                       [*Exit* DOL.]
In a new tune, new gesture, but old language. —
This fellow is sent from one negotiates with me
About the stone too, for the holy brethren
Of Amsterdam, the exil'd saints, that hope
To raise their discipline by it. I must use him
In some strange fashion now, to make him admire me.

1. *sanguine*] red cheeks.
2. *gudgeons*] easy dupes.
3. *gold-end-man*] a man who buys broken remnants of gold.

SCENE V.—*The same*

SUBTLE. [*Enter*] ANANIAS.

      Where is my drudge?   [*Aloud.*]

[*Enter*] FACE.

FACE.	Sir!
SUB.	Take away the recipient,

And rectify your menstrue from the phlegma.
Then pour it on the Sol, in the cucurbite,
And let 'em macerate together.

FACE.   Yes, sir.
And save the ground?

SUB.   No: *terra damnata*
Must not have entrance in the work.—Who are you?

ANA.   A faithful brother, if it please you.

SUB.   What 's that?
A Lullianist? a Ripley?[1] *Filius artis?*
Can you sublime and dulcify? Calcine?
Know you the sapor pontic? Sapor stiptic?
Or what is homogene, or heterogene?

ANA.   I understand no heathen language, truly.

SUB.   Heathen! You Knipperdoling?[2] Is Ars sacra,
Or chrysopoeia, or spagyrica,
Or the pamphysic, or panarchic knowledge,
A heathen language?

ANA.   Heathen Greek, I take it.

SUB.   How! Heathen Greek?

ANA.   All 's heathen but the Hebrew.

SUB.   Sirrah my varlet, stand you forth and speak to him
Like a philosopher: answer i' the language.
Name the vexations, and the martyrizations
Of metals in the work.

FACE.   Sir, putrefaction,
Solution, ablution, sublimation,
Cohobation, calcination, ceration, and
Fixation.

---

1. A follower of Raymond Lully (1235–1315) or George Ripley (d. *cir.* 1490), well-
  known alchemical writers.
2. An Anabaptist leader.

SUB.	This is heathen Greek, to you, now!— And when comes vivification?
FACE.	After mortification.
SUB.	What 's cohobation?
FACE.	'T is the pouring on Your *aqua regis*, and then drawing him off, To the trine circle of the seven spheres.
SUB.	What 's the proper passion of metals?
FACE.	Malleation.
SUB.	What 's your *ultimum supplicium auri*?
FACE.	Antimonium.
SUB.	This 's heathen Greek to you!—And what 's your mercury?
FACE.	A very fugitive, he will be gone, sir.
SUB.	How know you him?
FACE.	By his viscosity, His oleosity, and his suscitability.
SUB.	How do you sublime him?
FACE.	With the calce of egg-shells, White marble, talc.
SUB.	Your magisterium now, What 's that?
FACE.	Shifting, sir, your elements, Dry into cold, cold into moist, moist into hot, Hot into dry.
SUB.	This is heathen Greek to you still! Your *lapis philosophicus*?
FACE.	'T is a stone, And not a stone; a spirit, a soul, and a body: Which if you do dissolve, it is dissolv'd; If you coagulate, it is coagulated; If you make it to fly, it flieth.
SUB.	Enough. [*Exit* FACE.] This 's heathen Greek to you! What are you, sir?
ANA.	Please you, a servant of the exil'd brethren, That deal with widows' and with orphans' goods, And make a just account unto the saints: A deacon.
SUB.	O, you are sent from Master Wholesome, Your teacher?
ANA.	From Tribulation Wholesome, Our very zealous pastor.
SUB.	Good! I have Some orphans' goods to come here.

ANA.	Of what kind, sir?
SUB.	Pewter and brass, andirons and kitchenware.
	Metals, that we must use our med'cine on:
	Wherein the brethren may have a penn'orth
	For ready money.
ANA.	Were the orphans' parents
	Sincere professors?
SUB.	Why do you ask?
ANA.	Because
	We then are to deal justly, and give, in truth,
	Their utmost value.
SUB.	'Slid, you 'd cozen else,
	An if their parents were not of the faithful!—
	I will not trust you, now I think on it,
	Till I ha' talk'd with your pastor. Ha' you brought money
	To buy more coals?
ANA.	No, surely.
SUB.	No? How so?
ANA.	The brethren bid me say unto you, sir,
	Surely, they will not venture any more
	Till they may see projection.
SUB.	How!
ANA.	You 've had
	For the instruments, as bricks, and lome, and glasses,
	Already thirty pound; and for materials,
	They say, some ninety more: and they have heard since,
	That one, at Heidelberg, made it of an egg,
	And a small paper of pin-dust.
SUB.	What 's your name?
ANA.	My name is Ananias.
SUB.	Out, the varlet
	That cozen'd the apostles! Hence, away!
	Flee, mischief! had your holy consistory
	No name to send me, of another sound
	Than wicked Ananias? Send your elders
	Hither, to make atonement for you, quickly,
	And gi' me satisfaction; or out goes
	The fire; and down th' alembics, and the furnace,
	Piger Henricus, or what not. Thou wretch!
	Both *sericon* and *bufo* shall be lost,
	Tell 'em. All hope of rooting out the bishops,
	Or th' anti-Christian hierarchy shall perish,
	If they stay threescore minutes: the aqueity,

Terreity, and sulphureity
Shall run together again, and all be annull'd,
Thou wicked Ananias! [*Exit* ANANIAS.] This will fetch 'em,
And make 'em haste towards their gulling more.
A man must deal like a rough nurse, and fright
Those that are froward, to an appetite.

SCENE VI. — *The same*

SUBTLE. [*Enter*] FACE [*in his uniform, followed by*] DRUGGER.

FACE.   He 's busy with his spirits, but we 'll upon him.
SUB.   How now! What mates, what Bayards[1] ha' we here?
FACE.   I told you he would be furious. — Sir, here 's Nab
         Has brought you another piece of gold to look on;
         — We must appease him. Give it me, — and prays you,
         You would devise — what is it, Nab?
DRUG.   A sign, sir.
FACE.   Ay, a good lucky one, a thriving sign, doctor.
SUB.   I was devising now.
FACE.   [*Aside to* SUBTLE.] 'Slight, do not say so,
         He will repent he ga' you any more. —
         What say you to his constellation, doctor,
         The Balance?
SUB.   No, that way is stale and common.
         A townsman born in Taurus, gives the bull,
         Or the bull's head: in Aries, the ram, —
         A poor-device! No, I will have his name
         Form'd in some mystic character; whose *radii*,
         Striking the senses of the passers-by,
         Shall, by a virtual influence, breed affections.
         That may result upon the party owns it:
         As thus——
FACE.   Nab!
SUB.   He first shall have *a bell*, that 's *Abel*;
         And by it standing one whose name is *Dee*,[2]
         In a *rug*[3] gown, there 's *D*, and *Rug*, that 's *drug*

---

1. *Bayards*] Blind horses.
2. A reference to Dr. Dee, the famous magician and astrologer, who died in 1608.
3. *rug*] of coarse frieze.

	And right anenst him a dog snarling *er*; There 's Drugger, Abel Drugger. That 's his sign. And here 's now mystery and hieroglyphic!
FACE.	Abel, thou art made.
DRUG.	Sir, I do thank his worship.
FACE.	Six o' thy legs[4] more will not do it, Nab. He has brought you a pipe of tobacco, doctor.
DRUG.	Yes, sir: I have another thing I would impart——
FACE.	Out with it, Nab.
DRUG.	Sir, there is lodg'd, hard by me, A rich young widow——
FACE.	Good! a bona roba?[5]
DRUG.	But nineteen at the most.
FACE.	Very good, Abel.
DRUG.	Marry, she 's not in fashion yet; she wears A hood, but 't stands a cop.[6]
FACE.	No matter, Abel.
DRUG.	And I do now and then give her a fucus——
FACE.	What! dost thou deal, Nab?
SUB.	I did tell you, captain.
DRUG.	And physic too, sometime, sir; for which she trusts me With all her mind. She 's come up here of purpose To learn the fashion.
FACE.	Good (his match too!)—On, Nab.
DRUG.	And she does strangely long to know her fortune.
FACE.	God's lid, Nab, send her to the doctor, hither.
DRUG.	Yes, I have spoke to her of his worship already; But she 's afraid it will be blown abroad, And hurt her a marriage.
FACE.	Hurt it! 't is the way To heal it, if 't were hurt; to make it more Follow'd and sought. Nab, thou shalt tell her this. She 'll be more known, more talk'd of; and your widows Are ne'er of any price till they be famous; Their honour is their multitude of suitors. Send her, it may be thy good fortune. What! Thou dost not know?
DRUG.	No, sir, she 'll never marry Under a knight: her brother has made a vow.

4. *legs*] bows.
5. *bona roba*] handsome wench.
6. *'t stands a cop*] peaked (?) or straight on the top of her head, instead of tilted (?).

FACE.   What! and dost thou despair, my little Nab,
         Knowing what the doctor has set down for thee,
         And seeing so many o' the city dubb'd?
         One glass o' thy water, with a madam I know,
         Will have it done, Nab. What 's her brother? a knight?

DRUG.   No, sir, a gentleman newly warm in 's land, sir,
         Scarce cold in his one and twenty, that does govern
         His sister here; and is a man himself
         Of some three thousand a year, and is come up
         To learn to quarrel, and to live by his wits,
         And will go down again, and die i' the country.

FACE.   How! to quarrel?

DRUG.   Yes, sir, to carry quarrels,
         As gallants do; to manage 'em by line.

FACE.   'Slid, Nab, the doctor is the only man
         In Christendom for him. He has made a table,
         With mathematical demonstrations,
         Touching the art of quarrels: he will give him
         An instrument to quarrel by. Go, bring 'em both,
         Him and his sister. And, for thee, with her
         The doctor happ'ly may persuade. Go to:
         'Shalt give his worship a new damask suit
         Upon the premises.

SUB.   O, good captain!

FACE.   He shall;
         He is the honestest fellow, doctor. Stay not,
         No offers; bring the damask, and the parties.

DRUG.   I 'll try my power, sir.

FACE.   And thy will too, Nab.

SUB.   'T is good tobacco, this! What is 't an ounce?

FACE.   He 'll send you a pound, doctor.

SUB.   O no.

FACE.   He will do 't.
         It is the goodest soul!—Abel, about it.
         Thou shalt know more anon. Away, be gone.   [*Exit* ABEL.]
         A miserable rogue, and lives with cheese,
         And has the worms. That was the cause, indeed,
         Why he came now: he dealth with me in private,
         To get a med'cine for 'em.

SUB.   And shall, sir. This works.

FACE.   A wife, a wife for one on 's, my dear Subtle!
         We 'll e'en draw lots, and he that fails, shall have
         The more in goods, the other has in tail.

SUB.	Rather the less; for she may be so light
	She may want grains.
FACE.	Ay; or be such a burden,
	A man would scarce endure her for the whole.
SUB.	Faith, best let 's see her first, and then determine.
FACE.	Content: but Dol must ha' no breath on 't.
SUB.	Mum.
	Away you, to your Surly yonder, catch him.
FACE.	Pray God I ha' not staid too long.
SUB.	I fear it. [*Exeunt.*]

ACT III

SCENE I.—*The lane before Lovewit's house*

[*Enter*] TRIBULATION [WHOLESOME] *and* ANANIAS:

TRI.   These chastisements are common to the saints,
       And such rebukes we of the separation
       Must bear with willing shoulders, as the trials
       Sent forth to tempt our frailties.

ANA.   In pure zeal,
       I do not like the man; he is a heathen,
       And speaks the language of Canaan, truly.

TRI.   I think him a profane person indeed.

ANA.   He bears
       The visible mark of the beast in his forehead.
       And for his stone, it is a work of darkness,
       And with philosophy blinds the eyes of man.

TRI.   Good brother, we must bend unto all means
       That may give furtherance to the holy cause.

ANA.   Which his cannot: the sanctified cause
       Should have a sanctified course.

TRI.   Not always necessary:
       The children of perdition are oft times
       Made instruments even of the greatest works.
       Beside, we should give somewhat to man's nature,
       The place he lives in, still about the fire,
       And fume of metals, that intoxicate
       The brain of man, and make him prone to passion.
       Where have you greater atheists than your cooks?
       Or more profane, or choleric, than your glass-men?
       More anti-Christian than your bell-founders?
       What makes the devil so devilish, I would ask you,
       Sathan, our common enemy, but his being

Perpetually about the fire, and boiling
Brimstone and arsenic? We must give, I say,
Unto the motives, and the stirrers up
Of humours in the blood. It may be so,
When as the work is done, the stone is made,
This heat of his may turn into a zeal,
And stand up for the beauteous discipline
Against the menstruous cloth and rag of Rome.
We must await his calling, and the coming
Of the good spirit. You did fault, t' upbraid him
With the brethren's blessing of Heidelberg, weighing
What need we have to hasten on the work,
For the restoring of the silenc'd saints,
Which ne'er will be but by the philosopher's stone.
And so a learned elder, one of Scotland,
Assur'd me; *aurum potabile* being
The only med'cine for the civil magistrate,
T' incline him to a feeling of the cause;
And must be daily us'd in the disease.

ANA.   I have not edified more, truly, by man;
          Not since the beautiful light first shone on me:
          And I am sad my zeal hath so offended.
TRI.   Let us call on him then.
ANA.   The motion 's good,
          And of the spirit; I will knock first. [*Knocks.*] Peace be within!
              [*The door is opened, and they enter.*]

SCENE II. — *A room in Lovewit's house*

[*Enter*] SUBTLE, [*followed by*] TRIBULATION *and* ANANIAS.

SUB.   O, are you come? 'T was time. Your threescore minutes
          Were at last thread, you see; and down had gone
          Furnus acediae, turris circulatorius:
          Limbec, bolt's-head, retort, and pelican
          Had all been cinders. Wicked Ananias!
          Art thou return'd? Nay, then it goes down yet.
TRI.   Sir, be appeased; he is come to humble
          Himself in spirit, and to ask your patience,
          If too much zeal hath carried him aside
          From the due path.

SUB.   Why, this doth qualify!
TRI.   The brethren had no purpose, verily,
           To give you the least grievance; but are ready
           To lend their willing hands to any project
           The spirit and you direct.
SUB.   This qualifies more!
TRI.   And for the orphans' goods, let them be valu'd,
           Or what is needful else to the holy work,
           It shall be numb'red; here, by me, the saints
           Throw down their purse before you.
SUB.   This qualifies most!
           Why, thus it should be, now you understand.
           Have I discours'd so unto you of our stone,
           And of the good that it shall bring your cause?
           Show'd you (beside the main of hiring forces
           Abroad, drawing the Hollanders, your friends,
           From th' Indies, to serve you, with all their fleet)
           That even the med'cinal use shall make you a faction
           And party in the realm? As, put the case,
           That some great man in state, he have the gout,
           Why, you but send three drops of your elixir,
           You help him straight: there you have made a friend.
           Another has the palsy or the dropsy,
           He takes of your incombustible stuff,
           He 's young again: there you have made a friend.
           A lady that is past the feat of body,
           Though not of mind, and hath her face decay'd
           Beyond all cure of paintings, you restore
           With the oil of talc: there you have made a friend;
           And all her friends. A lord that is a leper,
           A knight that has the bone-ache, or a squire
           That hath both these, you make 'em smooth and sound
           With a bare fricace[1] of your med'cine; still
           You increase your friends.
TRI.   Ay, 't is very pregnant.
SUB.   And then the turning of this lawyer's pewter
           To plate at Christmas——
ANA.   Christ-tide, I pray you.
SUB.   Yet, Ananias!
ANA.   I have done.
SUB.   Or changing

---

1. *fricace*] rubbing.

His parcel gilt to massy gold. You cannot
But raise you friends. Withal, to be of power
To pay an army in the field, to buy
The King of France out of his realms, or Spain
Out of his Indies. What can you not do
Against lords spiritual or temporal,
That shall oppone[2] you?

Tri.   Verily, 't is true.
We may be temporal lords ourselves, I take it.

Sub.   You may be anything, and leave off to make
Long-winded exercises; or suck up
Your *ha!* and *hum!* in a tune. I not deny,
But such as are not graced in a state,
May, for their ends, be adverse in religion,
And get a tune to call the flock together:
For, to say sooth, a tune does much with women
And other phlegmatic people; it is your bell.

Ana.   Bells are profane; a tune may be religious.

Sub.   No warning with you? Then farewell my patience.
Slight, it shall down; I will not be thus tortur'd.

Tri.   I pray you, sir.

Sub.   All shall perish. I have spoke it.

Tri.   Let me find grace, sir, in your eyes; the man,
He stands corrected: neither did his zeal,
But as your self, allow a tune somewhere,
Which now, being tow'rd the stone, we shall not need.

Sub.   No, nor your holy vizard,[3] to win widows
To give you legacies; or make zealous wives
To rob their husbands for the common cause:
Nor take the start of bonds broke but one day,
And say they were forfeited by providence.
Nor shall you need o'er night to eat huge meals,
To celebrate your next day's fast the better;
The whilst the brethren and the sisters humbled,
Abate the stiffness of the flesh. Nor cast
Before your hungry hearers scrupulous bones;
As whether a Christian may hawk or hunt,
Or whether matrons of the holy assembly
May lay their hair out, or wear doublets,
Or have that idol, starch, about their linen.

2. *oppone*] oppose.
3. *vizard*] set expression of face.

ANA.   It is indeed an idol.
TRI.   Mind him not, sir.
            I do command thee, spirit (of zeal, but trouble),
            To peace within him! Pray you, sir, go on.
SUB.   Nor shall you need to libel 'gainst the prelates,
            And shorten so your ears[4] against the hearing
            Of the next wire-drawn grace. Nor of necessity
            Rail against plays, to please the alderman
            Whose daily custard you devour; nor lie
            With zealous rage till you are hoarse. Not one
            Of these so singular arts. Nor call yourselves
            By names of Tribulation, Persecution,
            Restraint, Long-patience, and such like, affected
            By the whole family or wood[5] of you,
            Only for glory, and to catch the ear
            Of the disciple.
TRI.   Truly, sir, they are
            Ways that the godly brethren have invented,
            For propagation of the glorious cause,
            As very notable means, and whereby also
            Themselves grow soon, and profitably, famous.
SUB.   O, but the stone, all 's idle to 't! Nothing!
            The art of angels, nature's miracle,
            The divine secret that doth fly in clouds
            From east to west: and whose tradition
            Is not from men, but spirits.
ANA.   I hate traditions;
            I do not trust them——
TRI.   Peace!
ANA.   They are popish all.
            I will not peace: I will not——
TRI.   Ananias!
ANA.   Please the profane, to grieve the godly; I may not.
SUB.   Well, Ananias, thou shalt overcome.
TRI.   It is an ignorant zeal that haunts him, sir:
            But truly else a very faithful brother,
            A botcher,[6] and a man by revelation
            That hath a competent knowledge of the truth.
SUB.   Has he a competent sum there i' the bag
            To buy the goods within? I am made guardian,

4. *And . . . ears*] Have your ears cut off in the pillory.
5. *wood*] assembly.
6. *botcher*] tailor. But the term was used generally of Puritans.

              And must, for charity and conscience' sake,
              Now see the most be made for my poor orphan;
              Though I desire the brethren, too, good gainers:
              There they are within. When you have view'd and bought
                  'em,
              And ta'en the inventory of what they are,
              They are ready for projection; there 's no more
              To do: cast on the med'cine, so much silver
              As there is tin there, so much gold as brass,
              I 'll gi' it you in by weight.
TRI.   But how long time,
              Sir, must the saints expect yet?
SUB.   Let me see,
              How 's the moon now? Eight, nine, ten days hence,
              He will be silver potate; then three days
              Before he citronise.[7] Some fifteen days,
              The magisterium[8] will be perfected.
ANA.   About the second day of the third week,
              In the ninth month?
SUB.   Yes, my good Ananias.
TRI.   What will the orphans' goods arise to, think you?
SUB.   Some hundred marks, as much as fill'd three cars,
              Unladed now: you 'll make six millions of 'em——
              But I must ha' more coals laid in.
TRI.   How?
SUB.   Another load,
              And then we ha' finish'd. We must now increase
              Our fire to *ignis ardens*;[9] we are past
              Fimus equinus, balnei, cineris,[10]
              And all those lenter[11] heats. If the holy purse
              Should with this draught fall low, and that the saints
              Do need a present sum, I have a trick.
              To melt the pewter, you shall buy now instantly,
              And with a tincture make you as good Dutch dollars
              As any are in Holland.
TRI.   Can you so?
SUB.   Ay, and shall bide the third examination.
ANA.   It will be joyful tidings to the brethren.

7. *citronise*] become the color of citron—a stage in the process of producing the stone.
8. *magisterium*] full accomplishment.
9. *ignis ardens*] fiery heat.
10. *Fimus . . . cineris*] Heat from horse-dung, warm bath, ashes.
11. *lenter*] milder.

Sub.	But you must carry it secret.
Tri.	Ay; but stay,
	This act of coining, is it lawful?
Ana.	Lawful!
	We know no magistrate: or, if we did,
	This 's foreign coin.
Sub.	It is no coining, sir.
	It is but casting.
Tri.	Ha! you distinguish well:
	Casting of money may be lawful.
Ana.	'T is, sir.
Tri.	Truly, I take it so.
Sub.	There is no scruple,
	Sir, to be made of it; believe Ananias;
	This case of conscience he is studied in.
Tri.	I 'll make a question of it to the brethren.
Ana.	The brethren shall approve it lawful, doubt not.
	Where shall 't be done?
Sub.	For that we 'll talk anon. [*Knock without.*]
	There 's some to speak with me. Go in, I pray you,
	And view the parcels. That 's the inventory.
	I 'll come to you straight. [*Exeunt* Trib. *and* Ana.] Who is
	it?—Face! appear.

SCENE III.—*The same*

Subtle. [*Enter*] Face [*in his uniform*].

Sub.	How now! good prize?
Face.	Good pox! Yond' costive cheater
	Never came on.
Sub.	How then?
Face.	I ha' walk'd the round
	Till now, and no such thing.
Sub.	And ha' you quit him?
Face.	Quit him! An hell would quit him too, he were happy.
	'Slight! would you have me stalk like a mill-jade,
	All day, for one that will not yield us grains?
	I know him of old.
Sub.	O, but to ha' gull'd him,
	Had been a mastery.

FACE.   Let him go, black boy!
        And turn thee, that some fresh news may possess thee.
        A noble count, a don of Spain (my dear
        Delicious compeer, and my party[1]-bawd),
        Who is come hither private for his conscience
        And brought munition with him, six great slops,[2]
        Bigger than three Dutch hoys,[3] beside round trunks,[4]
        Furnish'd with pistolets,[5] and pieces of eight,[6]
        Will straight be here, my rogue, to have thy bath,
        (That is the colour,) and to make his batt'ry
        Upon our Dol, our castle, our cinqueport,
        Our Dover pier, our what thou wilt. Where is she?
        She must prepare perfumes, delicate linen,
        The bath in chief, a banquet, and her wit,
        Where is the doxy?
SUB.   I'll send her to thee:
        And but despatch my brace of little John Leydens
        And come again myself.
FACE.   Are they within then?
SUB.   Numb'ring the sum.
FACE.   How much?
SUB.   A hundred marks, boy. [*Exit.*]
FACE.   Why, this is a lucky day. Ten pounds of Mammon!
        Three o' my clerk! A portague o' my grocer!
        This o' the brethren! Beside reversions
        And states to come, i' the widow, and my count!
        My share to-day will not be bought for forty——

[*Enter* DOL.]

DOL.   What?
FACE.   Pounds, dainty Dorothy! Art thou so near?
DOL.   Yes; say, lord general, how fares our camp?
FACE.   As with the few that had entrench'd themselves
        Safe, by their discipline, against a world, Dol,
        And laugh'd within those trenches, and grew fat
        With thinking on the booties, Dol, brought in
        Daily by their small parties. This dear hour,

1. *party*] partner.
2. *slops*] large breeches.
3. *Dutch hoys*] Passenger sloops.
4. *trunks*] trunk hose.
5. *pistolets*] a Spanish gold coin worth about 16s. 8d.
6. *pieces of eight*] a coin worth about 4s. 6d.

A doughty don is taken with my Dol;
And thou mayst make his ransom what thou wilt,
My Dousabel;[7] he shall be brought here, fetter'd
With thy fair looks, before he sees thee; and thrown
In a down-bed, as dark as any dungeon;
Where thou shalt keep him waking with thy drum;
Thy drum, my Dol, thy drum; till he be tame
As the poor blackbirds were i' the great frost,
Or bees are with a bason; and so hive him
I' the swan-skin coverlid and cambric sheets,
Till he work honey and wax, my little God's-gift.

DOL.   What is he, general?
FACE.   An adalantado,[8]
A grandee, girl. Was not my Dapper here yet?
DOL.   No.
FACE.   Nor my Drugger?
DOL.   Neither.
FACE.   A pox on 'em,
They are so long a furnishing! such stinkards
Would not be seen upon these festival days.—

[*Re-enter* SUBTLE.]

How now! ha' you done?
SUB.   Done. They are gone: the sum
Is here in bank, my Face. I would we knew
Another chapman who would buy 'em outright.
FACE.   'Slid, Nab shall do 't against he ha' the widow,
To furnish household.
SUB.   Excellent, well thought on:
Pray God he come.
FACE.   I pray he keep away
Till our new business be o'erpast.
SUB.   But, Face,
How camst thou by this secret don?
FACE.   A spirit
Brought me th' intelligence in a paper here,
As I was conjuring yonder in my circle
For Surly; I ha' my flies abroad. Your bath
Is famous, Subtle, by my means. Sweet Dol,
You must go tune your virginal, no losing

---

7. *My Dousabel*] i.e. *douce et belle*; sweetheart.
8. *adalantado*] a Spanish governor.

O' the least time. And—do you hear?—good action!
Firk like a flounder; kiss like a scallop, close;
And tickle him with thy mother-tongue. His great
Verdugoship[9] has not a jot of language;
So much the easier to be cozen'd, my Dolly.
He will come here in a hir'd coach, obscure,
And our own coachman, whom I have sent as guide,
No creature else. [*One knocks.*] Who 's that?   [*Exit* DOL.]

SUB.   It is not he?
FACE.   O no, not yet this hour.

[*Re-enter* DOL.]

SUB.   Who is 't?
DOL.   Dapper,
Your clerk.
FACE.   God's will then, Queen of Fairy,
On with your tire; [*Exit* DOL.] and, doctor, with your robes.
Let 's despatch him for God's sake.
SUB.   'T will be long.
FACE.   I warrant you, take but the cues I give you,
It shall be brief enough. [*Goes to the window.*] 'Slight, here
    are more!
Abel, and I think the angry boy, the heir,
That fain would quarrel.
SUB.   And the widow?
FACE.   No,
Not that I see. Away!   [*Exit* SUB.]

SCENE IV.—*The same*

FACE. [*Enter*] DAPPER.

FACE.   O, sir, you are welcome.
The doctor is within a moving for you;
I have had the most ado to win him to it!—
He swears you 'll be the darling o' the dice:
He never heard her highness dote till now.
Your aunt has giv'n you the most gracious words
That can be thought on.

9. *Verdugoship*] Verdugo is a Spanish name, but the precise allusion is uncertain.

| DAP. | Shall I see her grace? |
| FACE. | See her, and kiss her too. — |

[*Enter* ABEL, *followed by* KASTRIL.]

	What, honest Nab!
	Hast brought the damask?
NAB.	No, sir; here 's tobacco.
FACE.	'T is well done, Nab; thou 'lt bring the damask too?
DRUG.	Yes. Here 's the gentleman, captain, Master Kastril,
	I have brought to see the doctor.
FACE.	Where 's the widow?
DRUG.	Sir, as he likes, his sister, he says, shall come.
FACE.	O, is it so? Good time. Is your name Kastril, sir?
KAS.	Ay, and the best o' the Kastrils, I 'd be sorry else,
	By fifteen hundred a year. Where is this doctor?
	My mad tobacco-boy here tells me of one
	That can do things. Has he any skill?
FACE.	Wherein, sir?
KAS.	To carry a business, manage a quarrel fairly,
	Upon fit terms.
FACE.	It seems, sir, you 're but young
	About the town, that can make that a question.
KAS.	Sir, not so young but I have heard some speech
	Of the angry boys,[1] and seen 'em take tobacco;
	And in his shop; and I can take it too.
	And I would fain be one of 'em, and go down
	And practise i' the country.
FACE.	Sir, for the duello,
	The doctor, I assure you, shall inform you,
	To the least shadow of a hair; and show you
	An instrument he has of his own making,
	Wherewith, no sooner shall you make report
	Of any quarrel, but he will take the height on 't
	Most instantly, and tell in what degree
	Of safety it lies in, or mortality.
	And how it may be borne, whether in a right line,
	Or a half circle; or may else be cast
	Into an angle blunt, if not acute:
	And this he will demonstrate. And then, rules
	To give and take the lie by.
KAS.	How! to take it?

1. *angry boys*] roysterers, young bloods.

FACE.   Yes, in oblique he 'll show you, or in circle;[2]
           But ne'er in diameter.[3] The whole town
           Study his theorems, and dispute them ordinarily
           At the eating academies.
KAS.   But does he teach
           Living by the wits too?
FACE.   Anything whatever.
           You cannot think that subtlety but he reads it.
           He made me a captain. I was a stark pimp,
           Just o' your standing, 'fore I met with him;
           It 's not two months since. I 'll tell you his method:
           First, he will enter you at some ordinary.
KAS.   No, I 'll not come there: you shall pardon me.
FACE.   For why, sir?
KAS.   There 's gaming there, and tricks.
FACE.   Why, would you be
           A gallant, and not game?
KAS.   Ay, 't will spend a man.
FACE.   Spend you! It will repair you when you are spent.
           How do they live by their wits there, that have vented
           Six times your fortunes?
KAS.   What, three thousand a year!
FACE.   Ay, forty thousand.
KAS.   Are there such?
FACE.   Ay, sir,
           And gallants yet. Here 's a young gentleman
           Is born to nothing,—[*Points to* DAPPER.] forty marks a year
           Which I count nothing:—he 's to be initiated,
           And have a fly o' the doctor. He will win you
           By unresistible luck, within this fortnight,
           Enough to buy a barony. They will set him
           Upmost, at the groom porter's,[4] all the Christmas:
           And for the whole year through at every place
           Where there is play, present him with the chair,
           The best attendance, the best drink, sometimes
           Two glasses of Canary, and pay nothing;
           The purest linen and the sharpest knife,
           The partridge next his trencher: and somewhere
           The dainty bed, in private, with the dainty.

2. *in circle*] the lie circumstantial.
3. *in diameter*] the lie direct.
4. *groom porter's*] An officer of the royal household, having charge of the cards, dice, etc.
   He had the privilege of keeping open table at Christmas.

You shall ha' your ordinaries bid for him,
As playhouses for a poet; and the master
Pray him aloud to name what dish he affects,
Which must be butter'd shrimps: and those that drink
To no mouth else, will drink to his, as being
The goodly president mouth of all the board.

KAS.   Do you not gull one?

FACE.   'Ods my life! Do you think it?
You shall have a cast commander, (can but get
In credit with a glover, or a spurrier,
For some two pair of either's ware aforehand,)
Will, by most swift posts, dealing [but] with him,
Arrive at competent means to keep himself,
His punk, and naked boy, in excellent fashion,
And be admir'd for 't.

KAS.   Will the doctor teach this?

FACE.   He will do more, sir: when your land is gone,
(As men of spirit hate to keep earth long),
In a vacation, when small money is stirring,
And ordinaries suspended till the term,
He 'll show a perspective,[5] where on one side
You shall behold the faces and the persons
Of all sufficient young heirs in town,
Whose bonds are current for commodity;[6]
On th' other side, the merchants' forms, and others,
That without help of any second broker,
Who would expect a share, will trust such parcels:
In the third square, the very street and sign
Where the commodity dwells, and does but wait
To be deliver'd, be it pepper, soap,
Hops, or tobacco, oatmeal, woad,[7] or cheeses.
All which you may so handle, to enjoy
To your own use, and never stand oblig'd.

KAS.   I' faith! is he such a fellow?

FACE.   Why, Nab here knows him.
And then for making matches for rich widows,
Young gentlewomen, heirs, the fortunat'st man!
He 's sent to, far and near, all over England,

5. *perspective*] a magic glass.
6. *commodity*] The reference is to the "commodity" fraud, in which a borrower was
   obliged to take part of a loan in merchandise, which the lender frequently bought
   back by agents for much less than it represented in the loan.
7. *woad*] a plant used for a dye.

	To have his counsel, and to know their fortunes.
KAS.	God 's will, my suster shall see him.
FACE.	I 'll tell you, sir,
	What he did tell me of Nab. It 's a strange thing—
	(By the way, you must eat no cheese, Nab, it breeds melancholy,
	And that same melancholy breeds worms) but pass it:—
	He told me, honest Nab here was ne'er at tavern
	But once in 's life.
DRUG.	Truth, and no more I was not.
FACE.	And then he was so sick——
DRUG.	Could he tell you that too?
FACE.	How should I know it?
DRUG.	In troth, we had been a shooting,
	And had a piece of fat ram-mutton to supper,
	That lay so heavy o' my stomach——
FACE.	And he has no head
	To bear any wine; for what with the noise o' the fiddlers,
	And care of his shop, for he dares keep no servants——
DRUG.	My head did so ache——
FACE.	As he was fain to be brought home.
	The doctor told me: and then a good old woman——
DRUG.	Yes, faith, she dwells in Seacoal-lane,—did cure me,
	With sodden ale, and pellitory[8] o' the wall;
	Cost me but twopence. I had another sickness
	Was worse than that.
FACE.	Ay, that was with the grief
	Thou took'st for being cess'd[9] at eighteen-pence,
	For the waterwork.
DRUG.	In truth, and it was like
	T' have cost me almost my life.
FACE.	Thy hair went off?
DRUG.	Yes, sir; 't was done for spite.
FACE.	Nay, so says the doctor.
KAS.	Pray thee, tobacco-boy, go fetch my suster;
	I 'll see this learned boy before I go;
	And so shall she.
FACE.	Sir, he is busy now:
	But if you have a sister to fetch hither,
	Perhaps your own pains may command her sooner;

8. *pellitory*] a herb.
9. *cess'd*] assessed, taxed.

                   And he by that time will be free.
KAS.   I go.   [*Exit.*]
FACE.   Drugger, she 's thine: the damask!—[*Exit* ABEL.] Subtle and I
         Must wrastle for her. [*Aside.*] Come on, Master Dapper,
         You see how I turn clients here away,
         To give your cause dispatch; ha' you perform'd
         The ceremonies were enjoin'd you?
DAP.   · Yes, o' the vinegar,
         And the clean shirt.
FACE.   'T is well: that shirt may do you
         More worship than you think. Your aunt 's afire,
         But that she will not show it, t' have a sight of you.
         Ha' you provided for her grace's servants?
DAP.   Yes, here are six score Edward shillings.
FACE.   Good!
DAP.   And an old Harry's sovereign.
FACE.   Very good!
DAP.   And three James shillings, and an Elizabeth groat,
         Just twenty nobles.
FACE.   O, you are too just.
         I would you had had the other noble in Maries.
DAP.   I have some Philip and Maries.
FACE.   Ay, those same
         Are best of all: where are they? Hark, the doctor.

SCENE V.—*The same*

FACE, DAPPER. [*Enter*] SUBTLE, *disguised like a priest of Fairy* [*with a strip of cloth*].

SUB.   [*in a feigned voice.*] Is yet her grace's cousin come?
FACE.   He is come.
SUB.   And is he fasting?
FACE.   Yes.
SUB.   And hath cried "hum"?
FACE.   Thrice, you must answer.
DAP.   Thrice.
SUB.   And as oft "buz"?
FACE.   If you have, say.
DAP.   I have.
SUB.   Then, to her cuz,

Hoping that he hath vinegar'd his senses,
As he was bid, the Fairy queen dispenses,
By me, this robe, the petticoat of Fortune;
Which that he straight put on, she doth importune.
And though to Fortune near be her petticoat,
Yet nearer is her smock, the queen doth note:
And therefore, even of that a piece she hath sent,
Which, being a child, to wrap him in was rent;
And prays him for a scarf he now will wear it,
With as much love as then her grace did tear it,
About his eyes, [*They blind him with the rag.*] to show he is
    fortunate.
And, trusting unto her to make his state,
He 'll throw away all worldly pelf about him;
Which that he will perform, she doth not doubt him.

FACE. She need not doubt him, sir. Alas, he has nothing
But what he will part withal as willingly,
Upon her grace's word—throw away your purse—
As she would ask it:—handkerchiefs and all—
She cannot bid that thing but he 'll obey.—
If you have a ring about you, cast it off,
Or a silver seal at your wrist; her grace will send [*He throws
    away, as they bid him.*]
Her fairies here to search you, therefore deal
Directly with her highness: if they find
That you conceal a mite, you are undone.

DAP. Truly, there 's all.
FACE.   All what?
DAP.   My money; truly.
FACE. Keep nothing that is transitory about you.
[*Aside to* SUBTLE.] Bid Dol play music.—Look, the elves are
    come   [DOL. *enters with a cittern.*]
To pinch you, if you tell not the truth. Advise you.
                     [*They pinch him.*]
DAP. O! I have a paper with a spur-ryal[1] in 't.
FACE. *Ti, ti.*
They knew 't, they say.
SUB.   *Ti, ti, ti, ti.* He has more yet.
FACE. *Ti, ti-ti-ti.* I' the other pocket?
SUB.   *Titi, titi, titi, titi, titi.*
They must pinch him or he will never confess, they say.
                   [*They pinch him again.*]

1. *spur-ryal*] a gold coin worth 15s.

DAP.   O, O!

FACE.   Nay, pray you, hold: he is her grace's nephew
       Ti, ti, ti? What care you? Good faith, you shall care.—
       Deal plainly, sir, and shame the fairies. Show
       You are innocent.

DAP.   By this good light, I ha' nothing.

SUB.   *Ti, ti, ti, ti, to, ta.* He does equivocate she says:
       Ti, ti do ti, ti ti do, ti da; and swears by the light when he is
          blinded.

DAP.   By this good dark, I ha' nothing but a half-crown
       Of gold about my wrist, that my love gave me;
       And a leaden heart I wore sin' she forsook me.

FACE.   I thought 't was something. And would you incur
       Your aunt's displeasure for these trifles? Come,
       I had rather you had thrown away twenty half-crowns.
                                              [*Takes it off.*]
       You may wear your leaden heart still.—How now!

SUB.   What news, Dol?

DOL   Yonder 's your knight, Sir Mammon.

FACE.   God's lid, we never thought of him till now!
       Where is he?

DOL.   Here hard by. He 's at the door.

SUB.   And you are not ready now! Dol, get his suit.   [*Exit* DOL.]
       He must not be sent back.

FACE.   O, by no means.
       What shall we do with this same puffin[2] here,
       Now he 's o' the spit?

SUB.   Why, lay him back awhile,
       With some device.

[*Re-enter* DOL *with* FACE's *clothes.*]

                       —*Ti, ti, ti, ti, ti, ti.* Would her grace speak with me?
       I come.—Help, Dol!   [*Knocking without.*]

FACE.   [*speaks through the keyhole.*] Who 's there? Sir Epicure,
       My master 's i' the way. Please you to walk
       Three or four turns, but till his back be turn'd,
       And I am for you.—Quickly, Dol!

SUB.   Her grace
       Commends her kindly to you, Master Dapper.

DAP.   I long to see her grace.

SUB.   She now is set

---

2. *puffin*] a sort of sea-bird; used contemptuously of a puffed-up person.

At dinner in her bed, and she has sent you
From her own private trencher, a dead mouse,
And a piece of gingerbread, to be merry withal,
And stay your stomach, lest you faint with fasting:
Yet if you could hold out till she saw you, she says,
It would be better for you.

FACE.   Sir, he shall
Hold out, an 't were this two hours, for her highness;
I can assure you that. We will not lose
All we ha' done.——

SUB.   He must not see, nor speak
To anybody, till then.

FACE.   For that we 'll put, sir,
A stay in 's mouth.

SUB.   Of what?

FACE.   Of gingerbread.
Make you it fit. He that hath pleas'd her grace
Thus far, shall not now crinkle³ for a little.——
Gape, sir, and let him fit you.

                    [*They thrust a gag of gingerbread into his mouth.*]

SUB.   ——Where shall we now
Bestow him?

DOL.   I' the privy.——

SUB.   Come along, sir,
I must now show you Fortune's privy lodgings.

FACE.   Are they perfum'd, and his bath ready?

SUB.   All:
Only the fumigation 's somewhat strong.

FACE.   [*speaking through the keyhole.*] Sir Epicure, I am yours, sir,
          by and by.   [*Exeunt with* DAPPER.]

3. *crinkle*] turn aside from his purpose.

ACT IV

Scene I.—*A room in Lovewit's house*

[*Enter*] Face *and* Mammon.

Face.	O, sir, you 're come i' the only finest time.——
Mam.	Where 's master?
Face.	Now preparing for projection, sir. Your stuff will be all chang'd shortly.
Mam.	Into gold?
Face.	To gold and silver, sir.
Mam.	Silver I care not for.
Face.	Yes, sir, a little to give beggars.
Mam.	Where 's the lady?
Face.	At hand here. I ha' told her such brave things o' you, Touching your bounty and your noble spirit——
Mam.	Hast thou?
Face.	As she is almost in her fit to see you. But, good sir, no divinity i' your conference, For fear of putting her in rage.——
Mam.	I warrant thee.
Face.	Six men [sir] will not hold her down. And then, If the old man should hear or see you——
Mam.	Fear not.
Face.	The very house, sir, would run mad. You know it, How scrupulous he is, and violent, 'Gainst the least act of sin. Physic or mathematics, Poetry, state, or bawdry, as I told you, She will endure, and never startle; but No word of controversy.
Mam.	I am school'd, good Ulen.
Face.	And you must praise her house, remember that, And her nobility.

196

MAM.   Let me alone:
No herald, no, nor antiquary, Lungs,
Shall do it better. Go.

FACE.   [*Aside.*] Why, this is yet
A kind of modern happiness, to have
Dol Common for a great lady.   [*Exit.*]

MAM.   Now, Epicure,
Heighten thyself, talk to her all in gold;
Rain her as many showers as Jove did drops
Unto his Danaë; show the god a miser,
Compar'd with Mammon. What! the stone will do 't.
She shall feel gold, taste gold, hear gold, sleep gold;
Nay, we will *concumbere* gold: I will be puissant,
And mighty in my talk to her.—

[*Re-enter* FACE *with* DOL *richly dressed.*]

                                    Here she comes.
FACE.   To him, Dol, suckle him. This is the noble knight
I told your ladyship——

MAM.   Madam, with your pardon,
I kiss your vesture.

DOL.   Sir, I were uncivil
If I would suffer that; my lip to you, sir.

MAM.   I hope my lord your brother be in health, lady.

DOL.   My lord my brother is, though I no lady, sir.

FACE.   [*Aside.*] Well said, my Guinea bird.

MAM.   Right noble madam——

FACE.   [*Aside.*] O, we shall have most fierce idolatry.

MAM.   'T is your prerogative.

DOL.   Rather your courtesy.

MAM.   Were there nought else t' enlarge your virtues to me,
These answers speak your breeding and your blood.

DOL.   Blood we boast none, sir; a poor baron's daughter.

MAM.   Poor! and gat you? Profane not. Had your father
Slept all the happy remnant of his life
After that act, lien but there still, and panted,
He 'd done enough to make himself, his issue,
And his posterity noble.

DOL.   Sir, although
We may be said to want the gilt and trappings,
The dress of honour, yet we strive to keep
The seeds and the materials.

MAM.   I do see

	The old ingredient, virtue, was not lost,

       The old ingredient, virtue, was not lost,
       Nor the drug money us'd to make your compound.
       There is a strange nobility i' your eye,
       This lip, that chin! Methinks you do resemble
       One o' the Austriac princes.

FACE.   [*Aside.*] Very like!
       Her father was an Irish costermonger.

MAM.   The house of Valois just had such a nose,
       And such a forehead yet the Medici
       Of Florence boast.

DOL.   Troth, and I have been lik'ned
       To all these princes.

FACE.   [*Aside.*] I 'll be sworn, I heard it.

MAM.   I know not how! it is not any one,
       But e'en the very choice of all their features.

FACE.   [*Aside.*] I 'll in, and laugh.   [*Exit.*]

MAM.   A certain touch, or air,
       That sparkles a divinity beyond
       An earthly beauty!

DOL.   O, you play the courtier.

MAM.   Good lady, gi' me leave——

DOL.   In faith, I may not,
       To mock me, sir.

MAM.   To burn i' this sweet flame;
       The phoenix never knew a nobler death.

DOL.   Nay, now you court the courtier, and destroy
       What you would build. This art, sir, i' your words,
       Calls your whole faith in question.

MAM.   By my soul——

DOL.   Nay, oaths are made o' the same air, sir.

MAM.   Nature
       Never bestow'd upon mortality
       A more unblam'd, a more harmonious feature;
       She play'd the step-dame in all faces else:
       Sweet madam, le' me be particular——

DOL.   Particular, sir! I pray you, know your distance.

MAM.   In no ill sense, sweet lady: but to ask
       How your fair graces pass the hours? I see
       You're lodg'd here, i' the house of a rare man,
       An excellent artist: but what 's that to you?

DOL.   Yes, sir; I study here the mathematics,
       And distillation.

MAM.   O, I cry your pardon.

He 's a divine instructor! can extract
The souls of all things by his art; call all
The virtues, and the miracles of the sun,
Into a temperate furnace; teach dull nature
What her own forces are. A man, the emp'ror
Has courted above Kelly;[1] sent his medals
And chains, t' invite him.

DOL.   Ay, and for his physic, sir——
MAM.   Above the art of Aesculapius,
That drew the envy of the thunderer!
I know all this, and more.

DOL.   Troth, I am taken, sir,
Whole with these studies that contemplate nature.
MAM.   It is a noble humour; but this form
Was not intended to so dark a use.
Had you been crooked, foul, of some coarse mould,
A cloister had done well; but such a feature,
That might stand up the glory of a kingdom,
To live recluse is a mere solecism,
Though in a nunnery. It must not be.
I muse, my lord your brother will permit it:
You should spend half my land first, were I he.
Does not this diamond better on my finger
Than i' the quarry?

DOL.   Yes.
MAM.   Why, you are like it.
You were created, lady, for the light.
Here, you shall wear it; take it, the first pledge
Of what I speak, to bind you to believe me.

DOL.   In chains of adamant?
MAM.   Yes, the strongest bands.
And take a secret too.—Here, by your side,
Doth stand this hour the happiest man in Europe.

DOL.   You are contented, sir?
MAM.   Nay, in true being,
The envy of princes and the fear of states.

DOL.   Say you so, Sir Epicure?
MAM.   Yes, and thou shalt prove it,
Daughter of honour. I have cast mine eye
Upon thy form, and I will rear this beauty
Above all styles.

1. *Kelly*] The partner of Dee, the astrologer. He and Dee visited the emperor, Rodolph
   II, at Prague in 1584.

DOL.	You mean no treason, sir?
MAM.	No, I will take away that jealousy.
	I am the lord of the philosopher's stone,
	And thou the lady.
DOL.	How, sir! ha' you that?
MAM.	I am the master of the mastery.²
	This day the good old wretch here o' the house
	Has made it for us: now he 's at projection.
	Think therefore thy first wish now, let me hear it;
	And it shall rain into thy lap, no shower,
	But floods of gold, whole cataracts, a deluge,
	To get a nation on thee.
DOL.	You are pleas'd, sir,
	To work on the ambition of our sex.
MAM.	I am pleas'd the glory of her sex should know,
	This nook here of the Friars is no climate
	For her to live obscurely in, to learn
	Physic and surgery, for the constable's wife
	Of some odd hundred in Essex; but come forth,
	And taste the air of palaces; eat, drink
	The toils of empirics, and their boasted practice;
	Tincture of pearl, and coral, gold, and amber;
	Be seen at feasts and triumphs; have it ask'd,
	What miracle she is; set all the eyes
	Of court a-fire, like a burning glass,
	And work 'em into cinders, when the jewels
	Of twenty states adorn thee, and the light
	Strikes out the stars that, when thy name is mention'd,
	Queens may look pale; and, we but showing our love,
	Nero's Poppaea may be lost in story!
	Thus will we have it.
DOL.	I could well consent, sir.
	But in a monarchy, how will this be?
	The prince will soon take notice, and both seize
	You and your stone, it being a wealth unfit
	For any private subject.
MAM.	If he knew it.
DOL.	Yourself do boast it, sir.
MAM.	To thee, my life.
DOL.	O, but beware, sir! You may come to end
	The remnant of your days in a loath'd prison,
	By speaking of it.

2. *mastery*] the art of transmutation.

MAM.   'T is no idle fear.
We 'll therefore go with all, my girl, and live
In a free state, where we will eat our mullets,
Sous'd in high-country wines, sup pheasants' eggs,
And have our cockles boil'd in silver shells;
Our shrimps to swim again, as when they liv'd,
In a rare butter made of dolphins' milk,
Whose cream does look like opals; and with these
Delicate meats set ourselves high for pleasure,
And take us down again, and then renew
Our youth and strength with drinking the elixir,
And so enjoy a perpetuity
Of life and lust! And thou shalt ha' thy wardrobe
Richer than Nature's, still to change thyself,
And vary oft'ner, for thy pride, than she,
Or Art, her wise and almost-equal servant.

[*Re-enter* FACE.]

FACE.   Sir, you are too loud. I hear you every word
Into the laboratory. Some fitter place;
The garden, or great chamber above. How like you her?
MAM.   Excellent! Lungs. There 's for thee.   [*Gives him money.*]
FACE.   But do you hear?
Good sir, beware, no mention of the rabbins.
MAM.   We think not on 'em.   [*Exeunt* MAM. *and* DOL.]
FACE.   O, it is well, sir.—Subtle!

SCENE II.—*The same*

FACE. [*Enter*] SUBTLE.

          Dost thou not laugh?
SUB.   Yes; are they gone?
FACE.   All 's clear.
SUB.   The widow is come.
FACE.   And your quarreling disciple?
SUB.   Ay.
FACE.   I must to my captainship again then.
SUB.   Stay, bring 'em in first.
FACE.   So I meant. What is she?
          A bonnibel?

SUB.	I know not.
FACE.	We 'll draw lots:

FACE. You 'll stand to that?

SUB. What else?

FACE. O, for a suit,
To fall now like a curtain, flap!

SUB. To th' door, man.

FACE. You 'll ha' the first kiss, 'cause I am not ready.   [*Exit.*]

SUB. Yes, and perhaps hit you through both the nostrils.[1]

FACE. [*within.*] Who would you speak with?

KAS. [*within.*] Where 's the captain?

FACE. [*within.*] Gone, sir,
About some business.

KAS. [*within.*] Gone!

FACE. [*within.*] He 'll return straight.
But, master doctor, his lieutenant, is here.

[*Enter* KASTRIL, *followed by* Dame PLIANT.]

SUB. Come near, my worshipful boy, *my terrae fili*,
That is, my boy of land; make thy approaches:
Welcome; I know thy lusts and thy desires,
And I will serve and satisfy 'em. Begin,
Charge me from thence, or thence, or in this line;
Here is my centre: ground thy quarrel.

KAS. You lie.

SUB. How, child of wrath and anger! the loud lie?
For what, my sudden boy?

KAS. Nay, that look you to,
I am aforehand.

SUB. O, this is no true grammar,
And as ill logic! You must render causes, child,
Your first and second intentions, know your canons
And your divisions, moods, degrees, and differences,
Your predicaments, substance, and accident,
Series extern and intern, with their causes,
Efficient, material, formal, final,
And ha' your elements perfect?

KAS. What is this?
The angry tongue he talks in?

SUB. That false precept,
Of being aforehand, has deceiv'd a number,

---

1. *hit . . . nostrils*] "put your nose out of joint."

And made 'em enter quarrels oftentimes
Before they were aware; and afterward,
Against their wills.

KAS.   How must I do then, sir?

SUB.   I cry this lady mercy; she should first
Have been saluted. [*Kisses her.*] I do call you lady,
Because you are to be one ere 't be long,
My soft and buxom widow.

KAS.   Is she, i' faith?

SUB.   Yes, or my art is an egregious liar.

KAS.   How know you?

SUB.   By inspection on her forehead,
And subtlety of her lip, which must be tasted
Often to make a judgment. [*Kisses her again.*] 'Slight, she
    melts
Like a myrobolane.[2] Here is yet a line,
In *rivo frontis*,[3] tells me he is no knight.

DAME P.   What is he then, sir?

SUB.   Let me see your hand.
O, your *linea fortunae* makes it plain;
And *stella* here *in monte Veneris*.
But, most of all, *junctura annularis*.[4]
He is a soldier, or a man of art, lady,
But shall have some great honour shortly.

DAME P.   Brother,
He 's a rare man, believe me!

[*Re-enter* FACE, *in his uniform*.]

KAS.   Hold your peace.
Here comes t' other rare man.—'Save you, captain.

FACE.   Good Master Kastril! Is this your sister?

KAS.   Ay, sir.
Please you to kuss her, and be proud to know her,

FACE.   I shall be proud to know you, lady.   [*Kisses her.*]

DAME P.   Brother,
He calls me lady, too.

KAS.   Ay, peace: I heard it.
                                        [*Takes her aside.*]

FACE.   The count is come.

SUB.   Where is he?

2. *myrobolane*] a kind of dried plum, esteemed as a sweetmeat.
3. *rivo frontis*] frontal vein.
4. *junctura annularis*] These are the cant phrases of palmistry.

FACE.   At the door.
SUB.   Why, you must entertain him.
FACE.   What will you do
        With these the while?
SUB.   Why, have 'em up, and show 'em
        Some fustian book, or the dark glass.
FACE.   'Fore God,
        She is a delicate dabchick! I must have her.   [*Exit.*]
SUB.   [*Aside.*] Must you! Ay, if your fortune will, you must.—
        Come, sir, the captain will come to us presently:
        I 'll ha' you to my chamber of demonstrations,
        Where I 'll show you both the grammar and logic,
        And rhetoric of quarreling; my whole method
        Drawn out in tables; and my instrument,
        That hath the several scales upon 't shall make you
        Able to quarrel at a straw's-breadth by moonlight.
        And, lady, I 'll have you look in a glass,
        Some half an hour, but to clear your eyesight,
        Against you see your fortune; which is greater
        Than I may judge upon the sudden, trust me.   [*Exeunt.*]

SCENE III.—*The same*

[*Enter*] FACE.

FACE.   Where are you, doctor?
SUB.   [*within.*] I 'll come to you presently.
FACE.   I will ha' this same widow, now I ha' seen her,
        On any composition.

[*Enter* SUBTLE]

SUB.   What do you say?
FACE.   Ha' you dispos'd of them?
SUB.   I ha' sent 'em up.
FACE.   Subtle, in troth, I needs must have this widow.
SUB.   Is that the matter?
FACE.   Nay, but hear me.
SUB.   Go to.
        If you rebel once, Dol shall know it all:
        Therefore be quiet, and obey your chance.
FACE.   Nay, thou art so violent now. Do but conceive,

	Thou art old, and canst not serve——
SUB.	Who cannot? I?
	'Slight, I will serve her with thee, for a——
FACE.	Nay,
	But understand: I 'll gi' you composition.[1]
SUB.	I will not treat with thee. What! sell my fortune?
	'T is better than my birthright. Do not murmur:
	Win her, and carry her. If you grumble, Dol
	Knows it directly.
FACE.	Well, sir, I am silent.
	Will you go help to fetch in Don in state? [*Exit.*]
SUB.	I follow you, sir. We must keep Face in awe,
	Or he will overlook us like a tyrant.

[*Re-enter* FACE, *introducing*] SURLY *like a Spaniard.*

	Brain of a tailor! who comes here? Don John!
SUR.	*Senores, beso las manos a vuestras mercedes.*[2]
SUB.	Would you had stoop'd a little, and kist our *anos*.
FACE.	Peace, Subtle!
SUB.	Stab me; I shall never hold, man.
	He looks in that deep ruff like a head in a platter,
	Serv'd in by a short cloak upon two trestles.
FACE.	Or what do you say to a collar of brawn, cut down
	Beneath the souse, and wriggled with a knife?
SUB.	'Slud, he does look too fat to be a Spaniard.
FACE.	Perhaps some Fleming or some Hollander got him
	In d'Alva's time; Count Egmont's bastard.
SUB.	Don,
	Your scurvy, yellow, Madrid face is welcome.
SUR.	*Gratia.*
SUB.	He speaks out of a fortification.
	Pray God he ha' no squibs in those deep sets.
SUR.	*Por dios, senores, muy linda casa!*[3]
SUB.	What says he?
FACE.	Praises the house, I think;
	I know no more but 's action.
SUB.	Yes, the *casa*,
	My precious Diego, will prove fair enough
	To cozen you in. Do you mark? You shall
	Be cozened, Diego.

1. *composition*] recompense.
2. Spanish. "Gentlemen, I kiss your hands."
3. "Gad, sirs, a very pretty house."

FACE.   Cozened, do you see,
My worthy Donzel, cozened.

SUR.   *Entiendo.*[4]

SUB.   Do you intend it? So do we, dear Don.
Have you brought pistolets or portagues,
My solemn Don? [*To* FACE.] Dost thou feel any?

FACE.   [*Feels his pockets.*] Full.

SUB.   You shall be emptied, Don, pumped and drawn
Dry, as they say.

FACE.   Milked, in troth, sweet Don.

SUB.   See all the monsters; the great lion of all, Don.

SUR.   *Con licencia, se puede ver a esta senora?*[5]

SUB.   What talks he now?

FACE.   Of the senora.

SUB.   O, Don,
This is the lioness, which you shall see
Also, my Don.

FACE.   'Slid, Subtle, how shall we do?

SUB.   For what?

FACE.   Why, Dol's employ'd, you know.

SUB.   That's true.
'Fore heav'n I know not: he must stay, that's all.

FACE.   Stay! that he must not by no means.

SUB.   No! why?

FACE.   Unless you 'll mar all. 'Slight, he 'll suspect it;
And then he will not pay, not half so well.
This is a travell'd punk-master, and does know
All the delays; a notable hot rascal,
And looks already rampant.

SUB.   'Sdeath, and Mammon
Must not be troubled.

FACE.   Mammon! in no case.

SUB.   What shall we do then?

FACE.   Think: you must be sudden.

SUR.   *Entiendo que la senora es tan hermosa, que codicio tan a verla
      como la bien aventuranza de mi vida.*[6]

FACE.   *Mi vida!* 'Slid, Subtle, he puts me in mind o' the widow.
What dost thou say to draw her to 't, ha!
And tell her 't is her fortune? All our venture

---

4. "I understand."
5. "If you please, may I see the lady?"
6. "I understand that the lady is so handsome that I am as eager to see her as the good
   fortune of my life."

                    Now lies upon 't. It is but one man more,
                    Which on 's chance to have her: and beside,
                    There is no maidenhead to be fear'd or lost.
                    What dost thou think on 't, Subtle?
SUB.   Who, I? why——
FACE.   The credit of our house too is engag'd.
SUB.   You made me an offer for my share ere-while.
                    What wilt thou gi' me, i' faith?
FACE.   O, by that light
                    I 'll not buy now. You know your doom[7] to me.
                    E'en take your lot, obey your chance, sir; win her,
                    And wear her—out for me.
SUB.   'Slight, I 'll not work her then.
FACE.   It is the common cause; therefore bethink you.
                    Dol else must know it, as you said.
SUB.   I care not.
SUR.   *Senores, porque se tarda tanto?*[8]
SUB.   Faith, I am not fit, I am old.
FACE.   That 's now no reason, sir.
SUR.   *Puede ser de hazer burla de mi amor?*[9]
FACE.   You hear the Don too? By this air I call,
                    And loose the hinges. Dol!
SUB.   A plague of hell——
FACE.   Will you then do?
SUB.   You 're a terrible rogue!
                    I 'll think of this. Will you, sir, call the widow?
FACE.   Yes, and I 'll take her too with all her faults,
                    Now I do think on 't better.
SUB.   With all my heart, sir;
                    Am I discharg'd o' the lot?
FACE.   As you please.
SUB.   Hands. [*They shake hands.*]
FACE.   Remember now, that upon any change
                    You never claim her.
SUB.   Much good joy and health to you, sir,
                    Marry a whore! Fate, let me wed a witch first.
SUR.   *Por estas honradas barbas*[10]——
SUB.   He swears by his beard.
                    Dispatch, and call the brother too.   [*Exit* FACE.]

    7. *doom*] agreement.
    8. "Sirs, why so long delay?"
    9. "Can it be to make sport of my love?"
    10. "By this honored beard——"

SUR.   *Tengo duda, senores, que no me hagan alguna traycion.*[11]
SUB.   How, issue on? Yes, *praesto, senor.* Please you
        Enthratha the *chambratha,* worthy don:
        Where if you please the fates, in your *bathada,*
        You shall be soak'd, and strok'd, and tubb'd, and rubb'd,
        And scrubb'd, and fubb'd,[12] dear don, before you go.
        You shall in faith, my scurvy baboon don,
        Be curried, claw'd, and flaw'd,[13] and taw'd,[14] indeed.
        I will the heartlier go about it now,
        And make the widow a punk so much the sooner,
        To be reveng'd on this impetuous Face:
        The quickly doing of it is the grace.
                                        [*Exeunt* SUB. *and* SURLY.]

SCENE IV.—*Another room in the same*

[*Enter*] FACE, KASTRIL, *and* Dame PLIANT.

FACE.   Come, lady: I knew the doctor would not leave
         Till he had found the very nick of her fortune.
KAS.   To be a countess, say you?
FACE.   A Spanish countess, sir.
DAME P. Why, is that better than an English countess?
FACE.   Better! 'Slight, make you that a question, lady?
KAS.   Nay, she is a fool, captain, you must pardon her.
FACE.   Ask from your courtier to your inns-of-court-man.
         To your mere milliner; they will tell you all,
         Your Spanish jennet is the best horse; your Spanish
         Stoop is the best garb; your Spanish beard
         Is the best cut; your Spanish ruffs are the best
         Wear; your Spanish pavin the best dance;
         Your Spanish titillation in a glove
         The best perfume: and for your Spanish pike,
         And Spanish blade, let your poor captain speak.—
         Here comes the doctor.

[*Enter* SUBTLE *with a paper.*]

11. "I fear, sirs, that you are playing me some trick."
12. *fubb'd*] cheated.
13. *flaw'd*] cracked.
14. *taw'd*] soaked, like a hide being tanned.

SUB.   My most honour'd lady,
        For so I am now to style you, having found
        By this my scheme,[1] you are to undergo
        An honourable fortune very shortly,
        What will you say now, if some——
FACE.   I ha' told her all, sir,
        And her right worshipful brother here, that she shall be
        A countess; do not delay 'em, sir; a Spanish countess.
SUB.   Still, my scarce-worshipful captain, you can keep
        No secret! Well, since he has told you, madam,
        Do you forgive him, and I do.
KAS.   She shall do that, sir;
        I 'll look to it; 't is my charge.
SUB.   Well then: nought rests
        But that she fit her love now to her fortune.
DAME P. Truly I shall never brook a Spaniard.
SUB.   No?
DAME P. Never sin' eighty-eight[2] could I abide 'em,
        And that was some three years afore I was born, in truth.
SUB.   Come, you must love him, or be miserable;
        Choose which you will.
FACE.   By this good rush, persuade her,
        She will cry[3] strawberries else within this twelve month.
SUB.   Nay, shads and mackerel, which is worse.
FACE.   Indeed, sir!
KAS.   God's lid, you shall love him, or I 'll kick you.
DAME P.   Why,
        I 'll do as you will ha' me, brother.
KAS.   Do,
        Or by this hand I 'll maul you.
FACE.   Nay, good sir,
        Be not so fierce.
SUB.   No, my enraged child;
        She will be rul'd. What, when she comes to taste
        The pleasures of a countess! to be courted——
FACE.   And kiss'd and ruffled!
SUB.   Ay, behind the hangings.
FACE.   And then come forth in pomp!
SUB.   And know her state!

1. *scheme*] horoscope.
2. *eighty-eight*] i.e., since 1588, the year of the "Invincible Armada."
3. *cry*] sell on the street.

FACE. Of keeping all th' idolators o' the chamber
Barer to her, than at their prayers!
SUB.   Is serv'd
Upon the knee!
FACE.   And has her pages, ushers,
Footmen, and coaches——
SUB.   Her six mares——
FACE.   Nay, eight!
SUB. To hurry her through London, to th' Exchange,
Bet'lem,[4] the China-houses[5]——
FACE.   Yes, and have
The citizens gape at her, and praise her tires,[6]
And my lord's goose-turd bands, that rides with her!
KAS. Most brave! By this hand, you are not my suster
If you refuse.
DAME P.   I will not refuse, brother.

[Enter Surly.]

SUR. *Que es esto, senores, que non se venga?*
Esta tardanza me mata![7]
FACE.   It is the count come:
The doctor knew he would be here, by his art.
SUB. *En gallanta, madama, Don! gallantissima!*
SUR. *Por todos los dioses, la mas acabada*
Hermosura, que he visto en ma vida![8]
FACE. Is 't not a gallant language that they speak?
KAS. An admirable language! Is 't not French?
FACE. No, Spanish, sir.
KAS.   It goes like law French,
And that, they say, is the court-liest language.
FACE.   List, sir.
SUR. *El sol ha perdido su lumbre, con el*
Resplandor que trae esta dana! Valga me dios![9]
FACE. H' admires your sister.
KAS.   Must not she make curt'sy.
SUB. 'Ods will, she must go to him, man, and kiss him!
It is the Spanish fashion, for the women

4. *Bet'lem*] The madhouse was often visited for entertainment.
5. *China-houses*] shops with merchandise from China.
6. *tires*] head-dresses.
7. "Why does n't she come, sirs? This delay is killing me."
8. "By all the gods, the most perfect beauty I have seen in my life."
9. "The sun has lost his light with the splendor this lady brings, so help me God."

	To make first court.
FACE.	'T is true he tells you, sir:
	His art knows all.
SUR.	*Porque no se acude?*[10]
KAS.	He speaks to her, I think.
FACE.	That he does, sir.
SUR.	*Por el amor de dios, que es esto que se tarda?*[11]
KAS.	Nay, see: she will not understand him! Gull, Noddy.
DAME P.	What say you, brother?
KAS.	Ass, my suster,
	Go kuss him, as the cunning man would ha' you;
	I 'll thrust a pin i' your buttocks else.
FACE.	O no, sir.
SUR.	*Senora mia, mi persona muy indigna esta
	Allegar a tanta hermosura.*[12]
FACE.	Does he not use her bravely?
KAS.	Bravely, i' faith!
FACE.	Nay, he will use her better.
KAS.	Do you think so?
SUR.	*Senora, si sera servida, entremos.*[13]

[*Exit with* Dame PLIANT.]

KAS.	Where does he carry her?
FACE.	Into the garden, sir;
	Take you no thought: I must interpret for her.
SUB.	Give Dol the word. [*Aside to* FACE, *who goes out.*]
	—Come, my fierce child, advance,
	We 'll to our quarreling lesson again.
KAS.	Agreed.
	I love a Spanish boy with all my heart.
SUB.	Nay, and by this means, sir, you shall be brother
	To a great count.
KAS.	Ay, I knew that at first.
	This match will advance the house of the Kastrils.
SUB.	'Pray God your sister prove but pliant!
KAS.	Why,
	Her name is so, by her other husband.
SUB.	How!
KAS.	The Widow Pliant. Knew you not that?
SUB.	No, faith, sir;

10. "Why don't you draw near?"
11. "For the love of God, why this delay?"
12. "Madam, my person is unworthy to approach such beauty."
13. "Madam, at your service, let us go in."

        Yet, by the erection of her figure,[14] I guess'd it.
        Come, let 's go practise.
KAS.   Yes, but do you think, doctor,
        I e'er shall quarrel well?
SUB.   I warrant you.   [*Exeunt.*]

SCENE V.—*Another room in the same*

[*Enter*] DOL [*followed by*] MAMMON.

DOL.   [*in her fit of talking.*] *For after Alexander's death*——
MAM.   Good lady——
DOL.   *That Perdiccas and Antigonus were slain,*
        The two that stood, Seleuc' and Ptolomy——
MAM.   Madam—
DOL.   *Make up the two legs, and the fourth beast,*
        That was Gog-north and Egypt-south: which after
        Was called Gog-iron-leg and South-iron-leg——
MAM.   Lady——
DOL.   *And then Gog-horned. So was Egypt, too:*
        Then Egypt-clay-leg, and Gog-clay-leg——
MAM.   Sweet madam——
DOL.   *And last Gog-dust, and Egypt-dust, which fall*
        In the last link of the fourth chain. And these
        Be stars in story, which none see, or look at——
MAM.   What shall I do?
DOL.   *For, as he says,* except
        We call the rabbins, and the heathen Greeks——
MAM.   Dear lady——
DOL.   *To come from Salem, and from Athens,*
        And teach the people of Great Britain——

[*Enter* FACE *hastily, in his servant's dress.*]

FACE.   What 's the matter, sir?
DOL.   *To speak the tongue of Eber and Javan*——
MAM.   O,
        She 's in her fit.
DOL.   *We shall know nothing*——
FACE.   Death, sir,

14. *the . . . figure*] by her horoscope, with a pun on her bearing.

	We are undone!
Dol.	*Where then a learned linguist*
	Shall see the ancient us'd communion
	Of vowels and consonants——
Face.	My master will hear!
Dol.	*A wisdom, which Pythagoras held most high——*
Mam.	Sweet honourable lady!
Dol.	*To comprise*
	All sounds of voices, in few marks of letters.
Face.	Nay, you must never hope to lay her now.

[*They all speak together.*]

Dol.	*And so we may arrive by Talmud skill,*
	And profane Greek, to raise the building up
	Of Helen's house against the Ismaelite,
	King of Thogarma, and his habergions
	Brimstony, blue, and fiery; and the force
	Of king Abaddon, and the beast of Cittim:
	Which rabbi David Kimchi, Onkelos,
	And Aben Ezra do interpret Rome.
Face.	How did you put her into 't?
Mam.	Alas, I talkt
	Of a fifth monarchy I would erect
	With the philosopher's stone, by chance, and she
	Falls on the other four straight.
Face.	Out of Broughton!
	I told you so. 'Slid, stop her mouth.
Mam.	Is 't best?
Face.	She 'll never leave else. If the old man hear her,
	We are but faeces, ashes.
Sub.	[*within.*] What 's to do there?
Face.	O, we are lost! Now she hears him, she is quiet.

[*Enter* Subtle;] *upon* Subtle's *entry they disperse.*

Mam.	Where shall I hide me!
Sub.	How! What sight is here?
	Close[1] deeds of darkness, and that shun the light!
	Bring him again. Who is he? What, my son!
	O, I have liv'd too long.
Mam.	Nay, good, dear father,
	There was no unchaste purpose.
Sub.	Not? and flee me

1. *close*] secret.

	When I come in?
MAM.	That was my error.
SUB.	Error?

Guilt, guilt, my son; give it the right name. No marvel
If I found check in our great work within,
When such affairs as these were managing!

| MAM. | Why, have you so? |
| SUB. | It has stood still this half hour: |

And all the rest of our less works gone back.
Where is the instrument of wickedness,
My lewd false drudge?

| MAM. | Nay, good sir, blame not him; |

Believe me, 't was against his will or knowledge:
I saw her by chance.

| SUB. | Will you commit more sin, |

T' excuse a varlet?

| MAM. | By my hope, 't is true, sir. |
| SUB. | Nay, then I wonder less, if you, for whom |

The blessing was prepar'd, would so tempt heaven,
And lose your fortunes.

| MAM. | Why, sir? |
| SUB. | This will retard |

The work a month at least.

| MAM. | Why, if it do, |

What remedy? But think it not, good father:
Our purposes were honest.

| SUB. | As they were, |

So the reward will prove. [*A great crack and noise within.*] —
   How now! ay me!
God and all saints be good to us. ——

[*Re-enter* FACE.]

| | What 's that? |
| FACE. | O, sir, we are defeated! All the works |

Are flown *in fumo*, every glass is burst;
Furnace and all rent down, as if a bolt
Of thunder had been driven through the house.
Retorts, receivers, pelicans,[2] bolt heads,[3]
All struck in shivers!   [SUBTLE *falls down as in a swoon.*]
         Help, good sir! alas,

---

2. *pelicans*] an alembic of a particular shape.
3. *bolt heads*] a globular flask.

   Coldness and death invades him. Nay, Sir Mammon,
   Do the fair offices of a man! You stand,
   As you were readier to depart than he.   [*One knocks.*]
   Who 's there? My lord her brother is come.

MAM.   Ha, Lungs!

FACE.   His coach is at the door. Avoid his sight,
   For he 's as furious as his sister 's mad.

MAM.   Alas!

FACE.   My brain is quite undone with the fume, sir,
   I ne'er must hope to be mine own man again.

MAM.   Is all lost, Lungs? Will nothing be preserv'd
   Of all our cost?

FACE.   Faith, very little, sir;
   A peck of coals or so, which is cold comfort, sir.

MAM.   O, my voluptuous mind! I am justly punish'd.

FACE.   And so am I, sir.

MAM.   Cast from all my hopes——

FACE.   Nay, certainties, sir.

MAM.   By mine own base affections.

SUB.   [*seeming to come to himself.*] O, the curst fruits of vice and
    lust!

MAM.   Good father,
   It was my sin. Forgive it.

SUB.   Hangs my roof
   Over us still, and will not fall, O justice,
   Upon us, for this wicked man!

FACE.   Nay, look, sir,
   You grieve him now with staying in his sight.
   Good sir, the nobleman will come too, and take you,
   And that may breed a tragedy.

MAM.   I 'll go.

FACE.   Ay, and repent at home, sir. It may be,
   For some good penance you may ha' it yet;
   A hundred pound to the box at Bet'lem[4]——

MAM.   Yes.

FACE.   For the restoring such as—ha' their wits.

MAM.   I 'll do 't.

FACE.   I 'll send one to you to receive it.

MAM.   Do.
   Is no projection left?

FACE.   All flown, or stinks, sir.

---

4. *Bet'lem*] the lunatic asylum.

MAM. Will nought be sav'd that 's good for med'cine, think'st thou?
FACE. I cannot tell, sir. There will be perhaps
       Something about the scraping of the shards,
       Will cure the itch,—though not your itch of mind, sir. [*Aside.*]
       It shall be sav'd for you, and sent home. Good sir,
       This way, for fear the lord shall meet you.   [*Exit* MAMMON.]
SUB.   [*raising his head.*] Face!
FACE. Ay.
SUB.   Is he gone?
FACE.   Yes, and as heavily
       As all the gold he hop'd for were in 's blood.
       Let us be light though.
SUB.   [*leaping up.*] Ay, as balls, and bound
       And hit our heads against the roof for joy:
       There 's so much of our care now cast away.
FACE. Now to our don.
SUB.   Yes, your young widow by this time
       Is made a countess, Face; she 's been in travail
       Of a young heir for you.
FACE.   Good, sir.
SUB.   Off with your case,
       And greet her kindly, as a bridegroom should,
       After these common hazards.
FACE.   Very well, sir.
       Will you go fetch Don Diego off the while?
SUB.   And fetch him over too, if you 'll be pleas'd, sir.
       Would Dol were in her place, to pick his pockets now!
FACE. Why, you can do 't as well, if you would set to 't.
       I pray you prove your virtue.
SUB.   For your sake, sir.   [*Exeunt.*]

SCENE VI.—*Another room in the same*

[*Enter*] SURLY *and* Dame PLIANT.

SUR.   Lady, you see into what hands you are fall'n;
       'Mongst what a nest of villains! and how near
       Your honour was t' have catch'd a certain clap,
       Through your credulity, had I but been
       So punctually forward, as place, time,
       And other circumstance would ha' made a man;

For you 're a handsome woman: would you were wise too!
I am a gentleman come here disguis'd,
Only to find the knaveries of this citadel;
And where I might have wrong'd your honour, and have not,
I claim some interest in your love. You are,
They say, a widow, rich; and I 'm a bachelor,
Worth nought: your fortunes may make me a man,
As mine ha' preserv'd you a woman. Think upon it,
And whether I have deserv'd you or no.

DAME P.   I will, sir.
SUR.   And for these household-rogues, let me alone
          To treat with them.

[*Enter* SUBTLE.]

SUB.   How doth my noble Diego,
          And my dear madam countess? Hath the count
          Been courteous, lady? liberal and open?
          Donzel, methinks you look melancholic,
          I do not like the dulness of your eye;
          It hath a heavy cast, 't is upsee Dutch,[1]
          And says you are a lumpish whore-master.
          Be lighter, I will make your pockets so.
                          [*He falls to picking of them.*]
SUR.   [*throws open his cloak.*] Will you, don bawd and pick-purse?
             [*Strikes him down.*] How now! Reel you?
          Stand up, sir, you shall find, since I am so heavy,
          I 'll gi' you equal weight.
SUB.   Help! murder!
SUR.   No, sir,
          There 's no such thing intended. A good cart
          And a clean whip shall ease you of that fear.
          I am the Spanish don that should be cozened,
          Do you see? Cozened? Where 's your Captain Face,
          That parcel-broker, and whole-bawd, all rascal?

[*Enter* FACE *in his uniform.*]

FACE.   How, Surly!
SUR.   O, make your approach, good captain.
          I 've found from whence your copper rings and spoons
          Come now, wherewith you cheat abroad in taverns.
          'T was here you learn'd t' anoint your boot with brimstone,

1. *Dutch*] as if you had been drinking heavy Dutch beer.

Then rub men's gold on 't for a kind of touch,
And say, 't was naught, when you had chang'd the colour,
That you might ha't for nothing. And this doctor,
Your sooty, smoky-bearded compeer, he
Will close you so much gold, in a bolt's-head,
And, on a turn, convey i' the stead another
With sublim'd mercury, that shall burst i' the heat,
And fly out all *in fumo!* Then weeps Mammon;
Then swoons his worship. Or, [FACE *slips out.*] he is the Faustus,
That casteth figures and can conjure, cures
Plagues, piles, and pox, by the ephemerides.[2]
And holds intelligence with all the bawds
And midwives of three shires: while you send in——
Captain!—what! is he gone?—damsels with child,
Wives that are barren, or the waiting-maid
With the green sickness. [*Seizes* SUBTLE *as he is retiring.*]—
    Nay, sir, you must tarry,
Though he be scap'd; and answer by the ears, sir.

SCENE VII.—*The same*

[*Re-enter*] FACE [*with*] KASTRIL [*to*] SURLY [*and*] SUBTLE.

FACE.   Why, now 's the time, if ever you will quarrel
            Well, as they say, and be a true-born child:
            The doctor and your sister both are abus'd.
KAS.   Where is he? Which is he? He is a slave.
            Whate'er he is, and the son of a whore.—Are you
            The man, sir, I would know?
SUR.   I should be loth, sir.
            To confess so much.
KAN.   Then you lie i' your throat.
SUR.   How!
FACE.   [*To* KASTRIL.] A very arrant rogue, sir, and a cheater,
            Employ'd here by another conjurer
            That does not love the doctor, and would cross him
            If he knew how.
SUR.   Sir, you are abus'd.

2. *ephemerides*] astrological almanacs.

KAS.   You lie:
          And 't is no matter.
FACE.   Well said, sir! He is
          The impudent'st rascal——
SUR.   You are indeed. Will you hear me, sir?
FACE.   By no means: bid him be gone.
KAS.   Begone, sir, quickly.
SUR.   This is strange!—Lady, do you inform your brother.
FACE.   There is not such a foist[1] in all the town.
          The doctor had him presently; and finds yet
          The Spanish count will come here.—Bear up, Subtle.
                                                    [Aside.]
SUB.   Yes, sir, he must appear within this hour.
FACE.   And yet this rogue would come in a disguise,
          By the temptation of another spirit,
          To trouble our art, though he could not hurt it!
KAS.   Ay,
          I know—Away, [To his sister.] you talk like a foolish mauther.[2]
SUR.   Sir, all is truth she says.
FACE.   Do not believe him, sir.
          He is the lying'st swabber! Come your ways, sir.
SUR.   You are valiant out of company!
KAS.   Yes, how then, sir?

[Enter DRUGGER with a piece of damask.]

FACE.   Nay, here 's an honest fellow too that knows him,
          And all his tricks. (Make good what I say, Abel.)
          This cheater would ha' cozen'd thee o' the widow.—
                                          [Aside to DRUG.]
          He owes this honest Drugger here seven pound,
          He has had on him in twopenny'orths of tobacco.
DRUG.   Yes, sir. And he has damn'd himself three terms to pay me.
FACE.   And what does he owe for lotium?
DRUG.   Thirty shillings, sir;
          And for six syringes.
SUR.   Hydra of villainy!
FACE.   Nay, sir, you must quarrel him out o' the house.
KAS.   I will:
          —Sir, if you get not out o' doors, you lie;
          And you are a pimp.

1. *foist*] rascal.
2. *mauther*] girl.

Sur.	Why, this is madness, sir,
	Not valour in you; I must laugh at this.
Kas.	It is my humour; you are a pimp and a trig.[3]
	And an Amadis de Gaul, or a Don Quixote.
Drug.	Or a knight o' the curious coxcomb, do you see?

[*Enter* Ananias.]

Ana.	Peace to the household!
Kas.	I 'll keep peace for no man.
Ana.	Casting of dollars is concluded lawful.
Kas.	Is he the constable?
Sub.	Peace, Ananias.
Face.	No, sir.
Kas.	Then you are an otter, and a shad, a whit,
	A very tim.
Sur.	You 'll hear me, sir?
Kas.	I will not.
Ana.	What is the motive?
Sub.	Zeal in the young gentleman,
	Against his Spanish slops.
Ana.	They are profane,
	Lewd, superstitious, and idolatrous breeches.
Sur.	New rascals!
Kas.	Will you be gone, sir?
Ana.	Avoid, Sathan!
	Thou art not of the light! That ruff of pride
	About thy neck, betrays thee; and is the same
	With that which the unclean birds, in seventy-seven,
	Were seen to prank it with on divers coasts:
	Thou look'st like antichrist, in that lewd hat.
Sur.	I must give way.
Kas.	Be gone, sir.
Sur.	But I 'll take
	A course with you. ——
Ana.	Depart, proud Spanish fiend!
Sur.	Captain and doctor.
Ana.	Child of perdition!
Kas.	Hence, sir! — [*Exit* Surly.]
	Did I not quarrel bravely?
Face.	Yes, indeed, sir.
Kas.	Nay, an I give my mind to 't, I shall do 't.

---

3. *trig*] dandy.

FACE.   O, you must follow, sir, and threaten him tame:
          He 'll turn again else.
KAS.   I 'll re-turn him then.   [*Exit.*]
FACE.   Drugger, this rogue prevented us, for thee:
          We had determin'd that thou should'st ha' come
          In a Spanish suit, and ha' carried her so; and he,
          A brokerly slave, goes, puts it on himself.
          Hast brought the damask?
DRUG.   Yes, sir.
FACE.   Thou must borrow
          A Spanish suit. Hast thou no credit with the players?
DRUG.   Yes, sir; did you never see me play the Fool?
FACE.   I know not, Nab;—thou shalt, if I can help it.—   [*Aside.*]
          Hieronimo's old cloak, ruff, and hat will serve;
          I 'll tell thee more when thou bring'st 'em.
          [*Exit* DRUGGER. SUBTLE *hath whisper'd with* ANAN. *this while.*]
ANA.   Sir, I know.
          The Spaniard hates the brethren, and hath spies
          Upon their actions: and that this was one
          I make no scruple.—But the holy synod
          Have been in prayer and meditation for it;
          And 't is reveal'd no less to them than me,
          That casting of money is most lawful.
SUB.   True.
          But here I cannot do it: if the house
          Should chance to be suspected, all would out,
          And we be lock'd up in the Tower for ever,
          To make gold there for th' state, never come out;
          And then are you defeated.
ANA.   I will tell
          This to the elders and the weaker brethren,
          That the whole company of the separation
          May join in humble prayer again.
SUB.   And fasting.
ANA.   Yea, for some fitter place. The peace of mind
          Rest with these walls!   [*Exit.*]
SUB.   Thanks, courteous Ananias.
FACE.   What did he come for?
SUB.   About casting dollars,
          Presently out of hand. And so I told him,
          A Spanish minister came here to spy,
          Against the faithful——
FACE.   I conceive. Come, Subtle,

    Thou art so down upon the least disaster!
    How wouldst thou ha' done, if I had not helpt thee out?
SUB. I thank thee, Face, for the angry boy, i' faith.
FACE. Who would ha' lookt it should ha' been that rascal
    Surly? He had dy'd his beard and all. Well, sir.
    Here 's damask come to make you a suit.
SUB.   Where 's Drugger?
FACE. He is gone to borrow me a Spanish habit;
    I 'll be the count now.
SUB.   But where 's the widow?
FACE. Within, with my lord's sister; Madam Dol
    Is entertaining her.
SUB.   By your favour, Face,
    Now she is honest, I will stand again.
FACE. You will not offer it?
SUB.   Why?
FACE.   Stand to your word,
    Or—here comes Dol. She knows——
SUB.   You 're tyrannous still.

[*Enter* DOL *hastily.*]

FACE. —Strict for my right.—How now, Dol! Hast told her,
    The Spanish count will come?
DOL.   Yes; but another is come,
    You little lookt for!
FACE.   Who 's that?
DOL.   Your master;
    The master of the house.
SUB.   How, Dol!
FACE.   She lies,
    This is some trick. Come, leave your quiblins,[4] Dorothy.
DOL. Look out and see.   [FACE *goes to the window.*]
SUB.   Art thou in earnest?
DOL.   'Slight,
    Forty o' the neighbours are about him, talking.
FACE. 'T is he, by this good day.
DOL.   'T will prove ill day
    For some on us.
FACE.   We are undone, and taken.
DOL. Lost, I 'm afraid.
SUB.   You said he would not come,

4. *quiblins*] quibbles.

	While there died one a week within the liberties.
FACE.	No: 't was within the walls.
SUB.	Was 't so? Cry you mercy.

I thought the liberties. What shall we do now, Face?

FACE. Be silent: not a word, if he call or knock.
I 'll into mine old shape again and meet him,
Of Jeremy, the butler. I' the meantime,
Do you two pack up all the goods and purchase[5]
That we can carry i' the two trunks. I 'll keep him
Off for to-day, if I cannot longer: and then
At night, I 'll ship you both away to Ratcliff,
Where we will meet to-morrow, and there we 'll share.
Let Mammon's brass and pewter keep the cellar;
We 'll have another time for that. But, Dol,
Prithee go heat a little water quickly;
Subtle must shave me. All my captain's beard
Must off, to make me appear smooth Jeremy.
You 'll do it?

SUB. Yes, I 'll shave you as well as I can.

FACE. And not cut my throat, but trim me?

SUB. You shall see, sir. [*Exeunt.*]

5. *goods and purchase*] stolen goods, booty.

ACT V

SCENE I.—*Before Lovewit's door*

[*Enter*] LOVEWIT, [*with several of the*] Neighbours.

LOVE.   Has there been such resort, say you?
1 NEI.   Daily, Sir.
2 NEI.   And nightly, too.
3 NEI.   Ay, some as brave as lords.
4 NEI.   Ladies and gentlewomen.
5 NEI.   Citizens' wives.
1 NEI.   And knights.
6 NEI.   In coaches.
2 NEI.   Yes, and oyster-women.
1 NEI.   Beside other gallants.
3 NEI.   Sailors' wives.
4 NEI.   Tobacco men.
5 NEI.   Another Pimlico.[1]
LOVE.   What should my knave advance,
        To draw this company? He hung out no banners
        Of a strange calf with five legs to be seen,
        Or a huge lobster with six claws?
6 NEI.   No, sir.
3 NEI.   We had gone in then, sir.
LOVE.   He has no gift
        Of teaching i' the nose[2] that e'er I knew of.
        You saw no bills set up that promis'd cure
        Of agues or the tooth-ache?
2 NEI.   No such thing, sir!
LOVE.   Nor heard a drum struck for baboons or puppets?

---

1. *Pimlico*] A summer resort, where the citizens had cakes and ale.
2. *Of . . . nose*] Like a Puritan preacher.

5 NEI.   Neither, sir.
LOVE.   What device should he bring forth now?
          I love a teeming wit as I love my nourishment:
          'Pray God he ha' not kept such open house,
          That he hath sold my hangings, and my bedding!
          I left him nothing else. If he have eat 'em,
          A plague o' the moth, say I! Sure he has got
          Some bawdy pictures to call all this ging;³
          The Friar and the Nun; or the new motion⁴
          Of the knight's courser covering the parson's mare;
          The boy of six year old, with the great thing:
          Or 't may be, he has the fleas that run at tilt
          Upon a table, or some dog to dance.
          When saw you him?
1 NEI.   Who, sir, Jeremy?
2 NEI.   Jeremy butler?
          We saw him not this month.
LOVE.   How!
4 NEI.   Not these five weeks, sir.
6 NEI.   These six weeks, at the least.
LOVE.   You amaze me, neighbours!
5 NEI.   Sure, if your worship know not where he is,
          He 's slipt away.
6 NEI.   Pray God he be not made away. [*He knocks.*]
LOVE.   Ha! it 's no time to question, then.
6 NEI.   About
          Some three weeks since I heard a doleful cry,
          As I sat up a-mending my wife's stockings.
LOVE.   This 's strange that none will answer! Did'st thou hear
          A cry, sayst thou?
6 NEI.   Yes, sir, like unto a man
          That had been strangled an hour, and could not speak.
2 NEI.   I heard it, too, just this day three weeks, at two o'clock
          Next morning.
LOVE.   These be miracles, or you make 'em so!
          A man an hour strangled, and could not speak,
          And both you heard him cry?
3 NEI.   Yes, downward, sir.
LOVE.   Thou art a wise fellow. Give me thy hand, I pray thee.
          What trade art thou on?

---

3. *ging*] gang.
4. *new motion*] puppet show.

3 NEI.   A smith, an 't please your worship.
LOVE.   A smith! Then lend me thy help to get this door open.
3 NEI.   That I will presently, sir, but fetch my tools—   [*Exit.*]
1 NEI.   Sir, best to knock again afore you break it.

SCENE II.—*The same*

LOVEWIT, Neighbours.

LOVE.   [*Knocks again.*] I will.

[*Enter* FACE *in his butler's livery.*]

FACE.   What mean you, sir?
1, 2, 4 NEI.   O, here 's Jeremy!
FACE.   Good sir, come from the door.
LOVE.   Why, what 's the matter?
FACE.   Yet farther, you are too near yet.
LOVE.   I' the name of wonder,
What means the fellow!
FACE.   The house, sir, has been visited.
LOVE.   What, with the plague? Stand thou then farther.
FACE.   No, sir,
I had it not.
LOVE.   Who had it then? I left
None else but thee i' the house.
FACE.   Yes, sir, my fellow,
The cat that kept the buttery, had it on her
A week before I spied it; but I got her
Convey'd away i' the night: and so I shut
The house for a month——
LOVE.   How!
FACE.   Purposing then, sir,
To have burnt rose-vinegar, treacle, and tar,
And ha' made it sweet, that you should ne'er ha' known it;
Because I knew the news would but afflict you, sir.
LOVE.   Breathe less, and farther off! Why this is stranger:
The neighbours tell me all here that the doors
Have still been open——
FACE.   How, sir!
LOVE.   Gallants, men and women,
And of all sorts, tag-rag, been seen to flock here

In threaves, these ten weeks, as to a second Hogsden,
In days of Pimlico and Eye-bright.[1]

FACE.   Sir,
Their wisdoms will not say so.

LOVE.   To-day they speak
Of coaches and gallants; one in a French hood
Went in, they tell me; and another was seen
In a velvet gown at the window: divers more
Pass in and out.

FACE.   They did pass through the doors then,
Or walls, I assure their eye-sights, and their spectacles;
For here, sir, are the keys, and here have been,
In this my pocket, now above twenty days!
And for before, I kept the fort alone there.
But that 't is yet not deep i' the afternoon,
I should believe my neighbours had been double
Through the black pot, and made these apparitions!
For, on my faith to your worship, for these three weeks
And upwards, the door has not been open'd.

LOVE.   Strange.

1 NEI.   Good faith, I think I saw a coach.

2 NEI.   And I too,
I 'd ha' been sworn.

LOVE.   Do you but think it now?
And but one coach?

4 NEI.   We cannot tell, sir: Jeremy
Is a very honest fellow.

FACE.   Did you see me at all?

1 NEI.   No; that we are sure on.

2 NEI.   I 'll be sworn o' that.

LOVE.   Fine rogues to have your testimonies built on!

[*Re-enter third* Neighbour, *with his tools.*]

3 NEI.   Is Jeremy come!

1 NEI.   O yes; you may leave your tools;
We were deceiv'd, he says.

2 NEI.   He 's had the keys;
And the door has been shut these three weeks.

3 NEI.   Like enough.

LOVE.   Peace, and get hence, you changelings.

[*Enter* SURLY *and* MAMMON.]

1. A suburban tavern, eclipsed as a resort by Pimlico.

FACE.   [*Aside.*] Surly come.
        And Mammon made acquainted! They 'll tell all.
        How shall I beat them off? What shall I do?
        Nothing's more wretched than a guilty conscience.

SCENE III.—*The same*

SURLY, MAMMON, LOVEWIT, FACE, Neighbours.

SUR.   No, sir, he was a great physician. This,
        It was no bawdy-house, but a mere chancel!
        You knew the lord and his sister.
MAM.   Nay, good Surly.——
SUR.   The happy word, BE RICH——
MAM.   Play not the tyrant.—
SUR.   Should be to-day pronounc'd to all your friends.
        And where be your andirons now? And your brass pots,
        That should ha' been golden flagons, and great wedges?
MAM.   Let me but breathe. What, they ha' shut their doors,
        Methinks!   [*He and* SURLY *knock.*]
SUR.   Ay, now 't is holiday with them.
MAM.   Rogues,
        Cozeners, impostors, bawds!
FACE.   What mean you, sir?
MAM.   To enter if we can.
FACE.   Another man's house!
        Here is the owner, sir; turn you to him,
        And speak your business.
MAM.   Are you, sir, the owner?
LOVE.   Yes, sir.
MAM.   And are those knaves within, your cheaters!
LOVE.   What knaves, what cheaters?
MAM.   Subtle and his Lungs.
FACE.   The gentleman is distracted, sir! No lungs
        Nor lights ha' been seen here these three weeks, sir,
        Within these doors upon my word.
SUR.   Your word,
        Groom arrogant!
FACE.   Yes, sir, I am the housekeeper,
        And know the keys ha' not been out o' my hands.
SUR.   This 's a new Face.

FACE.   You do mistake the house, sir:
          What sign was 't at?
SUR.   You rascal! This is one
          Of the confederacy. Come, let 's get officers,
          And force the door.
LOVE.   Pray you stay, gentlemen.
SUR.   No, sir, we 'll come with warrant.
MAM.   Ay, and then
          We shall ha' your doors open.   [*Exeunt* MAM. *and* SUR.]
LOVE.   What means this?
FACE.   I cannot tell, sir.
1 NEI.   These are two o' the gallants
          That we do think we saw.
FACE.   Two o' the fools!
          You talk as idly as they. Good faith, sir,
          I think the moon has craz'd 'em all.—[*Aside.*] O me,

[*Enter* KASTRIL.]

          The angry boy come too! He 'll make a noise,
          And ne'er away till he have betray'd us all.
KAS.   [*knocking.*] What, rogues, bawds, slaves, you 'll open the door
            anon!
          Punk, cockatrice, my suster! By this light
          I 'll fetch the marshal to you. You are a whore
          To keep your castle——
FACE.   Who would you speak with, sir?
KAS.   The bawdy doctor, and the cozening captain,
          And puss my suster.
LOVE.   This is something, sure.
FACE.   Upon my trust, the doors were never open, sir.
KAS.   I have heard all their tricks told me twice over,
          By the fat knight and the lean gentleman.
LOVE.   Here comes another.

[*Enter* ANANIAS *and* TRIBULATION.]

FACE.   Ananias too!
          And his pastor!
TRI.   The doors are shut against us.
                               [*They beat too, at the door.*]
ANA.   Come forth, you seed of sulphur, sons of fire!
          Your stench it is broke forth; abomination
          Is in the house.
KAS.   Ay, my suster's there.

ANA.   The place,
It is become a cage of unclean birds.

KAS.   Yes, I will fetch the scavenger, and the constable.

TRI.   You shall do well.

ANA.   We 'll join to weed them out.

KAS.   You will not come then, punk devise,[1] my suster!

ANA.   Call her not sister; she 's a harlot verily.

KAS.   I 'll raise the street.

LOVE.   Good gentleman, a word.

ANA.   Satan avoid, and hinder not our zeal!
                      [*Exeunt* ANA., TRIB., *and* KAST.]

LOVE.   The world 's turn'd Bet'lem.

FACE.   These are all broke loose,
Out of St. Katherine's, where they use to keep
The better sort of mad-folks.

1 NEI.   All these persons
We saw go in and out here.

2 NEI.   Yes, indeed, sir.

3 NEI.   These were the parties.

FACE.   Peace, you drunkards! Sir,
I wonder at it. Please you to give me leave
To touch the door; I 'll try an the lock be chang'd.

LOVE.   It mazes me!

FACE.   [*goes to the door.*] Good faith, sir, I believe
There 's no such thing: 't is all *deceptio visus.*[2]—
[*Aside.*] Would I could get him away.

DAP.   [*within.*] Master captain! Master doctor!

LOVE.   Who 's that?

FACE.   [*Aside.*] Our clerk within, that I forgot!—I know not, sir.

DAP.   [*within.*] For God's sake, when will her grace be at leisure?

FACE.   Ha!
Illusions, some spirit o' the air!—[*Aside.*] His gag is melted,
And now he sets out the throat.

DAP.   [*within.*] I am almost stifled——

FACE.   [*Aside.*] Would you were together.

LOVE.   'T is i' the house.
Ha! list.

FACE.   Believe it, sir, i' the air.

LOVE.   Peace, you.

DAP.   [*within.*] Mine aunt's grace does not use me well.

---

1. *punk devise*] perfect harlot.
2. *deceptio visus*] optical illusion.

SUB.	[*within.*] You fool,
	Peace, you 'll mar all.
FACE.	[*speaks through the keyhole, while* LOVEWIT *advances to the door unobserved.*] Or you will else, you rogue.
LOVE.	O, is it so? Then you converse with spirits!—
	Come, sir. No more o' your tricks, good Jeremy.
	The truth, the shortest way.
FACE.	Dismiss this rabble, sir.—
	[*Aside.*] What shall I do? I am catch'd,
LOVE.	Good neighbours,
	I thank you all. You may depart. [*Exeunt* Neighbours.]—
	Come, sir,
	You know that I am an indulgent master;
	And therefore conceal nothing. What 's your medicine,
	To draw so many several sorts of wild fowl?
FACE.	Sir, you were wont to affect mirth and wit—
	But here 's no place to talk on 't i' the street.
	Give me but leave to make the best of my fortune,
	And only pardon me th' abuse of your house:
	It 's all I beg. I 'll help you to a widow,
	In recompense, that you shall gi' me thanks for,
	Will make you seven years younger, and a rich one.
	'T is but your putting on a Spanish cloak:
	I have her within. You need not fear the house;
	It was not visited.
LOVE.	But by me, who came
	Sooner than you expected.
FACE.	It is true, sir.
	'Pray you forgive me.
LOVE.	Well: let's see your widow. [*Exeunt.*]

SCENE IV.—*A room in the same*

[*Enter*] SUBTLE [*leading in*] DAPPER, [*with his eyes bound as before*].

SUB.	How! ha' you eaten your gag?
DAP.	Yes, faith, it crumbled
	Away i' my mouth.
SUB.	You ha' spoil'd all then.
DAP.	No!
	I hope my aunt of Fairy will forgive me.

SUB.   Your aunt's a gracious lady; but in troth
          You were to blame.
DAP.   The fume did overcome me,
          And I did do 't to stay my stomach. 'Pray you
          So satisfy her grace.

[*Enter* FACE *in his uniform.*]

                              Here comes the captain.
FACE.   How now! Is his mouth down?
SUB.   Ay, he has spoken!
FACE.   A pox, I heard him, and you too. He 's undone then.—
          [*Aside to* SUBTLE.] I have been fain to say, the house is
              haunted
          With spirits, to keep churl back.
SUB.   And hast thou done it?
FACE.   Sure, for this night.
SUB.   Why, then triumph and sing
          Of Face so famous, the precious king
          Of present wits.
FACE.   Did you not hear the coil
          About the door?
SUB.   Yes, and I dwindled[1] with it.
FACE.   Show him his aunt, and let him be dispatch'd:
          I 'll send her to you.   [*Exit* FACE.]
SUB.   Well, sir, your aunt her grace
          Will give you audience presently, on my suit,
          And the captain's word that you did not eat your gag
          In any contempt of her highness.   [*Unbinds his eyes.*]
DAP.   Not I, in troth, sir.

[*Enter* DOL *like the Queen of Fairy.*]

SUB.   Here she is come. Down o' your knees and wriggle:
          She has a stately presence. [DAPPER *kneels and shuffles
              towards her.*] Good! Yet nearer,
          And bid, God save you!
DAP.   Madam!
SUB.   And your aunt.
DAP.   And my most gracious aunt, God save your grace.
DOL.   Nephew, we thought to have been angry with you;
          But that sweet face of yours hath turn'd the tide,
          And made it flow with joy, that ebb'd of love.

1. *dwindled*] shrank with fear.

	Arise, and touch our velvet gown.
SUB.	The skirts,

SUB.   The skirts,
And kiss 'em. So!

DOL.   Let me now stroke that head.
Much, nephew, shalt thou win, much shalt thou spend;
Much shalt thou give away, much shalt thou lend.

SUB. [*Aside.*] Ay, much! indeed.—Why do you not thank her
    grace?

DAP. I cannot speak for joy.

SUB.   See, the kind wretch!
Your grace's kinsman right.

DOL.   Give me the bird.——
Here is your fly in a purse, about your neck, cousin;
Wear it, and feed it about this day sev'n-night,
On your right wrist——

SUB.   Open a vein with a pin
And let it suck but once a week; till then,
You must not look on 't.

DOL.   No: and, kinsman,
Bear yourself worthy of the blood you came on.

SUB. Her grace would ha' you eat no more Woolsack pies,
Nor Dagger frumety.

DOL.   Nor break his fast
In Heaven and Hell.

SUB.   She 's with you everywhere!
Nor play with costermongers, at mumchance, traytrip,
God-make-you-rich (when as your aunt has done it); but
    keep
The gallant'st company, and the best games——

DAP.   Yes, sir.

SUB. Gleek and primero; and what you get, be true to us.

DAP. By this hand, I will.

SUB.   You may bring 's a thousand pound
Before to-morrow night, if but three thousand
Be stirring, an you will.

DAP.   I swear I will then.

SUB. Your fly will learn you all games.

FACE.   [*within.*] Ha' you done there?

SUB. Your grace will command him no more duties?

DOL.   No:
But come and see me often. I may chance
To leave him three or four hundred chests of treasure,
And some twelve thousand acres of fairy land,

	If he game well and comely with good gamesters.
SUB.	There 's a kind aunt: kiss her departing part. —
	But you must sell your forty mark a year now.
DAP.	Ay, sir, I mean.
SUB.	Or, give 't away; pox on 't!
DAP.	I 'll gi' 't mine aunt. I 'll go and fetch the writings. [*Exit.*]
SUB.	'T is well; away.

[*Re-enter* FACE.]

FACE.	Where 's Subtle?
SUB.	Here: what news?
FACE.	Drugger is at the door; go take his suit,
	And bid him fetch a parson presently.
	Say he shall marry the widow. Thou shalt spend
	A hundred pound by the service! [*Exit* SUBTLE.]
	Now, Queen Dol,
	Have you pack'd up all?
DOL.	Yes.
FACE.	And how do you like
	The Lady Pliant?
DOL.	A good dull innocent.

[*Re-enter* SUBTLE.]

SUB.	Here 's your Hieronimo's cloak and hat.
FACE.	Give me 'em.
SUB.	And the ruff too?
FACE.	Yes; I 'll come to you presently. [*Exit.*]
SUB.	Now he is gone about his project, Dol,
	I told you of, for the widow.
DOL.	'T is direct
	Against our articles.
SUB.	Well, we will fit him, wench.
	Hast thou gull'd her of her jewels or her bracelets?
DOL.	No; but I will do 't.
SUB.	Soon at night, my Dolly,
	When we are shipt, and all our goods aboard,
	Eastward for Ratcliff, we will turn our course
	To Brainford, westward, if thou sayst the word,
	And take our leaves of this o'erweening rascal.
	This peremptory Face.
DOL.	Content; I 'm weary of him.
SUB.	Thou 'st cause, when the slave will run at wiving, Dol,
	Against the instrument that was drawn between us.

DOL.   I 'll pluck his bird as bare as I can.
SUB.   Yes, tell her
        She must by any means address some present
        To th' cunning man, make him amends for wronging
        His art with her suspicion; send a ring,
        Or chain of pearl; she will be tortur'd else
        Extremely in her sleep, say, and ha' strange things
        Come to her. Wilt thou?
DOL.   Yes.
SUB.   My fine flitter-mouse,[2]
        My bird o' the night! We 'll tickle it at the Pigeons,[3]
        When we have all, and may unlock the trunks,
        And say, this 's mine, and thine; and thine, and mine.
                                        [*They kiss.*]

[*Re-enter* FACE.]

FACE.   What now! a billing?
SUB.   Yes, a little exalted
        In the good passage of our stock-affairs.
FACE.   Drugger has brought his parson; take him in, Subtle,
        And send Nab back again to wash his face.
SUB.   I will: and shave himself?   [*Exit.*]
FACE.   If you can get him.
DOL.   You are hot upon it, Face, whate'er it is!
FACE.   A trick that Dol shall spend ten pound a month by.

[*Re-enter* SUBTLE.]

        Is he gone?
SUB.   The chaplain waits you i' the hall, sir.
FACE.   I 'll go bestow him.   [*Exit.*]
DOL.   He 'll now marry her instantly.
SUB.   He cannot yet, he is not ready. Dear Dol,
        Cozen her of all thou canst. To deceive him
        Is no deceit, but justice, that would break
        Such an inextricable tie as ours was.
DOL.   Let me alone to fit him.

[*Re-enter* FACE.]

FACE.   Come, my venturers,
        You ha' pack'd up all? Where be the trunks? Bring forth.

2. *flitter-mouse*] bat.
3. *Pigeons*] an inn at Brentford.

SUB. Here.
FACE. Let us see 'em. Where 's the money?
SUB.   Here,
In this.
FACE.   Mammon's ten pound; eight score before:
The brethren's money this. Drugger's and Dapper's.
What paper 's that?
DOL.   The jewel of the waiting maid's,
That stole it from her lady, to know certain——
FACE. If she should have precedence of her mistress?
DOL.   Yes.
FACE. What box is that?
SUB.   The fish-wives' rings, I think,
And th' ale-wives' single money. Is 't not, Dol?
DOL. Yes; and the whistle that the sailor's wife
Brought you to know an her husband were with Ward.[4]
FACE. We 'll wet it to-morrow; and our silver beakers
And tavern cups. Where be the French petticoats
And girdles and hangers?
SUB.   Here, i' the trunk,
And the bolts of lawn.
FACE.   Is Drugger's damask there,
And the tobacco?
SUB.   Yes.
FACE.   Give me the keys.
DOL. Why you the keys?
SUB.   No matter, Dol; because
We shall not open 'em before he comes.
FACE. 'T is true, you shall not open them, indeed;
Nor have 'em forth, do you see? Not forth, Dol.
DOL.   No!
FACE. No, my smock-rampant. The right is, my master
Knows all, has pardon'd me, and he will keep 'em.
Doctor, 't is true—you look—for all your figures:
I sent for him, indeed. Wherefore, good partners,
Both he and she, be satisfied: for here
Determines the indenture tripartite
'Twixt Subtle, Dol, and Face. All I can do
Is to help you over the wall, o' the back-side,
Or lend you a sheet to save your velvet gown, Dol.
Here will be officers presently, bethink you

---

4. A famous pirate.

	Of some course suddenly to scape the dock;
	For thither you 'll come else. [*Some knock.*] Hark you,
	thunder.
SUB.	You are a precious fiend!
OFFI.	[*without.*] Open the door.
FACE.	Dol, I am sorry for thee i' faith; but hear'st thou?
	It shall go hard but I will place thee somewhere:
	Thou shalt ha' my letter to Mistress Amo——
DOL.	Hang you.
FACE.	Or Madam Caesarean.
DOL.	Pox upon you, rogue,
	Would I had but time to beat thee!
FACE.	Subtle,
	Let 's know where you 'll set up next; I will send you
	A customer now and then, for old acquaintance.
	What new course have you?
SUB.	Rogue, I 'll hang myself;
	That I may walk a greater devil than thou,
	And haunt thee i' the flock-bed and the buttery. [*Exeunt.*]

SCENE V.—*An outer room in the same*

[*Enter*] LOVEWIT [*in the Spanish dress, with the* Parson. *Loud knocking at the door.*]

LOVE.	What do you mean, my masters?
MAM.	[*without.*] Open your door,
	Cheaters, bawds, conjurers.
OFFI.	[*without.*] Or we 'll break it open.
LOVE.	What warrant have you?
OFFI.	[*without.*] Warrant enough, sir, doubt not,
	If you 'll not open it.
LOVE.	Is there an officer there?
OFFI.	[*without.*] Yes, two or three for failing.
LOVE.	Have but patience,
	And I will open it straight.

[*Enter* FACE, *as butler.*]

FACE.	Sir, ha' you done?
	Is it a marriage? Perfect?
LOVE.	Yes, my brain.

FACE.   Off with your ruff and cloak then; be yourself, sir.
SUR.   [*without.*] Down with the door.
KAS.   [*without.*] 'Slight, ding¹ it open.
LOVE.   [*opening the door.*] Hold,
         Hold, gentlemen, what means this violence?

[MAMMON, SURLY, KASTRIL, ANANIAS, TRIBULATION *and* Officers *rush in.*]

MAM.   Where is this collier?
SUR.   And my Captain Face?
MAM.   These day-owls.
SUR.   That are birding² in men's purses.
MAM.   Madam Suppository.
KAS.   Doxy, my suster.
ANA.   Locusts.
         Of the foul pit.
TRI.   Profane as Bel and the Dragon.
ANA.   Worse than the grasshoppers, or the lice of Egypt.
LOVE.   Good gentlemen, hear me. Are you officers,
         And cannot stay this violence?
1 OFFI.   Keep the peace.
LOVE.   Gentlemen, what is the matter? Whom do you seek?
MAM.   The chemical cozener.
SUR.   And the captain pander.
KAS.   The nun my suster.
MAM.   Madam Rabbi.
ANA.   Scorpions,
         And caterpillars.
LOVE.   Fewer at once, I pray you.
1 OFFI. One after another, gentlemen, I charge you,
         By virtue of my staff.
ANA.   They are the vessels
         Of pride, lust, and the cart.
LOVE.   Good zeal, lie still
         A little while.
TRI.   Peace, Deacon Ananias.
LOVE.   The house is mine here, and the doors are open;
         If there be any such persons as you seek for,
         Use your authority, search on o' God's name,
         I am but newly come to town, and finding

1. *ding*] break.
2. *birding*] stealing.

	This tumult 'bout my door, to tell you true,

This tumult 'bout my door, to tell you true,
It somewhat maz'd me; till my man here, fearing
My more displeasure, told me he had done
Somewhat an insolent part, let out my house
(Belike presuming on my known aversion
From any air o' the town while there was sickness),
To a doctor and a captain: who, what they are
Or where they be, he knows not.

MAM.   Are they gone?

LOVE.   You may go in and search, sir. [MAMMON, ANA., *and* TRIB. *go
        in.*] Here, I find
The empty walls worse than I left 'em, smok'd,
A few crack'd pots, and glasses, and a furnace;
The ceiling fill'd with poesies of the candle,
And "Madam with a dildo"[3] writ o' the walls.
Only one gentlewoman I met here
That is within, that said she was a widow——

KAS.   Ay, that 's my suster; I 'll go thump her. Where is she?
                                              [*Goes in.*]

LOVE.   And should ha' married a Spanish count, but he,
When he came to 't, neglected her so grossly,
That I, a widower, am gone through with her.

SUR.   How! have I lost her then?

LOVE.   Were you the don, sir?
Good faith, now she does blame you extremely, and says
You swore, and told her you had ta'en the pains
To dye your beard, and umber o'er your face,
Borrowed a suit, and ruff, all for her love:
And then did nothing. What an oversight
And want of putting forward, sir, was this!
Well fare an old harquebusier[4] yet,
Could prime his powder, and give fire, and hit,
All in a twinkling!   [MAMMON *comes forth.*]

MAM.   The whole nest are fled!

LOVE.   What sort of birds were they?

MAM.   A kind of choughs,[5]
Or thievish daws, sir, that have pickt my purse,
Of eight score and ten pounds within these five weeks,
Beside my first materials; and my goods,
That lie i' the cellar, which I am glad they ha' left,

3. Probably a fragment of a song.
4. *harquebusier*] musketeer.
5. *choughs*] crow.

	I may have home yet.
LOVE.	Think you so, sir?
MAM.	Ay.
LOVE.	By order of law, sir, but not otherwise.
MAM.	Not mine own stuff!
LOVE.	Sir, I can take no knowledge

That they are yours, but by public means.
If you can bring certificate that you were gull'd of 'em,
Or any formal writ out of a court,
That you did cozen yourself, I will not hold them.

MAM. I 'll rather lose 'em.
LOVE.   That you shall not, sir,
By me, in troth; upon these terms, they 're yours.
What, should they ha' been, sir, turn'd into gold, all?
MAM.   No.
I cannot tell. — It may be they should. — What then?
LOVE. What a great loss in hope have you sustain'd!
MAM. Not I; the commonwealth has.
FACE.   Ay, he would ha' built
The city new; and made a ditch about it
Of silver, should have run with cream from Hogsden;
That every Sunday in Moorsfields the younkers,
And tits[6] and tom-boys should have fed on, gratis.
MAM. I will go mount a turnip-cart, and preach
The end o' the world within these two months. Surly,
What! in a dream?
SUR.   Must I needs cheat myself
With that same foolish vice of honesty!
Come, let us go and hearken out the rogues:
That Face I 'll mark for mine, if e'er I meet him.
FACE. If I can hear of him, sir, I 'll bring you word
Unto your lodging; for in troth, they were strangers
To me; I thought 'em honest as myself, sir.
                                        [*They come forth.*]

[*Re-enter* ANANIAS *and* TRIBULATION.]

TRI. 'T is well, the saints shall not lose all yet. Go
And get some carts——
LOVE.   For what, my zealous friends?
ANA. To bear away the portion of the righteous
Out of this den of thieves.

6. *tits*] wenches.

LOVE.	What is that portion?
ANA.	The goods sometimes the orphans', that the brethren
	Bought with their silver pence.
LOVE.	What, those i' the cellar,
	The knight Sir Mammon claims?
ANA.	I do defy

ANA.   I do defy
The wicked Mammon, so do all the brethren,
Thou profane man! I ask thee with what conscience
Thou canst advance that idol against us,
That have the seal? Were not the shillings numb'red
That made the pounds; were not the pounds told out
Upon the second day of the fourth week,
In the eighth month, upon the table dormant,
The year of the last patience of the saints,
Six hundred and ten?

LOVE.   Mine earnest vehement botcher,
And deacon also, I cannot dispute with you:
But if you get you not away the sooner,
I shall confute you with a cudgel.

ANA.   Sir!

TRI.   Be patient, Ananias.

ANA.   I am strong,
And will stand up, well girt, against an host
That threaten Gad in exile.

LOVE.   I shall send you
To Amsterdam, to your cellar.

ANA.   I will pray there,
Against thy house. May dogs defile thy walls,
And wasps and hornets breed beneath thy roof,
This seat of falsehood, and this cave of coz'nage!

                              [*Exeunt* ANA. *and* TRIB.]

[*Enter* DRUGGER.]

LOVE.   Another too?

DRUG.   Not I, sir, I am no brother.

LOVE.   [*beats him.*] Away, you Harry Nicholas! do you talk?

                              [*Exit* DRUG.]

FACE.   No, this was Abel Drugger. Good sir, go, [*To the* Parson.]
         And satisfy him; tell him all is done:
         He staid too long a washing of his face.
         The doctor, he shall hear of him at Westchester;
         And of the captain, tell him, at Yarmouth, or
         Some good port-town else, lying for a wind.   [*Exit* Parson.]

            If you can get off the angry child now, sir——

[*Enter* KASTRIL, *dragging in his sister.*]

KAS.   Come on, you ewe, you have match'd most sweetly, ha' you
           not?
          Did not I say, I would never ha' you tupt
          But by a dubb'd boy, to make you a lady-tom?
          'Slight, you are a mammet![7] O, I could touse you now.
          Death, mun[8] you marry with a pox!

LOVE.   You lie, boy;
          As sound as you; and I 'm aforehand with you.

KAS.   Anon!

LOVE.   Come, will you quarrel? I will feize[9] you, sirrah;
          Why do you not buckle to your tools?

KAS.   God's light,
          This is a fine old boy as e'er I saw!

LOVE.   What, do you change your copy now? Proceed;
          Here stands my dove: stoop at her if you dare.

KAS.   'Slight, I must love him! I cannot choose, i' faith,
          An I should be hang'd for 't! Suster, I protest,
          I honour thee for this match.

LOVE.   O, do you so, sir?

KAS.   Yes, an thou canst take tobacco and drink, old boy,
          I 'll give her five hundred pound more to her marriage,
          Than her own state.

LOVE.   Fill a pipe full, Jeremy.

FACE.   Yes; but go in and take it, sir.

LOVE.   We will.
          I will be rul'd by thee in anything, Jeremy.

KAS.   'Slight, thou art not hide-bound, thou art a jovy boy!
          Come, let us in, I pray thee, and take our whiffs.

LOVE.   Whiff in with your sister, brother boy.

                      [*Exeunt* KAS. *and* Dame P.]
                       That master
          That had receiv'd such happiness by a servant,
          In such a widow, and with so much wealth,
          Were very ungrateful, if he would not be
          A little indulgent to that servant's wit,
          And help his fortune, though were some small strain

---

7. *mammet*] puppet.
8. *mun*] must.
9. *feize*] beat.

Of his own candour.[10] [*Advancing.*] Therefore, gentlemen,
And kind spectators, if I have outstript
An old man's gravity, or strict canon, think
What a young wife and a good brain may do;
Stretch age's truth sometimes, and crack it too.
Speak for thyself, knave.

FACE.   So I will, sir. [*Advancing to the front of the stage.*]
    Gentlemen,
My part a little fell in this last scene,
Yet 't was decorum. And though I am clean
Got off from Subtle, Surly, Mammon, Dol,
Hot Ananias, Dapper, Drugger, all
With whom I traded; yet I put myself
On you, that are my country:[11] and this pelf
Which I have got, if you do quit me, rests,
To feast you often, and invite new guests.   [*Exeunt.*]

10. *candour*] fair reputation.
11. *country*] jury.

DOVER · THRIFT · EDITIONS

PLAYS

THE MIKADO, William Schwenck Gilbert. 64pp. 27268-0

FAUST, PART ONE, Johann Wolfgang von Goethe. 192pp. 28046-2

THE INSPECTOR GENERAL, Nikolai Gogol. 80pp. 28500-6

SHE STOOPS TO CONQUER, Oliver Goldsmith. 80pp. 26867-5

A DOLL'S HOUSE, Henrik Ibsen. 80pp. 27062-9

GHOSTS, Henrik Ibsen. 64pp. 29852-3

HEDDA GABLER, Henrik Ibsen. 80pp. 26469-6

THE WILD DUCK, Henrik Ibsen. 96pp. 41116-8

VOLPONE, Ben Jonson. 112pp. 28049-7

DR. FAUSTUS, Christopher Marlowe. 64pp. 28208-2

THE MISANTHROPE, Molière. 64pp. 27065-3

ANNA CHRISTIE, Eugene O'Neill. 80pp. 29985-6

BEYOND THE HORIZON, Eugene O'Neill. 96pp. 29085-9

THE EMPEROR JONES, Eugene O'Neill. 64pp. 29268-1

THE LONG VOYAGE HOME AND OTHER PLAYS, Eugene O'Neill. 80pp. 28755-6

RIGHT YOU ARE, IF YOU THINK YOU ARE, Luigi Pirandello. 64pp. (Not available in Europe or United Kingdom.) 29576-1

SIX CHARACTERS IN SEARCH OF AN AUTHOR, Luigi Pirandello. 64pp. (Not available in Europe or United Kingdom.) 29992-9

PHÈDRE, Jean Racine. 64pp. 41927-4

HANDS AROUND, Arthur Schnitzler. 64pp. 28724-6

ANTONY AND CLEOPATRA, William Shakespeare. 128pp. 40062-X

AS YOU LIKE IT, William Shakespeare. 80pp. 40432-3

HAMLET, William Shakespeare. 128pp. 27278-8

HENRY IV, William Shakespeare. 96pp. 29584-2

JULIUS CAESAR, William Shakespeare. 80pp. 26876-4

KING LEAR, William Shakespeare. 112pp. 28058-6

LOVE'S LABOUR'S LOST, William Shakespeare. 64pp. 41929-0

MACBETH, William Shakespeare. 96pp. 27802-6

MEASURE FOR MEASURE, William Shakespeare. 96pp. 40889-2

THE MERCHANT OF VENICE, William Shakespeare. 96pp. 28492-1

A MIDSUMMER NIGHT'S DREAM, William Shakespeare. 80pp. 27067-X

MUCH ADO ABOUT NOTHING, William Shakespeare. 80pp. 28272-4

OTHELLO, William Shakespeare. 112pp. 29097-2

RICHARD III, William Shakespeare. 112pp. 28747-5

ROMEO AND JULIET, William Shakespeare. 96pp. 27557-4

THE TAMING OF THE SHREW, William Shakespeare. 96pp. 29765-9

THE TEMPEST, William Shakespeare. 96pp. 40658-X

TWELFTH NIGHT; OR, WHAT YOU WILL, William Shakespeare. 80pp. 29290-8

ARMS AND THE MAN, George Bernard Shaw. 80pp. (Not available in Europe or United Kingdom.) 26476-9

HEARTBREAK HOUSE, George Bernard Shaw. 128pp. (Not available in Europe or United Kingdom.) 29291-6

PYGMALION, George Bernard Shaw. 96pp. (Available in U.S. only.) 28222-8

THE RIVALS, Richard Brinsley Sheridan. 96pp. 40433-1

THE SCHOOL FOR SCANDAL, Richard Brinsley Sheridan. 96pp. 26687-7

ANTIGONE, Sophocles. 64pp. 27804-2

OEDIPUS AT COLONUS, Sophocles. 64pp. 40659-8

OEDIPUS REX, Sophocles. 64pp. 26877-2